ALSO BY CLAY SAVAGE

The Last Getaway

THE

IDENTICAL

OPPOSITE

CLAY SAVAGE

Ocean Park Press

The Identical Opposite. Copyright © 2020 by Clay Savage

www.theclaysavage.com

Published by Ocean Park Press, Los Angeles, California

ISBN 978-1-7338806-2-6 (paperback)
ISBN 978-1-7338806-3-3 (ebook)

For Susan. For all the years.

CHAPTER ONE

Paula Hickman stood at her closed bedroom door, listening to the sound of her husband making a breakfast smoothie. The discordant churning of the blender wound down and then briefly whirred again, before at last falling silent—all those disparate parts combining so easily together to make a new, pleasing whole.

Paula closed her eyes. *If only it were all that simple.*

When Paula at last entered the kitchen, she watched her husband at the sink a moment before speaking. "You don't need to scrub like that if you're only going to put it in the dishwasher," she said.

"I've been adding chia seeds and they're annoying as hell to get off if I don't take care of it right away." Alan continued to use the scouring pad on the blender.

Paula stood with the granite island between them and nodded, though her husband still had his back to her.

He put the blender in the dishwasher. "There's a smoothie in the refrigerator for you," he said. "You're gonna have to stir it a bit."

"Okay," Paula said, trying to sound grateful.

Alan looked at his wife for the first time as he wiped his

hands with a dishcloth. "I'm surprised to see you up so early. How'd you sleep?"

"Truth or lie?"

He smiled with half his mouth. "Whichever will allow you to get through the day, I suppose."

"I slept fine."

Alan pulled a teabag from his thermos and dropped it into the trash under the sink.

"Are you leaving already?" Paula asked him.

"I'm already running late. I have office hours and I need to stop by the bakery before my first class."

Paula tried to recall the last time she'd been to The Little Delicious, the dessert bakery on Montana Avenue she'd opened three years ago to such great success. Had it been a few weeks since she'd gone in? A month? Six weeks? Lately, after doing so well for so long, her days and weeks tended to meld together like dripping wax, a slow collection of time only noticed when hardened into a sizable mass.

"...so he's coming back this morning to take another look at the convection oven," Paula heard her husband say, his voice poking through gaps in her constantly churning internal considerations.

"That's been a real mess, hasn't it?" she asked, snapping to attention.

Alan used his thumb to wipe up a drop of purple smoothie from the counter. "Let's just hope they fix it right this time."

Paula's brain worked like a sponge, soaking up the guilt pumping from deep within, before squeezing out streams of negative thoughts about the endless demands placed upon her husband. Seeing as how his current job as a global studies professor at UCLA kept him busy enough, the bakery (her bakery, truly) had become another leaky ship that Alan was tasked to keep afloat. Paula longed to help bail water, to work as hard as he did, but, regardless of the grinding effort she expended, she couldn't even muster the energy for matters as mundane as repairing a finicky convection oven.

"I know I should be going in this morning," Paula said, picking at the cuticle of her thumb, "but with Anthony moving in today I'm having a hard time focusing on—"

Alan's exasperated sigh stopped her short and brought her attention up from her thumb, which had begun to bleed. "What?" she asked, wide-eyed, sucking on the now-ragged cuticle.

"Is that why you got up so early? This whole Anthony thing?"

She hesitated. "Truth or lie?"

"We talked about this, Paula," Alan said, screwing the cap firmly onto his thermos as if to demonstrate his unwillingness to do so again.

Paula felt a familiar vibration in her chest, like a gathering of agitated bees. "His wife isn't going to know anyone here."

Alan nodded. "That's right, she won't."

"And she'll need me to show her around."

"I promise you she's not gonna be looking for an on-call tour guide of Santa Monica. And if she does, all you have to do is introduce her to my sister—then you won't be able to get a word in edgewise, even if you wanted to."

Paula smiled.

Alan reached for his cellphone on the counter behind him. "Speaking of Wendy, she called. She'd like to drop by this afternoon."

Paula's heartbeat pulsed in her wounded thumb. "Please tell me you talked her out of it."

"I did my best, but you know how she is. She's been very concerned about you."

"Of course she has."

Paula was well versed in Wendy Hickman's concern; her sister-in-law was perhaps the most concerned person to ever walk the face of the earth. You name it—women in Afghanistan, rural poverty, diabetes, black mold, stray dogs—whatever it was, Wendy felt its pain. But despite her sincere claims of empathy, when it came to Paula, she never could fully grasp the immutable fact that while downcast moods were merely weather, *depression* was climate change.

Alan glanced at the clock above the sink. "Look, if you're not up to meeting Anthony's family today, then don't. Go for a drive. Go to the gym. Even just a walk. You'll feel better, I promise. Anything but sitting in your room all day, brooding."

It was a well-established point. It was always going to be something. If not Anthony's family moving in across the street, then Wendy's inexhaustible impulse to help. Or the bakery, or whatever. The bees in Paula's chest moved into her throat and their buzzing filled her ears. "Maybe I'll go down to the beach," she gamely offered.

Alan's half-grin expanded to include the other side of his mouth. "Good idea. In the meantime, drink your smoothie and remember to—"

"Rinse the glass," Paula said. "The chia seeds are a bitch to get off."

"Perfect. See? One less thing to worry about."

Paula's faint smile maintained its basic shape as Alan brushed his shaggy black hair behind his ears (though he was halfway through his forties, Paula appreciated that her husband remained strikingly hip) and stuffed his keys into his olive-green satchel.

He headed for the garage door beside the walk-in pantry. "I'll call you after my last class, all right?"

Paula nodded her appreciation, and then she was alone. Too much alone. She retrieved the smoothie from the fridge and stirred it with the straw Alan had left in the glass for her, before sucking up the thickened frozen strawberries, blueberries, bananas, and protein powder. The chia seeds struck coldly against her teeth. Her throat constricted as she swallowed. Her stomach tightened.

She tried to remember if the housekeepers were scheduled to come, hoping they weren't. The always-cheerful cleaning crew from Maria's Maid Service had become yet another tributary of guilt in Paula's emotional ecosystem, and having them in the house made her anxious. She was always in the way, despite having close to six-thousand square feet in which to hide.

Heading for the living room window that faced the house across the street—*Anthony's house now*—her advance was halted by the sound of a horn, followed by a man yelling something in Spanish. Paula's eyes remained fixed on the curtain covering the window. On the other side of that curtain was Anthony Mills, unloading all of his worldly possessions, along with his wife's dreams of a new life in Southern California. Hannah was her name. She sounded perfect for Anthony—lawyer, onetime competitive swimmer, loving mother to Alex, who had to be, what, four by now? Five? God, that meant it'd been six years since Paula had last seen Anthony—astounding how fast time went by.

The bees swirled.

What about the secrets? Would Anthony be unpacking those

as well? Would the secrets of their time together twenty-five years earlier tumble out, bringing back the pain she'd kept hidden from Alan? If only she'd kept her mouth shut about the house coming up for sale. Of course, she had only mentioned it in passing during one of their increasingly infrequent email exchanges, giving it no more weight than a mention of the weather. How could she have anticipated any of this? Anthony hadn't said anything about relocating. He'd been firmly entrenched in San Francisco, a ten-year executive for HSH Technology Systems. Rich and happy, content with what he had and where he was.

But now he's here.

Turning away from the window, Paula returned to the security of her bedroom. She climbed back into bed and opened her laptop, the very one on which she'd most often communicated with Anthony. Spreading her fingertips across the keyboard, she noticed dark blood filling the edges of her thumbnail like caulking where she'd picked at the cuticle. The sight of it bothered her, but the warmth of the computer on her lap, along with the soft glow of the screen, worked as a sedative. Her body relaxed. The bees slowly scattered, taking with them the burden of being Paula. Online, she did not have any burdens at all. She was free to be someone else.

Slipping free from the confines of her reality, she opened her Facebook page and clicked on "Groups." Though her obsession had begun exclusively with depression support groups, she had, over the years, joined close to a hundred others—ranging from "Indian Food Lovers" to "Ocean Fish Liberation" to "Crossword Fanatics." The groups were a panacea. Every time she clicked to join a new one, she existed someplace else, as *someone* else, free of baggage, taking up uncomplicated residence in somebody else's mind.

Down the rabbit hole she fell, checking in on "friends" she'd never met, tagging pictures, posting comments, and having virtual debates with people she would never see face to face—people who believed they were communing with a slight redhead in Los Angeles named Jill Carlson. Jill was a mother of three, with two rescued pit bulls named Maui and Kona and a husband named Dave. Jill's husband had become a necessary construct once Paula joined a Christian military wives group. Dave, a career soldier in the Marines who had recently achieved the rank of sergeant-major, was stationed in Europe, and Jill wished she could afford to take the kids on her trip to visit him next June. The phantom Jill Carlson was always outgoing and supportive, and everyone wanted to be her friend. Paula loved Jill, too, and wished she could be more like her.

"Don't let them bully you guys," Jill typed to Kathy in Memphis.

"The community garden has a lease," Kathy wrote back. "We're not giving up without a fight."

"Good!" Jill typed. Jill Carlson always used a lot of exclamation points. "We had to fight for ours exactly the same way as GrowMemphis is doing!"

"Thanks, Jill. Listen, I gotta run and pick up my daughter."

"Okay, keep me posted!"

With Kathy gone, Paula tried to hold on to the waking dream of Jill Carlson, but she wafted away. Her eyes drifted to the remnants of the smoothie beside her bed. Suddenly annoyed, she picked up the filmy glass and headed for the kitchen, but the bees in her chest would not settle again. Their insistent vibrations took her back to the living room window, where she swept the curtain aside only enough to achieve a narrow view of the commotion across the street.

Two massive rectangles on wheels were parked at the curb of the five-bedroom English Tudor home, purchased for a rumored seven-and-a-half million dollars. There were four workers that Paula could see, unloading boxes big and small, bubble-wrapped tables, chairs, sofas, bureaus, and what looked to be a dog house designed to resemble Hogwarts. Up and down the ramps they moved, unloading more and more items. And then a lone figure off to the side of the house caught her eye and, for a moment, she held her breath as he stepped from the open garage to survey the movers with a weary expression, as if wishing them done and gone.

Seeing Anthony gave Paula no surge of anxiety. Her heart did not race, her palms did not sweat. In fact, seeing him *calmed* her—as though the reality of him was easier to bear than the thought of him. He wore Levis and had on a tight blue polo shirt. In the morning light, his close-cropped Afro glistened, the slight greying of his hair set off by the darkness of his skin. His lean, muscular arms hung at his sides, a coffee mug that was evidently close to empty held loosely in his right hand. His eyes moved impatiently from one corner of the yard to the other, from one truck to the other, darting from worker to worker.

"Anthony," she whispered, as if saying his name aloud cemented him in place.

And then she gasped, her heartbeat once again a drum pounding a quickened beat, as a woman moved across the lawn to stand next to Anthony. Paula tried to swallow, but her throat had been plugged. No air escaped her constricting lungs. Her soft blue eyes welled with tears, blurring her vision as she studied the woman as though she were a hologram, a trick of refracted light.

But no, she was real. She was standing there.

The glass slipped from Paula's shaking hand and exploded on the hardwood floor between her bare feet. But she did not move at all—did not even flinch.

The woman standing next to Anthony was her. She, herself, Paula Hickman, wife of Alan Hickman—every blonde hair upon her head, every freckle in its proper place, every length of bone and bend of flesh her own—leaned close to kiss the cheek of Anthony Mills, the man she had loved all those years before, before the madness had driven them apart.

Paula's lips quivered as she watched, as though she felt the kiss through the tears dropping into her mouth. A tremor ran the length of her body, but she could not look away.

She had the impulse to run, to bolt to safety. But there was no place to hide from what she saw before her. There was no doubt.

She was watching herself move in across the street.

CHAPTER TWO

Paula's mouth hung open, as if lamenting the death of her sanity. Wendy sat beside her on the back porch, holding her hand, their chairs pulled so close together that their knees touched. Paula did not look at her; the perpetual frown on Wendy's face only made the situation more unbearable.

"It's going to be fine," Wendy said, squeezing Paula's hand tighter, working hard to ground her. "There has to be an explanation for what you think you saw."

"I don't *think* I saw her," Paula said, still shaking with adrenaline. "I definitely saw her."

"But you've been so overwhelmed lately, maybe you've—"

"I haven't been overwhelmed," Paula said, pulling her hand free. "I've been fucking *underwhelmed*, if anything." She was on her feet, taking a few steps toward the pool, before she spun back around. "And please stop looking at me like that."

"Looking at you like what?"

"Like you're analyzing me."

"I'm not analyzing you," Wendy insisted. "I'm worried about you."

Despite Wendy's penchant for the dramatic, Paula could not fault her. The fact was, Paula was pretty damned worried about herself too. Ever since stumbling away from the front window hours earlier, in a narrowing haze of hyperventilation upon seeing herself with Anthony, she felt like the physical embodiment of a scream.

She looked down at the faint, white scars across her wrists. "I know what I sound like, Wendy," she said. "And I know what people say about me."

"Oh, to hell with people. I'll always protect you. You know that."

Paula looked up sharply. "Protect me from myself, you mean?"

"No, that's not what I mean."

"I'm not crazy."

"No," Wendy said. "I don't believe you are."

Paula's throat ached from the strain of tamping down her emotions. "It was me," she insisted. "Everything about her. *Everything.*"

Wendy considered her. "I'll do whatever I can to help you understand what's happening."

Paula turned to face her sister-in-law. "Then go across the street and see for yourself," she said, "and then come back and tell me that I'm perfectly sane."

But Wendy did not want to leave Paula alone with her delusions. Instead she called Alan's cell.

"You need to come home," she said, leaving a message. "Nobody's hurt," she added quickly, sounding no less emotional, "but there's been an issue with Paula and she's very upset. Call me right away. I'm going to stay with her, but I'm not sure how to handle all this."

Alan checked his messages after his last student conference of the morning, then immediately called his sister. "What's

Paula so upset over?" he asked, his clipped voice sounding more annoyed than concerned as he walked from his office on the second floor of Bunche Hall at UCLA, heading downstairs for his first of two classes that day.

Wendy stepped from Paula's bedroom, where she'd been dutifully sitting beside Paula's bed. "She's had some sort of… mental aberration, or something," she whispered into the phone.

"What the hell does that mean?"

Wendy relayed as best she could Paula's fantastical story concerning the physical appearance of Anthony Mills's wife. When she finished, Alan let out a sound that landed somewhere between a laugh and groan, as though the whole thing were so bizarre it was difficult to take seriously. "I don't know what to tell you," he said. "She's very stressed out about Anthony moving here, and she's been slipping back emotionally lately. I'm sure that has something to do with it."

"I agree. But this isn't just stress. It seems very real to her."

"I hope you haven't been winding her up, Wendy."

"I've been trying to keep her calm!" Wendy's voice was shrill in her own defense. "She asked me to go over and see the woman for myself, but I'm afraid to leave her alone."

"Okay, please, let's not turn the drama up to eleven on this. Where is she now?"

"She's in bed—she's been in bed, not saying anything at all for the past hour. I'm not being dramatic, Alan. I think she's having a serious problem here."

Alan sighed heavily into the phone and Wendy allowed him the time to think. "I'll have to cancel my classes," he said at last. "I'll be there as soon as I can."

Less than an hour later, Alan stood in the doorway of his

wife's bedroom. Paula lay on her side atop the unmade bed, her eyes closed. He had certainly been through this before, the cocooning of his wife in a sheath of silence. It was all so familiar, so dispiriting. Alan had long accepted that while each cocooning would eventually come to an end, she would not emerge transformed, full of new color. She would be the same old Paula. She lived life on a seesaw—up and down—each ascent into happiness the result of some new preoccupation (a bakery!), and each descent into the shadowlands of disconnection the result of a fatiguing loss of interest. He did not try to wake her.

"You can go home, Wendy," Alan said, returning to his sister in the living room, where she stood, peering through the window at the now-quiet house across the street.

"What did she say?" Wendy asked.

"She didn't say anything. She's asleep."

"I'm sure she's not sleeping."

"Then she's pretending and I'm gonna let her keep right on pretending until she's ready to talk. Now, I appreciate you taking care of her, but I'll take it from here."

Wendy pointed at the window. "You should go over there and say hello to Anthony. I think if you meet his wife and can tell Paula that she was mistaken, it'll help calm her down."

"You keep saying she has to calm down, but she's pretty fucking calm in there."

"Please don't swear at me."

"I didn't swear at *you*. I'm frustrated, all right? Will you let me have that, at least? Canceling class is not something I like to do, and I'm still not convinced it was necessary."

"I'm sorry, but she was—"

"Again, I'm not blaming *you*. I'm not blaming anyone. Let's let her rest for a while and then we can assess what's actually happening here."

"What about going over to say hello to Anthony?"

"I'll handle it."

"I mean, if you could see his wife before you talk with Paula it would—"

"I said, I've got it."

There were a few more back and forths over how to rightly handle the situation before Alan was able to convince his big sister that he had it all under control. She left him with a stabbing kiss on the cheek. Alan watched her through the front window as she crossed to her parked Mazda with the faded "Heal The Bay" sticker on the bumper. She paused at the driver's-side door, key in hand, and looked again at the English Tudor across the street.

"Keep going," Alan whispered.

But Wendy tucked the keys into her purse, turned and strode across the street.

"Goddammit," Alan huffed, but he was helpless to do anything more than that.

He'd spent his entire childhood learning over and over again that when something stuck in his sister's mind, it was impossible to dislodge. So he watched with a familiar annoyance as Wendy walked to the front door of Anthony's new home and rang the bell. As if sensing her brother's disapproving stare, she looked briefly back toward him, but her expression was impossible to read before the door swung open and she turned back. Blocked by his sister's larger frame, Alan could not see anything more than the edge of a woman's shoulder and a brief glimpse of blonde hair in the doorway as Wendy introduced herself. And then the woman stepped aside, and Anthony stepped from inside the house, giving Wendy a hug.

It'd been years since Wendy had last seen Anthony, and it couldn't have been more than once or twice that they'd ever shared each other's company. Alan wondered what the hell she could be saying to him as they chatted on the porch. Wendy gestured toward the house across the street and Anthony's stare followed suit, causing Alan to duck back from the window. He hated that she had made him feel like a spying child. Resigned to the notion of joining his overbearing sister outside, of acknowledging his own desire to avoid Anthony's arrival, Alan stepped back into the glare of the window. But he was too late to join in, as the party had already ended. Wendy was walking back to her car, the porch across the street empty, the front door closed.

Wendy pursed her lips and shook her head when she saw her little brother in the window, watching her. She climbed inside her car and turned over the motor. A second later the phone in Alan's pocket rang. "Well?" he said, answering.

"I told them Paula had the flu, so she couldn't come over to greet them, but that when you're all done playing hide and seek, you both look forward to getting together."

He ignored her taunt. "And his wife?"

"Hannah," Wendy said, her car pulling from the curb. "There's definitely a similarity—the blonde hair, the general body type—but that's all. I'm telling you, Alan, Paula's having a serious problem that needs to be addressed."

Alan did not argue her assessment as he watched his sister's car disappear up the street.

*

"You need to put something in your stomach," Alan said the following morning, standing by Paula's bed, holding another smoothie.

Paula followed his movements beneath heavy eyelids as he gently placed the glass on the table beside her. *Poor Alan*, she thought, *doing all he can to keep the rickety construction of our shared life from falling apart completely.* Everything, it seemed, was her fault. Paula's guilt was like a vital organ deep inside her, a second heart pumping a steady pulse of self-loathing.

"Have you taken something?" Alan asked. "Any of my Ambien?"

It was, all things considered, an absurd consideration— even in light of the fact that she hadn't left her bed in nearly twenty-four hours. Despite the unrelenting grip of her depression, Paula had never taken—had adamantly refused to take—any medication at all.

"No," she said, rolling away to face the opposite wall.

Her eyes remained open until she heard him quietly close the door when he left.

When Alan returned an hour later, the untouched smoothie had congealed into a thickened mass, filling the bedroom with the sour scent of slow decomposition.

"My sister keeps calling," he said, his annoyance brimming with full force. "She's very worried about you."

"My phone died," Paula mumbled, not looking at him as she pushed matted hair from her forehead.

"It smells like more than your phone died in here."

Paula's heart fluttered. "I'm sorry," she said.

"I know. So, are you going to get up today? I have to go to class—I can't cancel again."

The reality was that they'd slept in separate bedrooms for

the past six months and had not been intimate for nearly a year. She was quite used to being alone.

"There's no reason for you to miss your class," she said.

Alan said nothing further as he collected the untouched drink and left. He was in the kitchen, keys in hand, satchel draped over his shoulder, when Paula's voice turned him around.

"Why does the woman across the street look exactly like me," she said. "Yet somehow everyone else is convinced that she doesn't?"

"I'm not sure what you're expecting from me," he said. "I can't tell you something that I don't—she was out there this morning, Paula, and she's not—"

"I saw her!" Paula shouted. "I *saw* her!"

The refrigerator hummed and a few cubes dropped into the ice maker's bucket, breaking the silence between them.

"You're confused," Alan said.

Paula's face was pale, her eyes pink with exhaustion. "I'm confused by *why* this is happening, not whether it is."

It was all tied together, that much Paula had determined over her long, sleepless night. She wanted desperately to pour everything out, to let the demons free, but the spigot was rusted shut. It was as though Alan had not married the true Paula, but a pretend version, the one she had created in order to be happy. He had no experience with the real her, the one who had once loved Anthony Mills, the Paula who had caused so much damage in so many lives. Perhaps he would understand if she explained it that way. He, too, was living multiple lives, after all. One as the happily married man he presented to friends, another as the lonely husband behind closed doors, and yet a third as the charming professor to easily impressed freshmen. It's what everyone does, isn't it? Nobody presents their true self to the world; the only variation is the degree of difference between their various personas. Everyone's made up. To be self-invented is to be human.

"Paula? Are you still with me?"

"I need to talk with somebody," she said, leaning her hands on the center island, lost on an island of her own. "A doctor."

Alan stared at her. After years of refusing therapy, the notion of his wife voluntarily seeking a doctor was almost as preposterous as the idea of an identical version of her living across the street. "Was that an admission?" he asked. "Or an actual request?"

"Don't do that! Don't be flippant!"

Alan remained stoic. "If you'd like to see a doctor, of course I support that," he said. "It was just a little surprising to hear you suggest it, considering your prior stance on the matter."

She stood there, shaking. "I'm scared, Alan," she said, as a tear slid down her cheek.

Alan's expression softened as he moved around the island between them and hugged her tight. "It's going to be okay," he whispered. "We're gonna figure this out, I promise."

CHAPTER THREE

Paula inhaled deeply from her diaphragm. Stomach out on the slow intake, hold for the count of four, stomach in on the slow exhale through the mouth. In. Out. In. Out. "Conscious breathing," it was called, designed to keep the adrenaline level low and to calm nervous energy. Her breath, however, continued to shudder through her chest as she watched herself drive away.

Paula pulled her Lexus from the curb, three houses down from Anthony's, and followed a safe distance behind.

Anthony and Hannah were followers of schedules. Each of the past three days, Paula had watched them. Anthony left for work at seven-forty-five, and exactly thirty minutes later, Hannah backed her Audi SUV from the garage with their little boy in the backseat. This day was no different, save for the fact that today Paula was shadowing her.

Breathe.

After heading south, the Audi turned left onto Montana Avenue at Seventh Street and passed The Little Delicious. Paula's eyes came off Hannah's car as she slowed to look through the front window of the bakery. It was like viewing old home movies; the life going on inside The Little Delicious now another life that was both familiar and foreign.

A few cars filled in the spaces between Paula and the Audi, but she was in no danger of losing them. The Audi pulled to the curb a few blocks later in front of The Growing Child preschool. There were two spaces held open by a volunteering mother, who greeted the morning arrivals in a bright-yellow crossing-guard vest, flashing a smile full of white teeth. Paula had to continue on, stopping a half-block away, double parked. A passing car gave an irritated honk of disapproval, but Paula barely noticed. She looked back over her right shoulder and watched herself get out of the Audi to give the little boy a hug goodbye.

Breathe.

Paula and Alan had no children. Years ago she had longed for a child, but it had never happened, despite their often belabored efforts. "Probably for the best," the rationalization had gone. Alan had never been sure about being a father, and Paula was well aware of her own limitations. Anthony Mills, though, was different; he had always wanted kids.

He'd once told Paula that his own father had disappeared when his little brother Darius came along, claiming that their mother had fucked some guy she worked with at Ralph's supermarket and that he had no intention of raising some kid who wasn't his own blood. Anthony's mother had screamed and cried, insisting that she hadn't been with anybody else—not ever, in fact—but she got only a busted lip and swollen cheek in response.

"Poor black men were left behind by this country a long time ago," Anthony had told her. "And now too many of them are doing the same damn thing to the generations they created to take their place. It's like they've forgotten who they truly are."

"What do you mean, who they truly are?" she had asked, looking into his dark eyes as they'd lain in bed in Anthony's apartment near People's Park, a few blocks off the Berkley campus.

Anthony's chest rose and fell under the weight of her resting hand. "It doesn't matter. Someday I'm gonna have a house full of kids and they're never gonna forget."

Another horn blared its displeasure at Paula's double-parked Lexus, as the little boy of Anthony's dreams disappeared behind the wooden gate of The Growing Child.

That would be my son. He would look like that.

Paula continued to stare, the world momentarily muted, as her identical opposite climbed back into her Audi and drove away. This time, she did not follow. Her hands shook uncontrollably, making it impossible to hold the wheel. Another car horn blared, then another. With a darting glance into the rearview mirror, Paula shook free from her stupor and pulled forward. She did not return home, though. She intended to, and didn't even realize that she wasn't until she was halfway to Venice, where Anthony was already toiling away at RuskTech, living the life she might have shared.

*

It was close to eleven when Alan returned home from class that night, and he went, as he always did lately, straight to his room. Despite all the internal work she'd done over the hours he'd been gone, it took another half-hour for Paula to build her nerve and follow him upstairs. She stood at her husband's closed bedroom door, settling herself before softly knocking.

"Come in," Alan's tired voice came from the other side.

Paula gripped the doorknob and slowly entered. Her skin

was pickled with goose flesh as her robe hung open, revealing her breasts. The belt was barely tight enough to keep the robe from falling completely open and revealing the rest of her naked body.

Alan's shocked expression perfectly reflected the drama of the moment. He had finished his nightly rituals and was stripped down to his boxers, ready to lie down and read before drifting off to sleep. "What's this?" he asked.

Paula wasn't sure, exactly. The idea of coming to him had been almost reflexive, an instinctive response to an email Anthony had sent, wishing a speedy recovery from the flu. "If you're up to it," he'd written, "how about dinner on Saturday?"

Alan had not moved from his position next to the bed, his reading glasses still clutched in his hand. "I'm not sure this is a good idea," he said.

She stepped closer. "Neither am I, but let's do it anyway."

Their sex life had always been passionate, at least for the first half of their marriage. Right from the start, they'd been enticingly free with each other. Paula was thirty and Alan thirty-four when they met on a blind date at Finn McCool's Bar on Main Street in Santa Monica, both already experienced enough to have no interest in feigning demureness. The sex was always mutually expressive, intense. Paula had once confided to an envious friend, "Even when we make love, we still fuck each other. It's fantastic."

But now, as Paula stood exposed in front of her uncertain husband, it was as though they had no idea how to join together. They were once again strangers.

"Please, Alan," she said, shivering. "Don't leave me standing here like this."

She stepped forward and pressed her breasts against his naked torso.

"Ten months," Alan said as Paula pulled her robe fully open, the patch of pubic hair above her vagina tickling his upper thigh.

"I'm sorry." She touched her nose to his neck.

"There's that guilt again."

"Touch me," she said.

He placed his glasses on the bedside table and ran his fingertips down her pale shoulders. But as the robe slipped to the floor and his hands dropped to her back and then down to the soft flesh of her ass, it was Anthony Mills's touch that Paula felt. The sensation moved through her like warm water, slippery and soothing. She squeezed the receding form of her husband and tilted her head, allowing his lips to find her chest, all the while imagining he could hear the beat of her guilty heart, could sense her warming to the radiance of another man.

They fell onto the bed, Alan's hands now more insistent, his movements more aggressive. His body was heavy on hers, a weight she felt acutely, as though she were sinking to the bottom of a pool. She drifted deeper. The pressure around her increased, further isolating her. The more probing her husband became, the less of a connection Paula felt. And with each emphatic thrust of his hips, Alan seemed to be making the same point. His breath, minty with toothpaste, folded against her neck as he let himself go. But Paula could not. She stared at the ceiling, separate from the body she so freely gave away.

Her hands came off of her husband's back and hovered in the air as though reaching for something, something she had lost twenty-five years ago as a freshman at Berkeley—once she met her new roommate and everything turned to shit.

CHAPTER FOUR

IT WOULD BE testified by those freshmen girls who lived in the Unit 2 dormitory housing complex at Cal Berkley that the two roommates were an odd fit. But Allyson Clemens claimed it was never anything personal—it was merely that she immediately loathed (that was her word for it) everything her new roommate *represented*.

When asked by one of the detectives on the case to be more specific, Allyson said, "Her hair, for starters. I detested her hair. Its very blondness was bad enough, but that stupid bob haircut made me want to shave it off in her sleep. She probably thought it was a perfect match for her Ralph Lauren luggage. You can add that to your notes: I hated her Ralph Lauren luggage. Jesus, she was going to college, not taking a cruise on her father's yacht. Rich kids are always so entitled, you know?" Allyson shifted in the chair and furrowed her brow. "Look, there are some personality problems between us, that's it. I mean, like I said, her weird mood swings cause some issues. I tried my best to get to know her, to help her unclench a little bit, you know? But it never worked out. You mind if I smoke?"

"It's a small room," the detective said.

"It's a small cigarette," Allyson countered, and then shrugged her indifference.

"I'd like to clarify that you two got along for the most part, at first?" the detective asked.

"At first."

"But it's safe to say that right from the beginning, she liked you more than you liked her?"

Allyson's mouth twisted into a sideways smile. "Yes, that's safe to say."

*

Allyson Clemens was everything Paula was not. Her hair wasn't blonde, for starters. It was jet black, with wide streaks in places that were a deep blue, with purple highlights on the ends. While Paula wore a hair clip to keep her short bangs from falling across her forehead (where they invariably got greasier and greasier as the day wore on), Allyson had shaved the left side of her head to a peach-fuzz closeness. She had two piercings on her right eyebrow. It was obvious why Allyson would hate everything about her—from her red hair clip and moisturized skin, to her beige chino pants and ballet flats. But that was okay, because Berkeley was a new place, a new experience. Facing new challenges head on, with confidence, was why she'd applied in the first place.

That first night in the dorm, as the new roommates were falling asleep, both of them drunk, Allyson laughed. Her cackling voice cut through the dark room like a flash of lightning. "You're so lucky I was there," she said. "That guy was trying so hard to fuck you!" She raised herself onto her elbow and peered through the darkness. "You do realize if it weren't for me, you'd totally be peeing on a pregnancy stick tomorrow morning, right?"

Her question was met with a long silence, followed by a soft mewling of tears.

"Are you crying? Jesus, nothing happened, you're fine. He was an asshole, but you're still pure as fucking snow, so stop worrying about it. No little bunny rabbits died. The bunnies are still hopping!" She laughed into the darkness. "Welcome to college," she sighed, turning onto her side. "I hope you didn't forget to pack plenty of little bunnies."

*

"Is that why you nicknamed her Bunny?" the detective asked.

"That and the aforementioned blonde hair," Allyson said.

The detective flipped another page of his notepad and looked at her over the top of his reading glasses. "So, other than that first night, were there any other similar experiences that had a different outcome?"

"Wow! Is that, like, some weirdly polite cop way of asking me if Bunny was ever raped?"

The detective leaned forward in his metal chair, which creaked slightly. "Did she ever share any other experiences with you?"

"No. No other *experiences* that I'm aware of. That should go in the college catalogues. *Come for the education…stay for the rapes.* What a fucking culture we live in. Men suck."

"Some do, yes."

"Present company excluded, I'm sure."

The detective grinned without showing his teeth. "Okay," he said, crossing his arms against his barrel chest. "Let's talk about Anthony Mills. What's your impression of him?"

Allyson narrowed her eyes to petulant slits. "Considering I've been sleeping with him for the last few months, I'd say it's pretty positive."

"Has your relationship with Anthony caused any problems?"

"I take it you mean with Bunny? Yes, obviously. But, the problems are only on her end—her fault, I mean. She's had a thing for Anthony since they first met. I'm guessing it's because it would make her happy to piss off her family by being with a black guy."

"You mean sexually?"

"As long as they thought so, I'm sure that'd be good enough."

"Did she show any signs of aggression toward Anthony, prior to the events of last night?"

"It's not like I'm with her all the time. Why don't you ask her?"

"We're asking a lot of people, including Anthony, but right now I'm asking you."

Allyson rolled her eyes. "She can be a little dramatic, obviously. She hasn't been in a stable state of mind these past few months."

The detective nodded his understanding. "She's been partying a bit."

"That's an understatement."

"You two party together?" he asked.

Allyson fidgeted in her chair and absently rubbed the piercing in her brow, trying to figure out how honest she should be. "A little, yeah. She wasn't into it at first, but she sure as hell took to it pretty quick."

"What sort of drugs you guys do together?"

There was a slight hitch in Allyson's cool demeanor. "A little weed."

"Nothing stronger?"

"I mean, we did coke once, but she didn't like it. Neither did I, by the way. At most, maybe we sometimes like to parachute a little Molly. She said it helps with her social anxiety."

"Where did she get the drugs?"

"I'm sure as hell not her drug dealer, if that's what you're getting at. I told her to chill with all that shit. If I had realized what an obsessive personality she had, I never would have done anything with her."

"What about Anthony? Did he help her get the drugs?"

Allyson stared hard at the detective. "I'm beginning to feel uncomfortable with this. Maybe I should shut up and think about calling a lawyer."

The detective spread his hands wide, like a magician indicating he had nothing up his sleeve. "That's entirely up to you. But it would help everyone involved, yourself included, if you told me a little bit about Anthony and his relationship with your roommate."

Allyson rolled her eyes again. "Anthony isn't into Bunny at all. He tolerates her, that's all, because he's nice. And he's certainly never given her any drugs. He doesn't party, he barely even drinks. He's very focused on his grades, I mean, intensely, you know?"

"Is that how you would describe him?" the detective said. "Intense?"

"God, you are really trying to fuck with the black guy, aren't you? Everything's always gotta be his fault? No, I wouldn't describe him as intense. In fact, I already described him as being *nice*, if you remember. If I'd describe anybody as *intense*, it would be Bunny."

"What about Anthony's brother? How would you describe him?"

"Moving on to the next black dude, huh?" She continued to rub the short metal bar slicing through her brow. "I haven't spent enough time with him to have an opinion."

The detective took off his reading glasses and placed them on the table. "Okay," he nodded. "Take me through what happened last night, after you left the party."

*

Allyson and Anthony had walked down Telegraph Avenue, returning to campus amid a jostling stream of students in various states of drunkenness. Anthony clutched a plastic bag of ice to his cheek as water dripped down his arm, wetting the rolled-up sleeve of his crisp white shirt. His cheek sufficiently numbed, he moved the ice bag to the scratches along his jawline and neck.

"Darius is behind us," Allyson said, without glancing back.

"Is she with him?" Anthony asked, still seething.

"I don't think so, I didn't see her."

Anthony stopped abruptly, causing the flow of students behind them to collide and falter before stepping around. A few disjointed voices laughed and a red-eyed sophomore in a faded San Francisco 49ers t-shirt made a snide comment about Anthony's face being "jacked up." Anthony immediately flung the bag of ice at the kid, striking him in the back of his head.

"What the fuck's your problem?" the kid said, spinning around.

"My problem is you running your mouth," Anthony yelled.

"Yeah?" the kid challenged him. "What you gonna do?"

Anthony, who was four inches taller and a good thirty pounds heavier than the unsteady sophomore, took a step forward and Allyson grabbed his arm.

"Stop pulling on me!" he barked at her, yanking himself free as Allyson recoiled. By the time Anthony turned back, the kid in the t-shirt was gone, swallowed up by the meandering throng. The sting around the puffy edges of the fingernail scratches on Anthony's face reasserted itself, as if a row of fire ants were crawling down from his hairline, across his cheek and down his neck. "Dammit," he muttered, pressing his fingers lightly against his skin.

"Yo, Anthony," came his younger brother's voice behind them. "Why you trippin'?"

"This ain't your business," Anthony said, turning toward his brother as the flow of students moved around them, now giving him a wide berth.

"I ain't even talkin' about that drunk-ass motherfucker," Darius said. "I mean with Bunny. You didn't need to be yellin' at her like that."

Anthony stepped close to tower over his brother. "Oh, you got advice for me now?"

"I'm just sayin' you scared the shit out of her. That's why she did you like that."

Anthony grabbed his brother by the armpit and dragged him to the edge of the sidewalk, toward the front gate of an apartment building. "What the hell you doin'?" Anthony said, easily slipping back into the cadence of the East Oakland neighborhood where he'd grown up, and where his younger brother still lived with their mother and sister. "You actin' like a punk."

"Man, fuck you," Darius said.

Anthony grabbed his brother's throat. "You shouldn't even be here, D. And you sure as hell shouldn't be playin' with that fucked-up white girl."

"Oh, the white women only for you, huh?" Darius said,

jerking his head to the side, not willing to show any more aggression toward his brother than that.

Anthony, a familiar guilt rising up, loosened his hand but kept his fingers on his brother's neck. Acutely aware of the passing students, who were slowing down to get an earful of the developing drama, Anthony leaned close and lowered his voice. "You have no idea what's up. I got mad like I did because after I rejected her she accused me of raping her."

"Bullshit," Darius said, glancing sideways at the flow of white faces beside them.

"You gonna say I'm lying now? Bitch is crazy. Is that what you wanna hear me say? Is that the only way my words will finally get through to you? She's fucking crazy. And what do you think is gonna happen when her rich-ass family tries to find out who's been giving her all those fuckin' drugs? Who you think they're gonna look at? Your ass'll be back behind bars before you can take a goddamn breath. And this time it won't be juvie, D. You eighteen now, and they don't play. Not with black men accused of raping white women."

Anthony stared hard at his little brother, as if he could sear the warning into his brain, despite Darius's history of self-destructive defiance.

"She really said that?" Allyson said, stepping close.

Anthony kept his eyes on his brother. "Yeah, she really said that."

*

The detective studied Allyson a moment. "You never heard her say that before? She never mentioned anything about Anthony raping her?"

Allyson shook her head. "I would have known, I swear to God."

The detective nodded. "Okay, so, after their confrontation, did you take Darius home with Anthony?"

"No," Allyson said. "Anthony drove him alone. He said it wasn't a good idea for me to go. Oakland is kind of rough, I guess. And his family isn't all that welcoming to me, so…"

"Why didn't you go back to the dorm?"

"Seriously? I wasn't particularly interested in sleeping in the same room as Bunny. Anthony dropped me off at his apartment, told me to wait for him."

"How long was it before he came home?"

"An hour, I guess. I don't know, I fell asleep. Look, I can guarantee Anthony didn't rape anybody. Bunny is unstable, right? Let me talk to her. I can straighten this whole thing out."

The detective leaned back in his seat and again crossed his arms. He looked briefly at the rectangular mirror along the far wall and then sighed. "Your roommate is dead," he said, without emotion. "Her body was found on the sidewalk a few blocks from your dorm room. Somehow she came off the roof of a ten-story apartment building."

Allyson's mouth hung open. "That can't be true."

"I'm afraid it is. And we're trying to figure out how it happened." The detective reached along the table beside them and opened a manila folder. "But the more we look into it, the more questions we have. For instance, why did it take so long for Anthony to get back to his apartment after he took Darius home?" He took a piece of paper from the folder and slid it over to her. "We're also curious," he said, his eyes steadily on her, "why you insist on presenting yourself as Allyson Clemens, when your name is actually Paula Sullivan?"

The hard-exterior she had invented for herself softened in the ensuing silence. The detective waited, watching intently as the indifferent persona she had worked so hard to sustain slowly dissolved and the chimera of Allyson Clemens faded, leaving only Paula as she truly was.

Finally, Paula looked at the detective through her own eyes. "Bunny's really dead?" was all she said, as a tear dropped down her cheek.

CHAPTER FIVE

IT HAD BEEN two days since Paula had surprised Alan in his bedroom, and neither had fully addressed the awkwardness the unexpected sex had caused. The act had been just that, an act—something performed by rote muscle memory rather than with true passion. It had not been a breakthrough of emotion, but an unsettling reminder of how far apart they truly were. They had lain together until drifting off to sleep, but when Alan woke in the morning, Paula was back in her own room.

And now they sat beside each other on the long white couch in their living room, trying to pretend they were comfortable. Alan waited as Paula's eyes traced the finely printed notes filling the white space under each name, written with exacting detail in Alan's steady hand. Paper-clipped to the edge of the sheet were five business cards, each one a grenade pin waiting to be pulled. Her mouth was dry as she read the names and qualifications of the doctors he had found.

Paula licked her cracked lips. "I can't," she said softly.

"You can't what?"

"I can't see a man, a male doctor. I have to be comfortable and—"

"There are two women on that list," Alan pointed out.

Paula breathed deeply, tried to feign enthusiasm, but the plug had been pulled, draining the necessary energy. "Their offices are in hospitals."

Alan took the list and put it on the coffee table. "Yes, good hospitals," he said. "Very good, in fact. All these doctors came highly recommended. If you'd consider the—"

But he held the rest of his thought in his mouth when Paula turned her eyes up to him; they were clouded with a thickening mist of anxiety.

"I can't," she said again.

Alan did not argue. At the beginning of their relationship, when things had first started getting serious and the faint white scars across Paula's wrists could no longer go politely unmentioned, Alan had learned of her stay at the Newberry Mental Health Institute in Marin County—though the details (the ones Paula was willing to share, anyway) were rarely touched upon. He knew only that she'd been a patient at Newberry, following her freshman year at Berkeley, when she finally passed over the event-horizon of her depression and was sucked into an emotional black hole so dense it was a small miracle she'd escaped at all.

He had never questioned her, had never pressed for information that she was unwilling to share. He knew nothing of Bunny and Allyson, just as he knew nothing of Jill Carlson, who lived entirely in Paula's mind and online. And he certainly knew nothing of the profound love and profound pain she and Anthony had shared so long ago.

Paula had never mentioned to anyone that during the first few months of forced committal to Newberry, cut off from the outside world, she wondered if Anthony Mills's life had been destroyed as violently as Bunny's. In more unforgiving moments, when the meds had yet to numb her into submission, Paula imagined him in prison, convicted of rape—or worse, Bunny's murder. That's what people believed, after all—that Anthony had killed her.

In her isolation room, arms strapped to the bedrails, she'd picture Anthony's hands restrained, as hers were, only he would not be left alone. In her fevered imaginings she could not visualize the faces of the men administering their own brand of punishment. She saw only Anthony's face, strangely passive in its anguish, as he lost himself to the control of others. When the nightmarish images came to her, passing orderlies would glance through the window of her room and note how long she would thrash and scream before at last falling silent, exhausted.

It was eight months after the night Bunny died when Paula learned from Dr. Lawrence Stickley—the man who'd put her off male doctors forever—that all charges against Anthony had been dropped.

"Mr. Mills has moved on and resumed his education," Doctor Stickley said to her during therapy one day, almost as an afterthought. "But you are no more responsible for what happens to him moving forward than you are for the choices he made in the past. Can you see that? He's not taking on any responsibility for your well-being, so there's no reason for you to take any for his. Paula, are you listening? Are you paying attention?"

Paula's molasses gaze found Doctor Stickley and she nodded.

"Good. You're doing very well, Paula."

"You don't have to keep using my name," Paula said. "I know who I am."

"And Emily," he said. "Do you know who Emily is?"

Paula's stare remained steady. "Bunny," she said.

The doctor reminded her of Bunny's real name—Emily. Emily Jenkins. He never wanted to talk about Anthony; he always wanted to talk about Emily.

And now, looking at the list of doctors her husband had made, Paula shook off the memories of Newberry.

"Well, I'll keep looking," Alan said.

"No men," she said. "And no institutions."

"Okay." Alan was clearly trying to keep the process moving forward. "No institutions."

Paula leaned back, the chasm between her past and her present as wide as that between the idea of her marriage and its actual day-to-day reality. When she looked up, Alan was already on his feet, walking away.

*

It was almost five in the afternoon, about the time Alan typically left for UCLA and his Tuesday/Thursday class, when Paula was jolted upright by the sound of the doorbell. Her heart raced as she closed the lid of her laptop. For a moment she sat on the edge of the bed, motionless, listening. And then she eased her way to the bedroom door, where she gently pulled it open, only a crack. At once, the newly arrived voices mixed with the rush of blood pounding in her ears. Which of her two hearts was beating louder, her physical one or the phantom one, full of guilt?

She could not, at first, make out any of the words coming from the foyer as they intermingled with a halting, polite awkwardness. But there was no doubt whose voices they were. The realization that Anthony and Hannah were inside her home instantly overtaxed her endocrine system, turning her hands to ice. Her stomach dropped and she stifled the impulse to turn and hide. No. She could not hide forever. It was time to confront the inevitable. She inched her way through the door and walked slowly down the hallway, her breath hiccuping in her throat.

"The house is still a bit of a mess though," she heard Anthony say. "We're trying to get ourselves organized. Going through everything reminds me of that George Carlin bit about their stuff being shit and my shit being stuff. Pardon my language."

"How's Alex adjusting?" Alan asked. "I look forward to meeting him too."

"We would have brought him," Hannah Mills said, "but we hired a new nanny today and they're down at the beach, bonding, hopefully. The move's been hard on him."

Hearing Hannah's voice momentarily stopped Paula's advance.

"He'll be fine," Anthony said in a humorous, though dismissive tone. "When you're five, all it takes to make new friends is a shared graham cracker."

Alan and Anthony laughed, but Paula noticed that Hannah did not.

Relax. Breathe.

"There she is!" Anthony said, as Paula stepped around the corner.

Paula could not quite force a smile as she stared at her mirror image, standing beside Anthony—the strawberry blonde hair, the wide blue eyes, the narrow nose, and the chin that sloped to a point around a faint hint of a cleft that was undoubtedly more pronounced in a certain light.

"You're up!" Alan said, too jovially playing his role as happy husband.

"Literally, if not figuratively," Paula said, playing her role as well.

"I'm sorry to hear you've been so sick," Anthony said, stepping toward her.

Paula floated above the scene, unable to fully connect to what was happening, only landing in her body when Anthony's arms wrapped around her. She barely had time to react to the warm embrace before he pulled back to get a better look at her.

"Risking my health with the hug," Anthony said with a grin.

"No, I'm sure I'm fine. You're safe."

"Well, you look great, Paula." Anthony continued to smile.

"You, too." She forced herself to turn to Hannah. "And it's nice to finally get to meet you, Hannah. I don't want to put both of you at risk, so I'll just give you a little wave for now."

"I appreciate it," Hannah said, extending her hand for a delicate pat on Paula's arm.

She tried not to flinch when Hannah's flesh touched hers. It was like looking into a funhouse mirror. "Welcome to the neighborhood," she said.

"Thank you," Hannah said. "It's great to finally put a face to the name."

"I was just thinking the same thing," said Alan, pointedly studying his wife's reaction as she continued to stare at Hannah. "You've been doing some painting?" he quickly asked, drawing their attention to the blue paint staining Hannah's fingers.

Hannah rubbed the tips of her fingers along her palm. "I have. Not walls though. I'm using the guest house out back as an art studio."

"Work avoidance at its best," Anthony joked.

"You're an artist?" Alan asked. He placed his hand on the

base of Paula's back, breaking her trance before her stare burned a hole through Hannah's face.

"No, still just a lawyer. At least I think I am. I was, anyway."

"What she means by that is that she hated it," Anthony said. "That's actually what precipitated the move. When the opportunity at RuskTech came up we figured it was a good time to make some changes—now she'll have the opportunity to reinvent herself."

"That's great," Alan smiled helpfully, once again glancing toward his wife to see how she was holding up.

Paula remained awkwardly silent, breathing through a slightly open mouth. Tiny beads of perspiration collected at her hairline. Hannah asked a question about the street and Alan waxed on in his professorial way about how many of the homes in the neighborhood had been remodeled over the years. Gone were the three-bedroom, two-bath California cottages. Gone were the elderly natives that reflected the simpler requirements of another era. The new homes were grander in scale and more prideful in taste, as were their new occupants.

Paula's focus returned when Hannah said, "Tech money. Same money that changed the analog vibes of San Francisco. I understand they're calling this area Silicon Beach now?"

"That's what they say." Alan shrugged. "Evidently they've been pushing out a lot of the smaller businesses, not to mention the smaller homes."

Hannah's darting smile returned. "It's a shame, but it's all about lines of code. And once those ones and zeroes break free from the computers, they're like invasive little bugs that swarm over the land, eating up all the crops."

"There is some ego-driven bullshit in tech, I will give her that," Anthony said.

"That's because they tend to believe theirs is the only industry that can truly change the world," Hannah said.

"I still maintain that technology is changing the world for the better," Anthony insisted, taking his wife's argument with good nature. "It's not everyone's desire to turn the populace into soulless drones addicted to social media."

The small patches of perspiration on Paula's hairline had migrated to the slope of her neck below her jawline.

"What exactly are you doing at RuskTech?" Alan asked.

"Applications for augmented reality, focusing primarily on the medical field. Think, like, what Iron Man sees when he's in the suit. Now, imagine a surgeon putting in contact lenses that are able to overlay an image onto a patient as he's operating. It's really exciting. The company was actually started by an ex-video-gamer from the Netherlands, if you can believe it."

Alan's eyes widened. "Sounds like you're going to, I hate to say it, change the world."

"And there it is." Hannah smiled.

They all shared a knowing chuckle, except for Paula, who had barely registered the conversation. For her it was so utterly surreal, standing there with Anthony and her identical self, like a familiar television show that had been badly dubbed with foreign actors, everything slightly out of time. The longer she was with Hannah, the more she felt she was being buried. She swallowed a hard knot of saliva and lowered her chin to her chest.

"You okay, Paula?" somebody asked, though she wasn't sure who. She looked up quickly and sucked air in through her nostrils, afraid she might faint.

"I think maybe she's not quite over her flu," Alan tried, reaching out to steady her.

"You do look a little pale," Hannah agreed.

You look fucking pale! You're seeing yourself, Goddammit! We're the same fucking person! What would happen if I cut you right now? Would I bleed, too?

Paula tried desperately to suppress the startling thought. But even as she fought against it, there came a flashing impulse from somewhere deep in her lizard brain, a burning urge to reach out and grab Hannah, to shake her until she saw what was so clear. She stepped back, away from Hannah and away from the impulse, nearly losing her footing. She pitched sideways and replanted her feet to keep from toppling over.

"Whoa," Anthony said, moving forward. "Maybe you should have a seat for a second."

Paula twitched away like a cat. "No, I'm fine. Just a little lightheaded," she insisted. "I'm so sorry."

Anthony's hands continued to hover around her, guarding against a sudden collapse. "No apology required."

"I am gonna go lie down, I think."

"Of course," Anthony said. "Of course."

Perhaps there were more concerned words of encouragement offered, but Paula heard nothing more as she moved back up the hallway. The bees had returned, filling her head with their vibrato buzzing. Moving quickly to her bathroom, her knees pressed to the floor and her stomach convulsed as she vomited into the toilet. Her throat stung from the bile that spewed sourly from her mouth. She spit and retched but gained nothing more from the involuntary effort. Tears fell down her face, wetting her lips. But she could not steady herself, could not ease the trembling.

The bathroom door opened and Alan stepped in, crouching behind her. "You okay?"

"Not at all," Paula said, spitting again into the toilet.

"What happened out there?"

"Are they still here?"

"No."

Paula eased back onto her knees and then slid sideways to lean against the cabinet under the sink. "I panicked. I had some bad thoughts, and they frightened me."

"What sort of bad thoughts?"

She stared at him like a frightened little girl, mouth open, unable to find her voice.

Alan took her wrists and turned her white scars upward. "These kind of thoughts?"

"That hurts," she said, yanking her arms free.

"What kind of bad thoughts, Paula?"

Her breath rose and fell. "Thoughts about Hannah."

Alan's face twisted in undisguised disgust. "This is all inside your head," he said.

"You have no idea what's going on inside my head!" she shouted.

Alan stood and raised his hand, palm facing down at his wife. "Yes, I do. I've done my research. You're severely depressed and it's causing a delusion. For whatever reason, you've become fixated on this woman. That's all that's happening here. What you're seeing is nothing but a symptom of a disease. She's not you. So whatever *bad thoughts* you're having, leave Hannah Mills out of it."

Paula's teeth clenched. "I'm afraid she's already in."

Alan didn't blink. "I'm pointing out the reality of your situation. Keep digging your way down this rabbit hole, and the only place it's gonna end is back in the mental ward."

A scream rose in Paula's throat as Alan exited the bathroom. By the time he closed the garage door a few minutes later, off to the freedom of his class, Paula was raging through her bedroom, sweeping the top of her bureau clean with one arm, tearing her bedclothes off the bed, and venting her fury on everything within reach.

CHAPTER SIX

OVER THE NEXT few days, time drifted by in silence. Each morning, Paula stayed in her room, pretending to sleep until Alan left the house. And each night he ate dinner alone in the stillness of their kitchen. When their paths threatened to cross, Alan retreated to the small music studio attached to the back of the pool house, where he banged on his drums, reliving his teenage rock-star fantasies.

But then a breakthrough arrived. At last, Alan's penchant for precise research paid off. And if Paula could follow through as she'd promised, this day offered the promise of a way back together.

"I can drive you," Alan said, when Paula came into the kitchen, already dressed, on the morning of her appointment.

"You have your faculty brunch," she said, eyeing the smoothie on the counter beside a row of vitamin bottles.

"I don't have to go."

Paula gave an appreciative smile. "I'll be fine. What's all this?"

Alan shook his head at the vitamin bottles. "Wendy's selling some nutrition supplement program, once more demonstrating her knack for wasting both her time and her friends' money.

I bought some to keep her from telling me anything more about it."

"It's intended for me, I take it?"

"She suggested you talk about it with the doctor today. In fact, she insists it will change your whole body chemistry. You should approach it as a life support system," she said.

"She thinks I'm on life support?"

Alan chuckled. "Life, comma, support system."

Paula opened one of the bottles, shook out a pill, and swallowed it with a sip of her smoothie. "I feel better already."

Alan looked seriously at her. "I really do hope so, Paula."

*

Paula walked up the tree-lined sidewalk. It was a Saturday, so it had taken only twenty-five minutes to make the drive from Santa Monica to Pasadena, and she had some time to kill. During the week, it could take as long as an hour and a half to traverse the same distance, a reality of life in Los Angeles that should have eliminated Dr. Claire Horst from consideration right out of the gate, along with the others Alan had researched. But for an initial meeting, the distance was not a deal-breaker. *Claire* (Paula already resisted the impulse to call her Doctor Horst) worked out of a cozy office in an old brick building across from a city park. It was as far from the suffocating stench of an institution as Paula could get.

But now, walking up South Fair Oaks Avenue, she felt like she might throw up. She sought refuge from the sun under the green awning of a Starbucks. The toxic memory of being under a doctor's care was like an injection of poison, stressing her organs, confusing her senses. Taking a few moments to collect herself, she struggled to slip into the skin of Jill Carlson.

Jill is outgoing. Capable. Be her now. Fake it till you make it, and all that shit.

With the clock relentlessly ticking to her appointment time, she found her way back up Fair Oaks until she stood at the buzzer for the four-story brick building. She had imagined it being larger, more imposing. Scanning the directory, she was unable to find the listing for Dr. Claire Horst. The security system was ancient, the protective glass badly scratched and cloudy, obscuring the entire left side of names. She remembered the office number—310, the same as her home area code in Santa Monica. All you have to do is press the call button, she told herself. Wait for a dial tone and then enter the number; do as instructed and everything will work out as it should. Simple. Paula steadied her shaking hand and performed as required. Nothing happened. After a few more tries, she grew frustrated, irritated with herself for not bringing the phone number to call. She was standing there, stewing, when a young man with a thick beard and round glasses exited the building. She reached to catch the door before it shut.

She took the stairs to the third floor and settled herself before knocking.

Doctor Horst opened the door to the tiny office. "Hello, Paula," she said, smiling. "It's nice to put a face to the name. Please, come on in. I hope the drive out here wasn't too bad."

"No, it was fine," Paula said. "No traffic."

"Small miracles," the doctor said with a chuckle.

She was a petite woman, with short black hair that barely touched the tops of her ears and thick bangs that swept across her forehead. She wore khaki pants with a solid blue blouse. Paula was struck by how young she was. According to Alan's notes, Claire had graduated from Brown University eight years earlier, but Paula hadn't thought to do the math. Thirty, she figured. Other than an understated gold wedding ring, she wore no jewelry and had on minimal makeup. Paula imagined she worked out four days a week to maintain the narrowness of her hips, and she was not sure yet if the image was one she liked.

"It's warm out there, isn't it?" Doctor Horst asked. "Would you like a water?"

Despite the distant urge to use the bathroom, Paula said that she would.

Doctor Horst retrieved a bottle of water from a small refrigerator in the corner of the office. "I wish I had a dispenser—I hate using these bottles. I also have room temperature, if you'd prefer."

"Cold is fine, thank you, Doctor."

"You can call me Claire, if it makes you more comfortable."

"Thank you," Paula said.

The walls were red brick, with a few nicely framed prints. They were all in calming hues, depicting seascapes or abstract images. One was of a strangely elongated horse, its mane flowing, that Paula found amusing. A single chair faced a plush couch, with a small coffee table between. In the corner, an old-fashioned table lamp sat on an uncluttered desk. Overall, the room looked like it could be converted to a hipster coffee bar without too much trouble.

When the doctor lowered herself into the chair opposite the couch, her blouse hugged tightly to her belly, which rounded forward.

"How far along are you?" Paula asked, unconcerned at hazarding such a guess.

"Is it that obvious?" Doctor Horst asked, slumping slightly.

"Not so much. I didn't even notice until just now."

"Four and a half months. No morning sickness though. I'm lucky."

Paula smiled. Even if it proved to be successful, this particular relationship would have an end date. *My hands are full with the baby*, she imagined Doctor Horst saying at some point in the future. *But I can give you a referral to a great therapist in your area.*

"If you don't mind," Doctor Horst said, reaching for the notepad on the coffee table between them, "I'm going to take some notes. There's a lot to cover and I'd like to make sure I don't forget anything."

Paula didn't mind; she was mostly glad she no longer felt the urge to throw up.

Doctor Horst began by rehashing in slightly more detail what she'd already told Alan on the phone—her college experience, medical school, and her general approach to psychotherapy. All of which was barely absorbed by Paula.

"So, tell me a little more about the concerns that brought you here," the doctor said finally, the notepad on her lap ignored for the moment.

"We might have to narrow that down," Paula said. "We only have ninety minutes."

"Fair enough," Doctor Horst said, with a slight smile. "Your husband mentioned you've struggled with depression for a long time. Why don't you tell me about that?"

Paula gathered herself. Talking about her depression was easy enough, she supposed. There would be no simple way to explain the rest of it, though. How could she talk about the shock of seeing that her ex-lover was married to a woman that was identical to herself without sounding insane? When doctors didn't believe you were mentally stable, it led to dark places.

"My depression is part of who I am, I think," she began. "I

mean, some years have been better than others. In fact, until recently, I was doing very well, feeling more connected. Then, a few months ago, it turned. The distance between myself and the world around me grew. It's worse than it's been since I was much younger. I've tried to figure out what the trigger was, what changed, but I can't."

"Have you had physical problems? Any chronic issues that keep you from being active?"

"No, but I don't sleep well. I have terrible insomnia."

"Trouble falling asleep or staying asleep?"

"Falling."

Doctor Horst picked up the notepad and took out a pen. "What medications do you take?"

"I don't take anything."

Doctor Horst looked up. "Why is that? I mean, nothing to help you sleep?"

"I don't trust them."

"But you've also said that you haven't been feeling well. Is it your concern that being on medication might make you feel even worse?"

"Let's just say I've been far enough down that road already."

"But there have been major advancements with regard to prescription med—"

"I don't want to come off as rude, but you're gonna have to back off from pushing the pill angle, because I also don't trust doctors who are so eager to prescribe them."

Doctor Horst scribbled on the pad, but seemed to take no offense. "Your husband mentioned that you've had some unpleasant history with therapy?"

Paula repositioned herself on the edge of the couch. "Are you familiar with the Newberry Institute, up in Marin?"

"No, I'm not, I'm sorry. Were you a patient there?"

"For a year and a half. When I was in college, my first year. It was against my will."

"I see. What was the reason you were there?"

Paula's pulse quickened, her palms moistened. She would not talk about Bunny, not yet anyway, but she was pleased that the conversation had at last turned closer toward her time with Anthony. Perhaps there was a way in. "They said I was a danger to myself."

"And you didn't agree with their assessment?"

"No, I didn't." She turned her wrists outward and exposed the faint white scars. "I guess I was wrong about that, though."

Doctor Horst didn't flinch. "Do you feel like you might be a danger to yourself now?"

Paula shook her head, running her thumb across her opposite wrist.

"Have you harmed yourself since then?"

"I'm a completely different person now."

"You're very self-aware, Paula. Would you agree with that?"

"I'm *aware*, yes. I'm not so clear on the *self* part."

Doctor Horst seemed to not notice the attempt at humor. "What do you mean by that?"

Paula took a moment, then said, "I'm outside of my body too much. Always on the outside looking in."

"Do you feel like that right now?"

"Yes. It's very difficult to tell if I'm saying the things I want to be saying or merely saying the things I think you want me to say."

"That's a very good observation."

"I hope you're not going to keep doing that."

"Doing what?"

"Complimenting me on how astute I am."

"Point taken," Doctor Horst said, scribbling on the note-pad. "I want you to be comfortable here. Cognitive behavioral therapy is a process, and we'll have plenty of time to talk about whatever issues you're dealing with. But right now, I'd like to get a clearer picture of what your primary concerns are."

Paula liked her already—she was so unlike her memories of Doctor Stickley. For the first time since arriving, Paula smiled. "This is the beginning of a beautiful friendship, huh?"

Doctor Horst's lips separated, and for a moment Paula thought she was returning her smile. But she was not. "I'm not going to be your friend," she said. "That's not what you need. But if you'll agree to it, I am going to help you find your way back to your true self."

Paula leaned back into the plush cushions of the sofa. She could not tell if she was suddenly exhausted or merely relaxed. "Okay," she said, softly.

"So," Dr. Horst said. "Tell me what you'd most like to talk about."

Paula reset herself. *Fake it till you make it.* She was thinking once again as Jill Carlson. After a few false starts, she began slowly recounting her history with Anthony: how they'd met in college and fallen in love. She found it pleasing to talk about that part of her life, and the words came easier, quickly expanding from the limited scope she'd originally planned. Eventually, despite her initial reservations, she touched lightly on Bunny, giving only an outline sketch of her death and the salacious accusations of Anthony's involvement. It took almost an hour, with a long detour into her failing relationship with Alan, for her to finally arrive at the doorstep of Hannah Mills, her identical opposite.

Doctor Horst took all of this in with a benign silence, only nodding and occasionally scribbling on her notepad. She asked no questions, until faced with the suggestion of an identical woman living across the street from her newest patient.

"And others—your husband—have seen this woman as well?"

"Of course."

"And yet they see her differently than you do? I mean to say, not as identical to you?"

Paula's cheeks burned and she knew her face had flushed, that her neck was blooming with red and white patches. If she were older, she might write it off as the onset of menopause, but for now she accepted it as a physical reaction to either her own insanity, or everyone else's. "I recognize how fucking strange it is, if that's what you're getting at."

Doctor Horst maintained her detached calm as she talked at length about something called the *Syndrome of Subjective Doubles*. It was, she explained, one of many different kinds of delusional misidentification syndromes. But it was a positive, she insisted, that Paula was staying in touch with reality—other, of course, than having this one, very specific, delusion.

"So, you're saying I'm not completely psychotic?" Paula said, only half joking.

"Right now," the doctor gently continued, "I see no evidence of paranoia. Which means that in my medical opinion you're not schizophrenic, if that's what you mean by psychotic. You seem to be making good judgements. And hearing the way you're effectively communicating your concerns, and that you're conscious of the abnormality of your perceptions, I'd say your emotional response to all of this is appropriate. All good signs. But the question is, why is this happening? Well, there could be any number of underlying reasons for what you're perceiving to be—"

"I don't like that," Paula interrupted. "I'm not hallucinating. I'm telling you, she looks exactly like me."

"I should have been clearer, I'm sorry." She leaned forward in her chair. "There's a difference between a hallucination and a delusion, though both of them do involve an impaired relationship with reality. I believe that a woman named Hannah Mills exists, that she lives across the street from you. You're right, she is not a hallucination. And I understand how frustrating it must be for you to hear this, but I believe that *how* you are seeing her is a delusion."

"But it's not," Paula said, her irritation once again spiking.

"Okay," Doctor Horst said. "But you do know that it would be highly *unusual* for a woman who looks exactly like you to be living across the street and have no one else be aware of it?"

"Of course it's highly unusual! But unusual doesn't mean *impossible*."

"You're right, it doesn't." Doctor Horst set down her pen and pad. "I understand the reasons you're hesitant to talk about medication, but it's important you understand that prescriptive medicine has changed quite a bit in the past twenty—"

"I thought I made it clear that I won't—"

"Paula, I understand you had a scarring experience at Newberry. But what you're going through has to be addressed. If you'll just humor me for a second. No pressure. We're only talking, nothing more. You can do whatever you want with the information, but you need to know that there are many good new options out there. A person in your position, for example, could begin with SSRIs, which ease depression by increasing

levels of serotonin in the brain. And there are also mood sta-
bilizers we could try. There are even newer medications called
atypical antipsychotics that supplement—"

"I said no. If I'm destined to be miserable, it'll be on my
own terms."

Doctor Horst nodded. "You're not destined to be miserable, Paula. And I'm not asking you to give up any part of
yourself. I'm only discussing available options. Any doctor you
go to will at least give you a complete physical and—"

"Then I won't go to any more doctors. I mean it. No hospitals. No facilities. No goddamned *checkups*. Nothing. If you
continue to press me on this, I'll leave."

Doctor Horst looked kindly at her. "I don't want that for
you, Paula. Coming here today is a big deal. It's undoubtedly
a huge step out of your comfort zone. I want you to continue,
and to trust that I only have your best interest in mind. I won't
force you to do anything that makes you uncomfortable. You
have my promise. Do you trust me?"

Paula leaned back into the couch and stared.

"I don't trust anything anymore," she said at last.

CHAPTER SEVEN

DESPITE HER COMMITMENT to seeing Doctor Horst, Paula remained in freefall. She didn't go outside for five days, ignoring Alan's daily urging that she leave the house—return to The Little Delicious, perhaps. "Start a new routine," was how he put it.

"I wouldn't know how to explain my absence," she said, looking up from her laptop as he stood at the foot of her bed.

"You're the *boss*, Paula," Alan insisted. "It's your shop. You don't have to explain anything to anyone. And going back might help break up your negative thought patterns."

"Jesus, Alan," she said, closing the lid of her laptop as though slamming a door. "I already have a therapist."

"Touché."

"I didn't realize we were fencing each other," she said.

He curled his lips together and breathed through his nose. "I'm doing the best I can, here," he said.

"I know," she relented. "It may not come across, but I'm trying the best I can too."

He forced a sad smile. "We're a hell of a pair, aren't we?"

Once Alan left (or *retreated,* as Paula saw it), the stillness of the house pricked at her, excoriating her for keeping her husband at a distance, just as she had during their pathetic attempt at intimacy. She was ashamed for having made love imagining Anthony Mills inside of her instead of the man she now loved. Berating voices screamed inside her skull. Anthony never truly loved her, not the way Alan loved her. Anthony had loved Allyson, a woman who didn't really exist. But Alan was here, always here, and she kept pushing him away.

She went for a walk and texted Alan that he was right— being outdoors was a relief. The salty breeze caressed her face and soothed her mind. He responded only with a smiley face, evidently unable to find any actual words. She couldn't blame him. Whenever they talked lately, they always ran out of words. She walked the five blocks to the bluffs running along the edge of the city, overlooking the Pacific Ocean. There she stood for over an hour, staring at the horizon, imagining what peace felt like.

When she returned to her house, she was stunned to see yet another ghost from her past standing in the driveway across the street, smoking a cigarette. She considered turning away, pretending she hadn't seen him, but the impulse passed as quickly as it came. The man eyed her as she approached, giving no indication that he recognized her.

"Darius?" she said.

Anthony's little brother blew out a stream of smoke and snuffed the cigarette beneath his foot. "How you doin'?" he said, his deep voice a shocking counterpoint to his lithe body. It had been over a decade since she'd last seen him.

"It's Paula," she said.

Darius's face broke into a happy smile full of yellowing teeth. "Damn girl, I know who you are. But, shit, look at you. You changed."

"Only on the outside." She smiled back. "Though it has been a while."

"Like fifteen years, probably."

He extended his hand and they shook, his skin like pitted wood against hers.

"What are you doing here?" Paula asked.

Darius's smile evaporated. "That ain't decided yet. They still in negotiations."

"I take it your arrival wasn't universally appreciated."

"Hannah and I don't get along too well, but I need someplace to stay for a while, so there you go."

He lit another cigarette and fell into a silence that Paula couldn't stand. Gone was the puffed-up bravado of his youth, his ego seemingly wasted away with the rest of his once thickly muscled body. "Why don't you two get along?" she asked.

"For real? She ain't mentioned that I just got out of prison?"

"I haven't talked to her about anything like that."

"Yeah, okay," Darius chuckled. "Well, she worried about Alex being around me—she say my lifestyle ain't something he need to be exposed to, you know what I'm sayin'? But I been through the program and been clean for over a year, so it's all good. Besides, I got nothing but love for the little man."

"You're done with Oakland, huh?"

"For real, I'd go back if I could, but they too many elements up there that everyone agree would be a bad influence on *me*."

Paula smiled and Darius held out the pack of cigarettes. "You want one?"

"Don't smoke anymore."

"Santa Monica's real nice," Darius said, putting the pack back into his pocket and nodding across the street. "You got a nice place too. It's crazy expensive here, huh?"

"Yes. Emphasis on crazy."

"Oakland gettin' like that too. 'Bout as bad in the East Bay as it is in San Francisco. Our sister got two kids, and she livin' with our mom 'cause she can't afford nothin' else. Anthony paying for them though, same as he payin' for me." Darius laughed. "If it works out, I'm gonna be like the Fresh Prince up in here!"

The garage door opened behind them and they moved aside as Hannah backed out in her Audi SUV. She glanced only at Paula as she backed down the driveway, never once looking at Darius. Paula immediately recognized her expression as the very one she herself had given Alan so many times recently. The identical face staring back from behind the raised window was pale, exhausted looking. Hannah said nothing, gave no indication she realized she was being rude. Once on the street, she threw the SUV into gear and drove away, leaving the garage door up.

"I guess negotiations are over," Darius said, smoke again billowing over his lips.

*

"It was all a performance," Paula said.

"What do you mean by that?" asked Doctor Horst.

"When she and Anthony came over to my house, they tried to come off as happy, connected. Hannah seemed so comfortable in her skin, so self-possessed. But there was something wrong between them. A distance. I didn't recognize it at first, but it was there in the way they talked to each other. And then when she backed out of her garage, I recognized it, because it's the same face I see in the mirror every day."

"She seems to have lost some control over her life lately," said Doctor Horst. "That can be very upsetting. You can identify with that, can't you?"

"Yes."

"Do you still feel that you're in control of yourself?"

"It's hard to tell anymore," Paula said, sniffing, tears collecting in the corners of her eyes.

"Are you unhappy with Alan?" Doctor Horst asked, knitting her brows together. "The same way you believe Hannah is unhappy with Anthony?"

Paula took a sip of water. "He and I haven't spoken much this past week. I'm afraid we've been reduced to roommates whose paths rarely cross."

Doctor Horst nodded. "Part of my concern is that you're keeping lots of secrets from him. Your past relationship with Anthony, for example. That's a big part of your true self." She leaned forward, catching Paula's eyes, not allowing her to look away. "Not to mention your history during college and the death of your roommate. No matter how deeply it's buried, it's still there."

Paula wiped at her tears, leaving a shine of moisture in the dark circles under her eyes. "I'm not ready to talk about that with him," she said.

"And that's a way you're keeping control, right? By deciding what information is shared and what's kept private. Which is fine. But there are many unresolved emotions involved with that time in your life. It's important you work through those."

"It's not as if I haven't been trying," Paula said, hating that she suddenly felt so defensive.

"Have you ever kept a journal?"

Paula shook her head. "No."

"I'd like you to start. You don't have to show it to anybody. In fact, it's best if you don't. Not even me. It's only for you. But I'd like you to write down all the thoughts and emotions that you're struggling with. Write about being angry with your husband for not understanding what you're going through, and how you feel about suddenly having Anthony and Hannah in your life. Write about what you were feeling when you tore apart your room and the impulses you had to lash out at Hannah when you first met. The hard part is to be completely open and honest, especially about those moments that scare you. It's the thoughts you can't control that are most important to explore on paper. Really let go—don't censor yourself. Do you think you can do that?"

Paula sat back in the plush couch and wondered if she could.

CHAPTER EIGHT

"WHY CAN'T ANYONE else see what is so fucking obvious???" Paula scrawled in big letters across the top of the page. "Hannah Mills <u>IS IDENTICAL TO ME</u>! Everyone keeps telling me it's all in my head, but they're the ones who can't SEE. I can scream at Alan all goddamn day, but I will never be able to convince him! He sees what he sees!! WHY IS THIS HAPPENING? I've cried myself to sleep for too many nights, have prayed to a God I'm not sure exists (or cares about me if he does) until I'm exhausted. Send me a fucking sign as to what I'm supposed to do, God. Any sign will do. There are plenty of bushes in the yard that you could burn. I'll listen. I AM LISTENING! I've tried to occupy my mind with other things—Facebook, television—even the idea of returning to The Little Delicious. But Hannah and Anthony are all I can think about. I can't DO anything else if I am only thinking about them. Does Hannah TRULY not see what I see? I have visions of holding her down, shaking her until she tells me the truth.

"There's a REASON and I am going to find it. Hannah is the KEY."

*

The notion snuck up on Paula the way a cold sneaks up on a person—she had gone to bed in one state, and woke up in another. "Hannah," she wrote in her journal, "is a part of me, and I am a part of her. Together, we can end all of this. There can be no more hiding. Hannah will help me find the answers."

She left her bedroom once Alan left for the day. He wouldn't be home until after his night class, giving her plenty of time to do what she needed to do without having to explain why she was ignoring his command to leave Hannah Mills alone.

Digging further down the rabbit hole isn't what will lead back to the mental ward—it's doing nothing that will consume whatever remains of my sanity.

Paula stood at the living room window, staring across the street at the onetime red brick facade of the Mills home. The house had recently been painted a more contemporary taupe color. She watched as Anthony backed out of his garage and drove off for work, with Darius sitting in the passenger seat. It was simple deduction to conclude that Anthony had found a job for his wayward little brother—most likely at RuskTech. Who the hell else would hire an ex-con with a history of armed robbery and drug addiction? He could wash the floors perhaps, or pick up lunch—anything, Anthony surely believed, to keep his mind and hands occupied.

As Paula stood there, building her nerve, she felt an eddy of dread swirling up from her stomach into her chest. Her sympathetic nervous system waged that familiar evolutionary war between fight or flight—and fight was being pummeled into submission. How was she ever going to be able to confront Hannah directly? The Morse-code pulse in her neck transmitted a simple message: run. And then, as the eddy threatened to drown her, she breathed deeply, closed her eyes a moment and then opened them. She saw only blue sky through Jill Carlson's eyes

I'm Jill.

Jill was confident, always on point, always enthusiastic. Everything Jill did came with an exclamation point. Jill could march right across that street and demand that Hannah help her find the answers! Jill had no reservations at all!

The newly emboldened Jill Carlson walked across Georgina Avenue, and before she realized it, she was on the Mills's porch, ringing the doorbell. A moment later the door opened and she was greeted by a wide, smiling face tucked under a wild bush of dark hair. "Can I help you?" the woman asked.

With the question, the fantasy of Jill Carlson slipped away. Paula realized at once that this was all a huge mistake. She should not have come. Alan was right—Hannah was not going to be an ally. Hell, even if she wanted to, she couldn't help decipher the mystery of why all this was happening any more than Alan could. But the realization that she should have left Hannah alone came too late and Paula wondered how she could have been so foolish.

"Ma'am?"

"Hi," she stammered.

"Can I help you?"

Paula somehow managed a smile. "Yes, is Hannah home?"

"Can I tell her who's asking?" the dark-haired young woman asked.

"Paula," she said, her own voice a shock, like a glass breaking in her hand. "Paula Hickman. I live across the street."

"Oh! I'm sorry, come in. I'm Lisa, Alex's nanny. I'll let her know you're here."

As the nanny went off in search of her boss, Paula remained

in the entry hall. Seven or eight moving boxes were stacked neatly along the wall of the living room. A plastic sword and shield lay on the floor near the couch, the only indication that a child shared the house. Paula took it all in, like a masked intruder in the midst of a crime.

"She said to come on back," Lisa said, returning. "She's in her studio."

She led Paula through the great room and out to the back patio. At the far end of the flagstones, lying in a warm patch of sunshine outside his Hogwarts doghouse, lay a muscular collection of brown fur—a sleeping ridgeback, his legs stretched out, exposing his belly to the sky. Showing an impressive dexterity, the massive dog flipped onto its stomach, his ears pricked and his watery eyes trained on the unexpected visitor, as though deciding if she was worth a bark.

"That's Edgar," Lisa informed Paula, continuing to smile in her overly friendly way. "He's huge, but gentle. Anyway, she's right through there," she said, pointing toward the open door of the ivy-covered studio, tucked into the corner of the lushly landscaped yard. "It was nice meeting you. I'm sure I'll see you around."

"Yes, thank you. Nice meeting you, too."

Paula left Lisa and traversed the last twenty steps alone, breathing in the almost medicinal scent of the freshly mowed lawn, the sun hot against her cheeks, her palms slick with nervous sweat. The corner of her left eye twitched and she tapped it with her fingertips. She turned back to the house, unable to shake the sensation of being watched. But there was no sign of Lisa. Other than Edgar, who paid her no mind, she was alone. Still, she could not shake the feeling. Perhaps it was only that she was outside her body, watching. Always watching. She took a shallow breath, then another, and stepped into the studio.

Hannah stood at an easel propped up beneath an open window, painting, her back to the door. "Hello, Paula," she said, not turning, her brush continuing across the canvas.

"I'm sorry to stop by unannounced," Paula said, stopping just inside room. Sunlight streamed through the windows, making the white paint on the walls glow.

Hannah set down her brush and reached for a bottle of Grey Goose Vodka set amongst the shriveled tubes and stained cans of paint on the table beside her. She poured three inches into a waiting glass and then turned to smile at Paula. She showed no teeth. "But you were announced," she said. "Lisa told me you were here."

"I meant that I hadn't—"

"It's fine. Care to join me in a drink?"

It was not yet noon.

"No, thank you," Paula said, feeling the same dizziness she'd experienced being with Hannah the first time—a kind of vertigo, brought on by the dissonance of sharing space with an identical version of herself. Hannah swallowed an inch of vodka and set the glass back down.

"You look like you're already ready to leave," she said.

"I feel like I'm intruding."

"That's interesting. I often feel the same way."

"I'm sorry?"

Hannah waved her off. "Come and tell me what you think." It sounded like a dare.

Paula followed as Hannah moved to a series of paintings propped up on a folding table. The first canvas was filled with the black waters of a lonely sea, rolling waves the color of a bruise, an empty lifeboat in its dark center. The second was brighter, but equally as startling—a decrepit barn nearly swallowed whole by a golden field of untended wheat. The third, the largest of them, and the most ambitious, was grey and distressed—a rusty swing set, a lone seat dangling from a broken chain, forgotten in the yard of a tenement building.

Hannah stood beside her, their shoulders almost touching. "If you're silently wondering, they're meant to be clichés," she said. "I'm making a comment."

"They're wonderful."

"They're something, anyway," Hannah said.

Paula turned to the new painting on the easel, its colors not yet taking any definitive shape. She glimpsed a half-smoked joint resting on the horizontal support and immediately diverted her eyes. "What do you call this one?" she asked.

Hannah let out a dismissive grunt. "Painting them is difficult enough without having to actually name them."

Paula chuckled dryly as her discomfort grew. "I used to fantasize about becoming an artist," she said. "But I could never do something like this."

"Of course you could," Hannah said, speaking with authority as she reached again for her glass of vodka. "It's impossible to fail as an artist. If it's not up to some imagined standard, all you have to do is call it *abstract*, and you're home free. Hell, even if it's awful, your work might still be discovered after you die and found to be worth millions."

"Such is the life of the unknown master," Paula offered, gamely trying to play along, despite Hannah's barely disguised—what? Annoyance? Animosity? Plain-old drunkenness?

Hannah swallowed another inch of booze. "I guess you don't have to wait, do you?"

Paula's forced cheerfulness faded. "What do you mean?"

Hannah's lips were wet with vodka as they parted into an

almost cruel grin. "I mean, you're already worth millions, aren't you? A lot more than that, actually. How much is the Sullivan Manufacturing fortune worth these days?"

Paula's cheeks flushed—her body shook. It was impossible not to feel as though she were under attack. "I haven't kept track," she said.

Hannah walked to the window and stared out at the yard. "That must be nice, having so much that you don't need to keep track. It's close to a billion dollars, by the way. At least, that was the best estimate I found."

Paula stared at the back of Hannah's head. "I'm not in charge of the trust," she said, unsure how else to respond.

Hannah turned and eyed her with suspicion. "I'm sure there's a story in there someplace. Or would you prefer to keep that a secret too?"

A chasm had suddenly opened up between them. If Paula moved forward, she'd fall right over the edge. *I'm not keeping any secrets,* she thought, but the lie stayed on her tongue, dying from exposure. "Are you upset with me?" she asked.

"I don't even *know* you, Paula," Hannah said. And then all pretense of friendliness dropped from her expression like a switch had been thrown. "Or should I call you Allyson?"

The question came like a gunshot across the crevasse, striking Paula in the chest. She didn't answer. Couldn't answer. It was all she could do to keep from staggering from its impact. *How could she have found out about Allyson? Anthony wouldn't have told her.* For twenty-five years they had honored the pact to keep the past buried. Telling Hannah would serve no purpose.

Hannah's expression darkened. "The real irony of learning about your sordid history with my husband is that I was actually worried you'd have no interest in being my friend if you knew the person *I* really am."

"That's because we're the same," Paula said, distantly, as if talking only to herself.

"Who's the same?" Hannah shot back, her voice growing sharper. "Me and you? Or me and Allyson? You know, Anthony's sister once mentioned his college girlfriend, but I had no idea you were the same person. She said it was that first love of his, that *crazy* love, she called it, that opened his heart to dating women of my particular pigmentation."

Paula found her voice, though it was barely a whisper. "I'm not Allyson anymore…."

Hannah's lips snapped like two rubber-bands pulled taught. "But that poor girl is still dead, isn't she? What was the name you gave her?"

Jesus. She knows everything! And that means that Alan will soon know it, too.

"Bunny," Paula said.

Hannah raised her glass. "Yes. Bunny. So here's to Bunny, and to Allyson and to Paula and to Darius and to Anthony and to your husband. I'd drink to myself as well, but it's still a bit confusing to me where I fit in." She downed the last of the vodka and then tossed the glass onto the cluttered table. "I can't believe this shit. What sort of fucked-up game are you two playing? Just old friends, nothing more! What other secrets do you two share? Murder? I mean, does it go that deep? Could it possibly be that twisted? Because that's what Darius told me people used to say—that poor little Bunny didn't kill herself, that you two conspired to cover up her murder!"

Darius. Of course. He always was a fuck up. And now he's blown everything all to hell. Nausea crept in relentlessly, like carsickness—Paula helpless to staunch its onslaught, everything moving, despite her wish to remain still. "Her name was Emily," she said.

"Oh, well, it's certainly important we cleared that up. Thank you! So let's clear this up, too—are you fucking my husband? Is that why we moved here? Because you two are still—"

"No," Paula said, her vision blurred behind gathering tears.

A bitter laugh spilled from Hannah's lips. "If you are, please realize that Anthony's appetites are not so easily sated. You wouldn't be the only one fucking him, I'm sure. I may be his main course, but he does love his side dishes."

As her tears fell, Paula made no sound, unable to emotionally digest what she was being told. She flinched as Hannah lashed out, kicking over the easel, sending it flying, unfinished joint and unfinished painting tumbling to the floor. "I don't want any part of this!" she yelled. "So leave me the hell alone!" And then Hannah's eyes deepened, her jawline jutted forward. "Do you understand that, Paula? Or Allyson? Or whatever the fuck you're calling yourself these days. Get out! Leave! Now!" Her nose flared as she stared expectantly. Her cheeks widened and her entire face shifted in the shafts of light coming through the window, the contours rearranging themselves like the pieces of a jigsaw puzzle falling into place.

"Don't do this," Paula begged, frightened by the transformation.

Hannah's eyes were darker than before—no longer a mirror image of hers—two more puzzle pieces finding their proper place. Paula brought her hands up, as if to protect herself.

"Get out!" the stranger yelled again.

Paula shuffled backward, unsteady, away from the new person staring her down. The woman who had been Hannah

Mills was gone—replaced by a woman with harsher features and wispier blonde hair shrouding a narrower face. With a burst of adrenaline, Paula broke free and ran from the studio. Bounding through the yard, she nearly tripped over an agitated Edgar, whose block head bobbed up and down as he arrived to investigate the commotion. Paula shuffled around the dog and lost her footing, her left ankle twisting as she fell hard to her knees. Her hands jutted forward and the skin on the fleshy pads of her palms skidded along the red bricks, drawing blood, the pain reaching all the way to her elbows. Edgar barked wildly.

"Are you okay?" she heard Alex's nanny say.

Paula's head twisted upward, toward the voice, but her vision was clouded, unable to focus. With blood trickling down her shins, she regained her bearings, pulling free from the concerned nanny, and bolted into the house. Running blindly, she cut back through the living room, yanked open the front door, and ran for the safety of her home.

*

Paula hid in her room for the rest of the day, but the terrifying reality of Hannah Mills relentlessly sought her out. *Nothing matters anymore*, Hannah screamed at her. *You can't hide from this, you bitch! You're exposed! This is who you truly are!* Paula wept and shook on the bed, curled up into herself. But there was no comfort, no safe haven inside her shattered mind.

So leave it. Save yourself. Get out while you still can. Do it.

Okay. That option was always on the table. She could end it all so easily. But first, that cordoned-off section of her mind that always got in the way would have to be drowned, choked to death, silenced for good. She left the bed and went upstairs to Alan's room. She knew where he kept his stash, she'd smelled its skunk odor enough times to know what he was up to, what he did to escape. And then from Alan's bedroom she went to the kitchen. *Yes. That'll help too.* She pulled the bottle of vodka from the freezer.

You see, Hannah? You and I are identical after all!

Paula had not consumed a drop of alcohol in twenty-five years, and the effects of the booze mixed with the marijuana eased the wearying weight of the body she longed to be freed from. But even as her defenses weakened, her mind raged— words poured onto the journal on her lap, the tip of the black pen striking hard on the paper, filling the pages until her fingers ached and her hand cramped beyond use.

Hannah, do you hear me? Do you understand that I don't want any part of this either?

The walls closed in on her like the lid of a coffin as her energy gave out. She sat on the floor of the living room, the last light of day receding, darkness swallowing the world. Hours passed. The darkness grew deeper, heavier. She mumbled to the God who had abandoned her, and to Alan, who'd done the same—off to class, happily engaged with a world she played no part in.

As the clock ticked on and the hours slipped away, she could no longer decipher the strung-out ideas pricking at her. She was lost in the darkness, even from herself. It was then, at the very end of whatever emotional rope she had been able to cling to, that her long-buried impulse solidified, no longer a bursting cloud of emotion, but solid ground on which she could firmly stand.

The house now ringing with an oppressive silence, she went into the kitchen. Her mind had imploded, leaving her to move on instinct. She drew a knife from the drawer beside the sink and ran the length of the serrated blade along her palm, as if testing its sharpness. But she was not testing anything—she was absent, her body void of consciousness. Her fingers folded together, clamping down on the knife, the blade tearing open the flesh of her palm. Harder she squeezed, as blood dripped down her wrist. Her opposite hand came off the handle and found the blade as well. The knife gouged deep, opening her up. Startling pain brought her to her knees, and the knife clanked free on the hardwood floor.

Paula stared at the pulsing wounds on her palms. Smearing the blood along the faint scars on her wrists, she made no effort to staunch its flow. She shivered as the viscous liquid flowed down her arms and onto the floor. The pain was real, she was pleased by that. She raised her eyes to the fallen knife glistening in the faint light, and, with a concentrated effort, picked it back up.

CHAPTER NINE

SHE SAT SLUMP-SHOULDERED, as if she'd fallen asleep. Her head was rolled forward, hands in her lap. Dew-dampened hair stuck stiffly to her scalp, though the breeze fluttered a few blonde strands across her ghostly-pale forehead. Neither of the two joggers noticed her sitting alone on the park bench facing the horizon; they made their way through fog so thick that not even the grand Ferris wheel at the end of the pier could be seen. Passing behind the woman, their conversation focused on the vagaries of raising teenaged girls.

"They posted it online, she saw it last night," one of them said.

"Why didn't they invite her?" the other asked.

"The dynamic of the group has changed so much since middle school…."

It was early, a few minutes before six thirty. A few cars made their way along Ocean Avenue, headlights glowing in the damp air, and an occasional weekend-warrior zipped down the bike lane adjacent to the park—but for the most part, the city's edge was shrouded in silence.

Reaching the north end of the park, the two women jogged back toward the pier, this time following the winding path next to the low fence guarding the panoramic view above the Pacific Coast Highway, a hundred fifty feet below. Faces stinging in the cold, throats aching from the frigid intake of air, their conversation lagged, as did their pace. Neither was speaking when they again approached the woman on the bench.

They might have not noticed anything peculiar at all— might have kept right on going, laboring to finish their workout—if not for the rust-colored stain fouling the silent woman's lap, and the pool of dark blood at her feet.

CHAPTER TEN

ALAN'S HEAD WAS filled with the detritus of a fitful sleep. He rarely accepted the invitations of his students, preferring to go straight home after a long day of grading papers, faculty meetings, conferences, and lecturing. But lately there was little comfort to be found at home, so when the offer had been made the night before, Alan had surprised everyone by agreeing to join his class for a Friday night drink at Barney's Beanery in Westwood.

Climbing from his bed, he sucked the film from his tongue and went to relieve his distended bladder. He was dehydrated and wobbly when he left the bathroom in search of orange juice to rehydrate and increase his blood sugar.

Flipping the light switch in the kitchen, he did not notice the blood smeared on the floor like ink blots from some sinister Rorschach test. He was focused on pulling a glass from the cupboard and opening the refrigerator. His mouth watered as he poured the cold orange juice. But as he raised the glass, the sound of the doorbell stopped him short. He took a quick sip and crossed to the entry hall, acutely aware that he wore only pajama bottoms and a ratty t-shirt. The doorbell continued to ring, and Alan suppressed a spike of irritation at its impatience at such an early hour.

He looked through the peephole and was, all at once, wide awake. "What's going on?" he said to not any particular one of the four uniformed police officers standing on his porch.

"Mr. Hickman?" a man in a suit said, stepping between the officers. His voice was calm, casual even. His boyishly round face would have made him look like a teenager dressed in his big brother's suit, if not for the receding hairline, which aged him severely.

Alan's gaze drifted to the six patrol cars idling in the middle of the street, their lights flashing like red and blue buoys adrift in the fog. "Yes?" he said.

"My name's Detective William Kerr. Your wife is Paula Hickman?"

The fog seeped into Alan's mind. "I don't understand. What's all this about?"

It was then that Alan saw Anthony Mills stepping forward between two patrol cars, his mouth moving as though trying to form words it couldn't quite manage. In the faint morning light, his eyes blazed.

"Is your wife home, sir?" Detective Kerr asked.

"Yes, of course," Alan stuttered. "I mean, I assume so."

"You're not sure if your wife is home?" the detective asked, eyebrows raised.

"I haven't seen her this morning," Alan said. The familiar anger he held for Paula, and the drama she fomented, reasserted itself after the silent indifference of the past few weeks. "We sleep in separate bedrooms," he added, without elaboration.

"Do you mind if we come in?" Detective Kerr asked. "We'd like to ask her a few questions."

Alan hesitated. Whatever the reason for the arrival of the police on his doorstep, for the pained look upon Anthony

Mills's face, it was a safe assumption that nothing would ever be the same. He moved aside and the police loomed even larger, stepping into his home. His hangover was not gone, but the influx of adrenaline had definitely diminished its effects as the uniformed invaders moved past him.

"Please see if Paula is here," Detective Kerr said.

"Is she in trouble for something?" Alan asked, still trying to make sense of the surreal scene unfolding in his living room.

"Detective?" one of the heretofore silent cops called out. "Take a look at this."

"What do you got?" Detective Kerr said, the only person in the room still looking at Alan.

The officer was bent over, his flashlight trained on the floor. "Looks like blood."

"Jesus," Alan said, his instinctive move toward the offending matter stopped by a firm hand on his arm.

"Let's take it easy," said the officer who had grabbed him.

Alan yanked himself free but made no further movement. "Can someone explain to me what the hell this is all about?" he said.

"Is it only you and your wife in the home, sir?" another officer asked.

"Yes."

"Any children in the home?"

"I just told you it's only us. We don't have any kids."

"Are there any weapons in the house, sir?" the officer asked.

Alan shook his head. "I don't own any guns, if that's what you mean."

Two officers left the room, unsnapping their holsters and pulling out their nine-millimeter Glocks as they went.

The reality of the blood on his floor staggered Alan. Trying to distance himself, he said, "I didn't notice that blood until you pointed it out. Is Paula hurt?"

"Her bedroom?" Detective Kerr said, ignoring Alan's comment.

Alan pointed to the hallway beside the kitchen. "Right through there," he said. "I'll get her."

The officer who had grabbed Alan's arm now placed a firm hand on his chest. "We'll take care of it," he said.

Alan's mind raced as the sergeant and the officer walked cautiously toward the closed bedroom door. Over the past month it was as if the room had become haunted, tormenting Alan with the potential of harm if he entered. Perhaps Paula would burst through the door, a wild animal fighting for freedom, or maybe she was gone, having fled after whatever the hell had transpired to bring the Santa Monica Police Department to their home.

He returned his gaze to the floor, to the blood. There was quite a bit of it, and he was astonished that he could have missed it. Last night, so inebriated that he'd left his car at UCLA and taken an Uber home, it was understandable. But this morning he must have walked right over it. He glanced down to see if there was any evidence of some hidden violence staining the soles of his bare feet. Nothing.

It came to him like the blow of a hammer—Paula had not yet made an appearance because she was no longer alive. After so many threats to her sanity, after so many dark months piled up on each other, she had finally done what she seemed destined to do. He straightened his spine, his chest expanded, his eyes searching out the ceiling, as if he could see her spirit rising, at last freed from the bonds of misery.

He was not saddened by the idea of Paula succeeding at the

suicide she'd long ago failed to complete. He was not shaken, but strangely calm. *This is how it will be from now on. No more arguing. No more drama. No more Paula.* A twinge of pain shook him—a shock of self-loathing for his lack of proper emotion—before the hammer struck again. *Why would so much wary attention be paid to the death of an emotionally distant woman who barely left her house? Holy shit. Did Paula do something to Hannah? Was that the reason for the pain animating Anthony's face?*

"We've got a knife in the kitchen," one of the returning officers announced.

More guns were drawn and the officer beside Alan moved his heavy hand to his shoulder, his other hand now gripping his arm, above the elbow, immobilizing him. "Why are you looking for my wife?" Alan asked, but they all acted as though they hadn't heard him.

The sergeant and the officer, guns drawn, stood at either side of Paula's closed bedroom door.

"Paula?" the sergeant called out. "This is the Santa Monica Police. We're going to open the door, do you understand?"

There was no response. The sergeant pressed the handle down, slowly pushed the door wide. His partner entered first. The only light in the room came from the soft glow of a cell phone, resting in Paula's lap. She sat on the side of her bed, wearing the same clothes she'd had on the night before. Her hands were distended, stiff with dried blood—a dark stain that wound its way down her forearms, a few dried tributaries reaching her elbows.

She looked up at the uniformed men pointing their guns at her.

"What did I do?" she asked.

CHAPTER ELEVEN

"**Detective Melendez?**" **The** lead Crime Scene Investigator called out as he poked his head around the edge of the three-sided screen hiding the vacated body of Hannah Mills from the long lenses of the media trucks parked along Ocean Avenue. "I'm all finished."

Detective Danny Melendez closed the small notebook he'd been studying, the pages of which were quickly filling up with his painstakingly specific notes and diagrams detailing the disposition of the dead woman on the bench. He tucked the notebook into a pocket of the tailored jacket that fit snugly around his thick shoulders and ran his hand over the top of his bald head. With a mixture of annoyance and understanding, he glanced at the growing collection of gawkers and reporters sequestered behind barricades and strips of yellow tape, all straining to figure out what he himself had not yet been able to comprehend.

The CSI, a lanky man in his mid-fifties with purple pads of crepe skin beneath his tired eyes, stretched his neck as Melendez stepped behind the screen. "Somebody was very intent," he said.

"It is quite the mess," Detective Melendez agreed.

Hannah was starkly pale, the sharp angles of her face even more pronounced, her vacant eyes fixed eternally in her skull. A putrid stench of dried blood, stale sweat, and slow decomposition wafted around her body like a halo of biological destruction.

"I agree with your initial assessment," the CSI said. "Blunt force trauma to the back of the head knocked her unconscious and then she bled to death from the sliced wrists."

"Defensive wounds?"

"No evidence of skin under the nails, no bruising on the arms, no ligature marks anywhere. No signs of any struggle at all." He leaned close to the body and used the tip of a pen to point at the bloodied hair stuck stiffly to the back of Hannah's head. "The contusion on the skull isn't very large, irregular in shape, moving downward. I'd guess the assailant most likely came up from behind, struck her from a standing position."

Melendez nodded. "Or it was somebody she knew, they argued, and the assailant surprised her with a sudden attack when she turned away."

The CSI put the pen back into his coat pocket and pulled the blue gloves from his hands. "You're the detective, not me."

Melendez looked back to Hannah and cocked his head. "Thoughts on the wrists?"

"Skin tissue is torn, not a clean cut. A knife probably, serrated, fairly dull blade. I'm guessing it was done with some hesitation."

"We'll see if it matches the knife found at the Hickman house. Try to put a rush on the DNA if you can."

"Hopefully next week we'll have it for you. The coroner can take her whenever you're ready and we'll see what they have to say after the autopsy."

The CSI agent left and Melendez stood motionless, staring at Hannah for a long while.

"Here you go," a voice came from behind him, breaking his concentration.

Detective Melendez looked over his shoulder to see his partner handing him a tube of Coppertone sunscreen. "Thanks," he said. "You lock the car back up? There's clearly a lot of criminal activity around here."

"Just heard from Menville," Detective Kerr said, ignoring Melendez's dark joke, as they walked from the bench and stood at the railing overlooking the bluffs. "The Hickman woman still isn't talking, just sitting in the holding cell, staring at the wall. She's a real head case, evidently. The blood we found in her house looks to be her own."

"Her own?" Melendez asked.

"Cut her own hands, right across the palms. Tore 'em up pretty good."

"A struggle over a knife, you figure? One with a serrated edge?"

Detective Kerr shrugged. "Possible. We'll see once we have a shot at her."

"I'm gonna go out on a limb here and say Hannah Mills already took a shot at her and came out the loser."

Behind the two detectives, a team from the coroner's office—their arrival noted in a log by a uniformed officer standing nearby—began the painstaking process of removing Hannah's body. Melendez, who had already been attending to the crime scene for close to five hours, squinted up at the sun breaking through the fog and squeezed a milky dot of lotion into his palm, which he rubbed over the top of his brown scalp.

"How's the media spinning this?" he asked, wiping the residual lotion through his black mustache.

Detective Kerr glanced over to the reporters mingling behind the barrier of yellow tape and then up to the three news helicopters hovering above. "They're all over the Hickman angle," he said, sounding impressed by their thoroughness. "Evidently they own The Little Delicious on Montana, so there's that storyline to push."

"I like that place," Melendez said. "They got some mighty tasty chocolate eclairs over there."

"Well, enjoy them while you can. If this thing continues to go in the direction it's headed, The Little Delicious isn't gonna last much longer."

Melendez looked down at the officers combing through the heavy brush and outcropping of rocks on the side of the bluffs, searching for a murder weapon that may or may not have been tossed over the railing. "That would be a real shame," he said.

*

"Hannah Mills evidently sent a text to Paula last night," Alan said, his stale breath clouding the face of his cellphone. He hadn't brushed his teeth that morning and his mouth was uncomfortably hot. He sat hunched over on a wooden bench in the hallway of the Santa Monica Police Station, distant voices echoing around him, his forehead resting heavily in his palm.

"What did it say?" Jacob Russo, the executor of the Sullivan estate, asked on the other end of the line from Connecticut.

"That's all they told me, that there was some sort of communication between them late last night." Alan sat up, his face slick with perspiration. "I have no idea why—they barely knew each other."

"What about Anthony? God, what he's going through is unimaginable, especially with that little boy."

"I haven't talked to him. Haven't even seen him since this morning when they came to find Paula and he…" Alan rubbed his eyes and Jacob waited. "He looked like you'd expect."

"What has he said to the police?"

Alan glanced up the hallway and dropped his voice. "Are you asking if he accused Paula of killing his wife?"

"I'm only trying to get as much information as I can."

"I don't have any other information, Jacob. All I can tell you is that she's not under arrest, she's here only for questioning. But after they took her out of the house, they locked it down. I wasn't allowed to take anything but my wallet and my keys. Last I heard, they were getting a search warrant for a murder weapon."

"Jesus," Jacob sighed into the phone. "Did Paula say anything to them?"

"I doubt it. She was practically comatose when they took her in for questioning."

"That actually works in our favor. Did they at least get her medical attention?"

"They had a doctor here, yeah. He bandaged her hands— the cuts were pretty deep."

"Thank God it wasn't her wrists this time."

"Yeah," Alan said, rubbing his eyes again.

"All right, Lincoln Childress should be there any minute. Make sure you do everything as he instructs from this moment forward. I'll be there tomorrow."

"I'm sorry, Jacob." Alan looked up as two cops walked by.

"What are you sorry for?"

"I couldn't control her. She's been having…issues, lately. She's been…I wasn't the husband I should have been."

"We're all familiar with Paula's issues," Jacob said, gently. "I'm sure you did everything you could to help her."

Despite knowing the truth, Alan did not argue with the assessment.

"Sit tight and wait for Lincoln," Jacob said. "I'll see you tomorrow morning."

Alan had time to walk to the end of the hallway and buy a crappy cup of coffee from a vending machine before he was confronted by the hard-charging leader of the cavalry.

"Alan Hickman," the lawyer's assured voice called out, arriving a good ten strides before the rest of him. "Lincoln Childress."

Lincoln was everything Alan imagined a lawyer kept on retainer by an estate worth a billion dollars to be—late fifties, with thick brown hair, cut short and flecked with grey notes that matched his tailored suit; his impressive height, six-foot-four, an apt reflection of his imposing demeanor. Lincoln Childress, Alan would quickly discover, was always above it all.

"Thank you for coming so quickly," Alan said, tossing the full cup of coffee into a nearby trashcan and extending a welcoming hand.

"What the hell are you doing here?" Lincoln said, with a firm grip on Alan's hand. It was immediately apparent that the handshake would not be finished until he decided so.

"I'm sorry?" Alan asked, his hand swallowed whole by his lawyer's.

"If you're not under arrest, then go home."

His hand at last freed, Alan said, "They asked me to stick around."

"Oh. I see. Did they ask nicely? Because that would certainly make a difference."

Alan was not accustomed to being condescended to, but he was exhausted and had little resolve to stand up for himself. "I thought I should be here for Paula."

"You're a good husband," Lincoln said, offering a slight smile that Alan could not tell was sincere or not. "But this is the last place you should be. Go find a bar, get yourself a drink, and don't say a word to anyone. *Anyone*, understand? I have your number and I will call you once your house has been cleared and you're able to return home."

Alan was hit by the realization that he was happy to be absolved of responsibility. He did not have to stay; he was no longer the only one able to protect Paula. Everything he'd done and said since he'd learned that Hannah had been found dead in the park—that his wife was a suspect in her murder—he had done as though programmed to respond accordingly: a robot performing a task he'd been wired for, no other motivation required. And now, with Lincoln Childress's edict, it was as though he'd been unplugged, the last bit of electricity cycling thorough his system before he would shut down completely. "How much trouble is she in?" he asked.

Lincoln patted him on the shoulder. "Go to the end of the hallway, turn left and take the stairs to the underground garage."

"I parked in the lot across the street."

Lincoln squinted at him. "Have you never watched Dateline? There's a throng of media out there waiting to talk with anyone dumb enough or attention-starved enough to do so— usually those two traits go hand in hand. I don't believe you're either. Am I reading you correctly?"

"You are," Alan nodded.

"My associate, Heather, is waiting for you in the garage. She'll get you past the press without being spotted. She a pretty brunette, early thirties, drives a black BMW. That's like wearing camouflage in Los Angeles. And Alan?"

"Yes?"

"Don't even talk to her about this."

CHAPTER TWELVE

Paula flexed her hand, stretching the skin of her bandaged palm, sending a jolt of pain from her wound to the tips of her fingers. Once the almost electrical sensation subsided, she repeated the action with the opposite hand, sending another tremor of concentric circles outward. Like a metronome keeping time, the pain came and went.

The door to her tiny cell clanged open, but she did not turn to look. Her eyes stayed on the opposite wall, hands continuing to slowly open and close, radiating that exquisite pain.

"Paula?" an unfamiliar voice said.

She had grown accustomed to the voices of the officers who'd come to speak with her in the interrogation room, before they'd brought her here. They were like dark shadows come to life from her past, when she last sat in a police interrogation room, twenty-five years ago, in Berkeley. She had not spoken to any of the officers, or to the two detectives who followed.

"Jacob Russo sent me," this new voice said.

At the mention of the name, Paula stopped flexing her hands. She looked up at the tall man in the grey suit, her mind adjusting to the information slowly, the way one's eyes adapt to sudden darkness.

"Is he mad at me?" she said to Lincoln Childress.

"What a peculiar question," Lincoln answered, looking as though he took it quite seriously. "Do you mind if I have a seat? Five hours ago I was standing on the eleventh hole at the Estancia Club in Scottsdale. I'm a bit tired."

"Sorry to ruin your game."

"Ah, you actually did me a favor," he said, waving her off. "I was already nine over par and would have lost all my money to the most annoying playing partner you could ask for."

Paula slid over a few unnecessary inches and the lawyer unbuttoned his coat and sat beside her. "Jacob is concerned about you, that's all," he said.

She became hyper-aware of her bare feet and the sheetless bed the two of them shared. Her shoes and clothes had been taken as evidence and she wore only a jail-issued yellow jumper.

"Everyone's worried I'm going to kill myself," she said.

"I understand you might have given it a go last night. Is that how you got those cuts?"

Paula held up her bandaged hands. "Evidently my aim isn't very good."

Lincoln smiled, but she couldn't tell if it was authentic or not.

"Why don't you tell me about it," he said.

"I don't remember," she began, haltingly. "I wasn't seeing things clearly last night."

"Were you medicated?"

She stared at her feet. "Of a kind, I guess. Yeah."

"Mm-hmm. Go ahead."

"I was very emotional. Not entirely rational. I've been having a few issues lately."

"So I've heard. Right now, let's talk about what you do remember."

"Only bits and pieces. But if I intended to kill myself, I'm sure I would have done it."

"Do you remember getting a text from Hannah Mills?"

Paula shook her head. "Why do people keep asking me about her?"

Lincoln studied her, taking inventory of every crease on her face, every movement of her eyes and mouth. "I'll tell you why," he said. "But first I need to ask—do you trust me, Paula?"

She nodded. "If Jacob sent you, I do."

Lincoln considered her kindly. "Good. I hope you'll feel the same way tomorrow."

*

Paula screamed as she thrashed against the restraints binding her arms to her torso, her voice reverberating down the hallway. The two orderlies assigned to deliver her to the one available bed in the seventy-four bed psychiatric facility on the fourth floor of the UCLA Medical Center ignored her pleas, their demeanor one of placid, though determined, professionalism. A few disembodied voices, unencumbered with civility, shouted their displeasure at the new arrival as she was hustled past their locked rooms.

Neck muscles straining, Paula twisted her head sideways and saw a gaping eye, a giant squid's eye, pressed to the window of a door, the accompanying voice flinging a fuselage of invectives at her. Her vision blurred, the back of her throat filling with mucus. The orderlies placed her in room 415 and made certain the soft restraints binding her arms and legs were well fastened to the rails of the bed. Paula continued screaming, her voice spewing harshly from her throat as her body writhed—her hips jutting toward the ceiling before slamming back to the mattress.

"You're safe, Paula," a man's voice came to her. "You're not in any danger here."

Paula's tears were stuck in her throat, stopping any actual words of protest from rising. All she could do was squeal and yelp and hiss like a trapped animal.

"My name is Doctor Santini," the voice said. "I'm going to give you something to help you relax."

Her eyes widened as a needle punctured the straining muscle of her upper arm. She stared at the man bending over her, his face so close, and saw instead Doctor Lawrence Stickley of the Newberry Institute.

And then the thrashing ceased. Her breathing softened as it flowed easily now from her chest. She drifted, a feather wafting back and forth on a current of air before alighting. Her energy lagged, her eyes lost focus. At the very edge of consciousness, a single thought animated her hazy mind.

Hannah Mills is dead.

CHAPTER THIRTEEN

"A FIFTY-ONE-FIFTY PSYCH hold lasts seventy-two hours," Lincoln Childress explained, the ice cubes in his glass of scotch clinking together like tiny chimes. "We'll get her stabilized, make sure she's in no danger of suicide, and then we'll get her home."

The home Paula was presently away from had been picked over by investigators for the previous twelve hours, infusing it with a lingering aura of suspicion. Luminal had been sprayed on surfaces where blood traces weren't already clear to the naked eye, and the ashy remnants of magnetic fingerprint-powder-soiled counters, drawers, doorhandles, and sinks—each splotch the mark of some faceless CSI looking for evidence that the dead woman found in the park had been in the home of the (by all accounts) crazy woman she had texted the night before.

Alan, halfway to drunk, sat wearily on the sofa opposite Lincoln, looking distracted by Lincoln's assistant, Heather. The tall brunette in the form-fitting business suit stood beside the front window facing Georgina Avenue, peeking through the curtains at the small village of interested parties from all of the major networks. The reporters were camped out in the street, their cameras on swivels, turning back and forth from the Hickman home to the Mills home—opposing sides on the tennis court of public opinion. Each and every theory as to what had happened to Hannah Mills was being whacked back and forth on television, online, and in the papers, every armchair detective trying their best to score a point in the minds of interested spectators. It was undoubtedly a fascinating match to watch—except for those closest to the action.

"She's going to hate you for sending her there," Alan said, slurring a bit.

"Perhaps," Lincoln said.

Heather turned away from the commotion outside. "Not if Jacob Russo expresses his approval of the committal. Mr. Russo holds a certain position in Paula's eyes, it seems."

"You think she killed Hannah Mills?" Alan asked, looking at Heather.

"What we think is irrelevant," Lincoln answered for her. "What matters now is what the police think and whether they have enough evidence to arrest her, and, ultimately, if the district attorney feels there's enough to convict her."

"It won't be for lack of trying," Alan said, briefly closing his eyes. "They took every knife and pair of scissors in the house."

"Then we'll learn soon enough if they've found any forensic evidence germane to the investigation. In the meantime we'll plan accordingly."

"So you're assuming they will eventually arrest her for murder?" Alan asked.

"I'm not assuming anything. But I am preparing for everything."

"Including a plea of not guilty by reason of insanity?"

"Courts in the state of California use the M'Naghten Rule," Lincoln explained. "It's a standard that establishes whether a defendant knew the nature of the crime, or understood right from wrong, at the time it was committed." He took a sip of scotch. "We could argue that, as a result of a previously untreated mental illness, Paula had an irresistible impulse that caused the inability to control her actions."

"I applaud your lawyer-speak. But do you truly think that's what happened?"

"What we think—"

"Is irrelevant," Alan interrupted, standing. "Yes, you've established that."

He went to the opposite side of the window from Heather and peeled the drapes back enough to see the bright lights of the media trucks casting long shadows across his lawn. The remaining dark spaces were filled with neighbors he had never spoken to, all of them undoubtedly talking in excited tones about the chilling death of the newest resident of Georgina Avenue.

"I think she did it," Alan said with a sigh, looking out the window.

Heather gave her boss a worried glance, but Lincoln raised a calming hand. "You've been having some trouble in your marriage lately," he said.

Alan looked back to him. "Who told you that?"

"You did."

Alan shook his head. "Jesus, you're smug."

"That could be argued. But am I correct?"

Truth or lie, Alan thought. That was the game Paula and he played so often. Which answer would be easiest to get past, so they could get on with their days? "We've been having our difficulties, yes," he said, deciding on the truth.

Lincoln softened his tone. "Married life is not for the faint of heart."

Alan returned to the couch and took another deep swallow of booze. "I'm afraid your opinions on the vagaries of marriage will not be appreciated, councilor. You have no standing with the court. I see no wedding ring on your finger."

Lincoln weighed his response before saying, "I'm not the marrying kind."

Alan raised his glass, offering a toast. "To George Cukor, then."

"I'm sorry?"

"Movie director," Alan said, clearly enjoying having the upper hand. "*Gone With The Wind*, among many others. Including *The Marrying Kind,* about a couple getting a divorce. It tries to answer the question of whether or not their love for each other is truly gone."

Lincoln nodded. "How does it end?"

Alan took another drink. "I won't ruin it for you. Not that you have any interest in such a life, as it might require you to have an actual opinion. Too real for you, I imagine."

Lincoln considered him, before saying, "To each of them it seemed that the life he led was the only real life, and the one his friend led was a mere illusion."

Alan stared at him beneath heavy eyelids. "Howdy Doody?"

Lincoln did not smile. "Leo Tolstoy. *Anna Karenina.* I won't ruin the ending for you."

Alan laughed. "God, you're such a *type*, Lincoln. Free from all constraints, so unencumbered from the responsibility of a lifelong commitment. I'd say you're not married because you couldn't find anyone you love as much as yourself." He glanced at Heather. "Leaving you free to do as you please." He toasted Lincoln for a second time, "All hail the non-marrying kind."

Heather grinned wanly and Lincoln continued to study

Alan. "My parents were happily married for forty-seven years," he said, finally. "Quite the role models, they were. Especially for such an impressionable young boy as I once was. And there was a time I longed for it. To have what my wonderful parents had. But from the time I was old enough to desire *such a life*, as you call it, I'd been convinced that I would never have it, that marriage was only for other people—ones not like me. But eventually I found myself in a committed relationship that lasted for seventeen years, right up until he died of cancer, a mere four months before the Supreme Court ruled that we were, after all, worthy of *such a life*." He raised his glass to return Alan's toast. "I once was the marrying kind, Mr. Hickman. But that time has passed."

Alan's expression shifted, his mind clearly reassessing what it knew to be true.

"Interesting, isn't it?" Lincoln went on. "How one small piece of new information can alter one's perception?"

Alan held his gaze only long enough to shore up the slipping sands of his ego, before at last lowering his eyes in defeat.

"Get some sleep, Alan," Lincoln said, kindly. "And do yourself a favor—don't watch the news. And for all that's holy, stay offline. You don't need the opinion of every nut-job in America. Ours will suffice." He stood and looked to Heather. "What time will Jacob be in?"

"His plane lands in twenty minutes. He'll call on the way to the hotel and we'll arrange to meet back here at nine tomorrow morning."

Lincoln glanced at Alan, still sitting on the couch. "Make it ten. Alan, we'll see you then, to discuss what will happen next."

Alan looked up, bleary eyed. "How can you possibly know what's going to happen next?" he asked.

"I don't." Lincoln set down his unfinished glass of scotch. "And that's precisely the reason we're going to be prepared for everything."

CHAPTER FOURTEEN

Years ago, Doctor Marcus Santini had treated a schizo-phrenic homeless woman named Gloria Rodriquez. Two days after leaving Resnick Neuropsychiatric, Gloria was stabbed to death by an unknown assailant as she waited outside a homeless shelter in downtown Los Angeles. Doctor Santini thought about her as he refilled his coffee mug in the doctor's lounge, a news report concerning the murder of Hannah Mills and his newest patient, the suspect Paula Hickman, droning on from a corner TV. There had been no news reports about the murder of Gloria Rodriquez.

"…police so far have not made any arrests," the reporter was saying, standing directly downstairs from where Doctor Santini was sipping his third cup of coffee, despite it only being a little past seven am. "Santa Monica police have said only that Paula Hickman remains a person of interest. A hospital spokesman would not comment on reports that Mrs. Hickman had attempted suicide, offering no information on whether or not she is even being treated in the Resnick Psychiatric ward here in the UCLA medical plaza. What we have confirmed is that the two women, who lived directly across the street from each other, had been…"

"Doctor Santini?"

The doctor turned from the TV, toward the nurse poking her head around the door.

"Yes, Marcia?"

"Doctor Claire Horst is on the phone for you. She says it's concerning your request for information on Paula Hickman."

*

At exactly eight in the morning, Lincoln Childress returned to the Santa Monica Police Station at the request of Detective Danny Melendez. The two men had met the night before and had immediately found that they disliked each other immensely. In fact, it had taken no more than two minutes of conversation before Detective Melendez had first warned Lincoln, "Don't take that condescending tone with me, sir."

So when the detective heard that the tall lawyer in the thousand-dollar suit had returned for round number two, he made sure to keep him waiting. Fifteen minutes after being informed of his presence, Melendez greeted Lincoln with a professional, if not polite, handshake.

"Thank you for coming down, Mr. Childress," he said, his other hand holding a chocolate donut. "Sorry for the early hour."

"Not a problem," Lincoln said as Melendez took a bite of his sugary breakfast. "I was up at five-thirty for my daily workout."

Melendez chewed slowly. "There's a few things we'd like to confirm with you," he said.

"I'll do what I can."

"We did some looking into Paula Hickman. She's got quite a history."

"She's had a difficult life, yes."

"As has Anthony Mills."

"Is that right?"

Detective Melendez took another bite of his donut. "It's odd that neither you nor Alan Hickman mentioned anything last night about their unfortunate history together. Or did it slip your mind that Paula Hickman was Paula Sullivan before they got married? The same woman Anthony once knew as Allyson Clemens? The same Allyson Clemens who was there the last time somebody close to him died?"

Lincoln did not hesitate to answer. "Mr. Hickman didn't mention it because he's not aware of the exact nature of the relationship between his wife and Mr. Mills, nor of the unfortunate *suicide* of the distraught young lady in Berkeley that you referred to. We will be discussing that with him today. It is not, however, necessary for me to discuss it with you, as it has no direct bearing on Hannah Mills's death."

"I don't think Mr. Mills would agree with you," Detective Melendez answered. "Seeing how his wife was murdered so soon after he moved across the street from an ex-lover with mental issues."

"Mr. Mills is under a tremendous strain. I imagine it is very difficult for him to see anything clearly at the moment."

"Lot of that going around. Evidently, Paula isn't able to see things very clearly herself. I do wonder what she'll say when the fog eventually clears."

"I can tell you exactly what she'll say," Lincoln smiled. "No comment."

"Seems bad things happen when those two get together, doesn't it?"

"Perhaps you should be asking Mr. Mills that question, rather than focusing on my client."

"Thank you for the advice. But right now we're focusing on the knife we found on the floor of your client's kitchen."

"Discovered in plain view," Lincoln calmly allowed. "But if you decide to come back for anything else, make sure you bring another warrant."

"Hmm," Melendez nodded in agreement. "We'd like to talk with Alan Hickman again."

"I'll arrange it," Lincoln said. "Anything else I can do for you?"

"Yes, there's one more thing I'm curious about," Detective Melendez said, putting the last of the donut into his mouth. "What sort of workout do you do, anyway?"

*

Most of what Paula knew of her mother and sister came from Jacob Russo, her father's lawyer, closest friend, and administrator of the Sullivan Trust. That was because her father, Kenneth Sullivan, had rarely spoken of his wife—Diane was her name— or of Allyson, Paula's sister, who died alongside her mother. Allyson was seven at the time of the accident—old enough, Paula imagined, to understand the horror of what was happening. For many years she wondered whose screams it was that eyewitnesses reported hearing, her mother's or her sister's. Paula, of course, was too young at the time of the accident to retain any memory of the family car rolling over or of the fire that engulfed it; only a dream-like recall remained, an amalgam from all the years she had envisioned that night. It was as if it hadn't truly happened at all, at least not to her; as though the memory belonged to a different person entirely.

As a child, whenever she pressed her father for information, he responded with short, precise answers, without elaboration.

He often cried when he spoke about it and on one occasion raised his voice to her in anger. She had asked why he'd chosen her to unbuckle and free from the burning car, rather than her mother or older sister. The sound of her father's voice in that moment haunted her still, though the anguished words themselves were lost to the hazy memory of time.

Paula had loved her father with a severe intensity, their painful history receding into the background hum of their relationship, and she forgave him for the silence between them, just as she forgave him when he shot himself in the head, unable, in the end, to forgive himself for the last glass of gin he'd swallowed before climbing behind the wheel of the family car on New Year's Eve.

But Jacob Russo was always there for her, spanning the emotional gaps that her father left. He had held Paula as a baby, a pretty little girl with the wispy blonde hair—angel's hair, her mother had called it. And he had held her when she was seven years old, when she shook uncontrollably from the unrelenting nightmare of her mother and sister screaming her name as flames engulfed them. And he held her six years later as she wept over the death of her father. So much pain in her life, so much loss.

Sitting with Lincoln and Alan in Alan's kitchen, sipping a cup of English Breakfast tea, Jacob recalled all of the times he'd been summoned to protect and care for the girl he had come to love as his own—the daughter that destiny had chosen to be his. He was eighty-one now, his once athletic frame eroded away, his hair white from half a life spent worrying about the only surviving member of his best friend's family. "It was my understanding she was doing better lately," he said. He set down his cup of tea on the granite center island. "I'd hoped the bakery was doing her some good. Emotionally, I mean."

"I think it did, at first," Alan said, elbows leaning on the counter opposite Jacob. "But honestly, it never sparked any real passion in her. But, yeah, things were going well, relatively speaking. And then a few months ago her depression returned, or, I don't know, reasserted itself. I mean, it was always there, lurking. Anyway, one day it was obvious she had…disconnected. I did everything I could to help her, but until the delusion about Hannah Mills looking identical to her began, she refused to even consider treatment. Our relationship has been strained by it, to say the least."

Jacob's own marriage had ended twenty-five years earlier, shortly after he'd left his wife's fiftieth birthday party on the Upper East Side. After a heated argument with her in front of the stunned party guests, he'd flown across the country to attend to Paula's detainment in connection to the death of her college roommate and her eventual forced placement into the Newberry Mental Health Institute. He wondered if he was witnessing the slow death of another marriage at the altar of little Paula.

Lincoln Childress remained silent, waiting for Jacob to say what needed to be said. "Alan," Jacob began, "we need to discuss some things that will be difficult for you to hear."

Alan sighed. "I find it hard to believe that anything will be more difficult than what I've been dealing with the past twenty-four hours."

Jacob maintained his intention to be direct and unapologetic. He and Alan had, over the years, developed a "friendship of necessity," as they called it. While very different in so many ways, they were bonded by their mutual desire to take care of Paula, and both men accepted that there were areas that would remain secret from the other—the necessarily private spaces carved out in marriage, for example, would be respected by

Jacob. In turn, the necessarily private inner workings of an entity as far-reaching as the Sullivan Manufacturing Corporation would remain hidden from Alan. Despite their respective roles having been well defined in the prenuptial agreement Alan had signed eleven years earlier, there remained a grey area for Jacob to weigh carefully—where his responsibilities to the Sullivan estate ended, and where Alan's right to information as Paula's husband began.

"After Paula lost so much as a child," Jacob went on, "my greatest fear has always been that I would act in some manner that would cause her to lose trust in me, to pull away. To the outside world, and certainly to my ex-wife, Paula had long been reduced to just another asset of the Sullivan Manufacturing Corporation I had to manage. But to me, she is the most important component of my life's work. And to maintain my position of trust in Paula's life, I agreed to keep hidden what she did not wish to be found."

Lincoln Childress shifted his weight on the stool beside him, and Jacob realized he was failing in his attempt to be forthright.

"When Paula went to college," he continued, turning to the heart of the matter, "it was her first time away from home, first time alone in the world. For reasons I did not initially understand, she changed her look dramatically and her entire personality followed suit. It was later explained to me that her doing so was a protective measure, a way to prevent the world from seeing how damaged she was. Becoming someone new was like slipping into armor. At Berkeley, she adopted the name of her older sister, Allyson—yet another psychological trick to feel less alone. It was as Allyson that she met Anthony Mills and the nature of their relationship deepened."

Alan stood upright, then leaned forward, as though Jacob's words could not reach him fast enough. "Deepened how?"

"They became a couple."

"You mean they were lovers?"

"Yes," Jacob continued. "And in the course of their relationship, Paula's roommate—a girl named Emily Jenkins—became quite infatuated with both of them. Ms. Jenkins came to fall in love with Anthony as well."

"What the fuck are you trying to tell me?" Alan asked, his impatience no doubt acerbated by the exhaustion and emotional upheaval of the previous twenty-four hours.

Jacob held up a hand. "Following an altercation involving Anthony, Emily Jenkins died. The exact circumstances surrounding her death remain unclear and, to many, suspicious. Ms. Jenkins had accused Anthony of raping her and the police suspected him of throwing her off the roof of a building, though the case was eventually closed as a suicide. But there were those that believed Paula had lied to protect Anthony—and still others who believed that she was somehow directly involved in Ms. Jenkins' death."

"Come on," Alan said, slowly processing the ramifications of Jacob's admission. His eyes darted between Lincoln and Jacob as though waiting for them to say it was all a joke. When no such admission came, he placed both hands heavily onto the island and lowered his head. He was quiet for almost a minute, then looked at Jacob. "Was she?"

"Excuse me?" said Jacob.

"Was Paula—did she kill her roommate?"

"Of course not," Jacob said, indignant at the mere suggestion.

"Of course not? How can you be so goddamned sure?"

"The accusations were all proven to be unfounded. Anthony

Mills was cleared of all charges. Paula was merely going through a difficult time and was acting out, which put her in the sights of those looking for answers. She had nothing to do with it."

"Well, shit," Alan said. "So, Paula takes on a new persona and her roommate, who loved Anthony, ends up dead. And now, after Paula comes to believe that Hannah, who *also* loved Anthony, has taken over her persona, she ends up dead as well."

"And there's the rub," Lincoln Childress said.

"You knew about all this?" Alan challenged him.

"I was aware of her history, yes."

"Well, fuck you too, then," Alan said, pushing himself away from the island.

"Alan," Jacob said. "Let's keep this from getting—"

"That's the reason she was sent to Newberry?"

"Yes," Jacob said. "She attempted suicide because of the stress surrounding the death of her roommate and the investigation. Placing her in Newberry was for her own protection."

Alan gave him a pained, disbelieving expression. "Or was it for the protection of Sullivan Manufacturing?" He looked at Lincoln. "Must have been your idea."

"No," Lincoln said. "That was before my time."

"The decision was mine," said Jacob. "When the police finally excluded her from their investigation, I used every means I could to keep her true identity from being made public—yes, for the protection of the company. Once the entire episode was behind us, I even arranged for the remainder of Anthony's education to be paid in full, and he agreed to keep quiet."

"You bribed him," Alan said.

"I helped an innocent young man who had lost his scholarship," Jacob insisted. "The offer came only after the police investigation was completed. You were never told because Paula preferred it that way."

"Anything to keep the golden goose happy," Alan said. "Sitting, as she is, on all those golden eggs."

"I did what was necessary to defend the interests of Sullivan Manufacturing. My means to that end could rightly be debated, but my personal motives in regards to Paula's well-being do not require any defense."

"Nor do they require an attack," Lincoln said in his lawyerly way. "Until recently, it was not information that had any bearing on the life you and Paula share, Alan."

Alan looked sharply to Lincoln. "As a general rule, the most successful man in life is the man who has the best information—Benjamin Disraeli."

"Understood, Professor," Lincoln said, giving him the victory this time, distracted as he was by the cellphone ringing in his coat pocket. "Hello?" he answered, stepping toward the hallway before stopping to turn back and face Alan. "Yes, he's here with me now." His expression gave nothing away as he listened. "Of course," he said, checking his watch. "We can be there in half an hour."

"What is it?" Jacob asked.

"I'm not sure," Lincoln said, placing the phone back in his pocket. "Evidently there's an issue with Paula's psychiatrist that needs to be straightened out."

CHAPTER FIFTEEN

A SLOW-MOVING ORDERLY went about his business in the day room, restocking scattered board games and collecting a few fallen playing cards, as the three men passed down the long hallway. A few patients sat in plush chairs, staring off as if asleep with their eyes open. Others sat around squared tables, coloring, reading, working crossword puzzles and word-searches with barely a word shared between them.

Alan had been told that Paula was still in her room, not yet ready to join the other residents of the ward. But still he looked for her, imaging her sitting among the pathetic collection of broken humans, not quite able to accept that she fit right in.

"Right this way, gentlemen," the accompanying nurse said, ushering Alan, Jacob, and Lincoln into the cramped office of Doctor Marcus Santini.

The doctor had longish dark hair that brushed the top of his collar, rimless glasses, and a round face presently set in a tired frown. "Hello, Mr. Childress," he said, standing from his desk to shake the tall lawyer's hand first. "Mr. Hickman," he nodded.

Jacob jutted his hand forward in an effort to hurry the formalities along. "Jacob Russo," he said.

"Yes, thank you for coming down so quickly."

"You have some information about Paula's doctor?" Jacob asked.

"I placed a call to Doctor Horst when we got some troubling results back from Paula's blood work," Santini explained. "Along with the THC and alcohol, there were also traces of benzodiazepine, phenobarbital, and beta-adrenergic blockers."

"What the hell are those?" Alan asked.

"They're from a class of central-nervous-system depressants often used to treat anxiety," Doctor Santini explained.

"Okay, hold on," Alan said. "That has to be a mistake, there's no way. She wouldn't take anything stronger than an aspirin."

"By her own admission, she was also drunk and stoned," Lincoln pointed out.

"That was the first time she ever got into my things," Alan said, sounding defensive and defiant all at once. "I guarantee you, in all the years we've been together. But these other drugs, I can't explain at all."

Doctor Santini looked as confused as Alan did. "There's no mistake," he said. "Your wife was mixing some very dangerous medications, which would undoubtedly have had an effect on her mindset and behavior."

Alan turned his head from side to side, as if trying to find a better angle on what he was being told. "No," he insisted. "That's just not possible."

"This psychiatrist she was seeing—" Jacob said.

"Doctor Horst," Santini nodded. "Yes, she was listed as her physician on the intake paperwork."

"I had no other name to give," Alan said. "Paula hasn't seen a general practitioner for several years."

"I understand," Doctor Santini said, softening a bit. "But I'm afraid there's some more confusion there as well."

With a soft knock on the door, an older woman entered. Her gray hair was pulled into a ponytail, a sunburst of loose strands sticking out at odd angles. "Sorry I'm late," she said. "I had some calls to make and was just told you had arrived."

"No, your timing is perfect," Doctor Santini said. "Thank you for coming. Gentlemen, this is Doctor Claire Horst."

"Can you shed some light on what's going on?" Jacob asked.

"I'm afraid I can't," Doctor Horst said. "Paula's not a patient of mine."

"What're you talking about?" Alan asked.

"I was surprised to hear from Doctor Santini that I was somehow involved with all of this," she answered as the crease in her forehead—undoubtedly gained from years spent in thoughtful reflection, listening to the problems of a parade of patients—deepened. "I've been seeing so much about this very sad situation on the news, but, the fact is, I've never met your wife."

"That's not true at all," Alan challenged her. "I spoke with you directly and set the first appointment."

"Yes, I remember. But Paula never showed up. I called and left several messages and never heard back. It's not unusual for patients to have second thoughts and I assumed when I hadn't heard anything that you had chosen a different doctor."

All eyes were on Alan, who was at a total loss. "I never got any messages," he said.

Doctor Horst said, "I recall you said your wife was hesitant to begin therapy. I can only assume she didn't want to disappoint you and erased the messages before you received them."

"Is it possible there's a different Claire Horst?" Lincoln asked, ever the lawyer, always trying to find a logical explanation.

"No, we've looked," Doctor Santini said.

"Then where the hell has she been going every Saturday for the past month?" Alan asked.

"That's what we'd like to find out," Doctor Santini said. "It's my hope that seeing Doctor Horst here, the real Doctor Horst, it will be impossible for Paula to maintain whatever delusion she's been under."

*

Paula's silence was like cement slowly filling a hole. The longer the doctors sat with her, the more impenetrable she became. She lay on her bed, the soft restraints of the past twenty-four hours no longer required. Her head was turned toward them, her eyes open, focused solely on the gray-haired woman sitting beside her bed, claiming to be Claire Horst.

"I understand how confusing all of this must be," the woman was saying. "I'm confused too. But if we talk to each other, we can work together to figure out where the confusion is coming from."

"Everyone is here for you," Doctor Santini said, though he remained only a shimmer of color in Paula's peripheral vision. "You're completely safe here."

They sat there for another hour, their voices soothing, caring, but were unable to make a crack in the hardening cement. The only sign that Paula heard what they said came when a single tear welled up in her eye and dropped down the slope of her cheek.

CHAPTER SIXTEEN

ALAN WAS GLAD to be rid of Lincoln Childress and Jacob Russo. He drove home from the hospital alone, consumed by thoughts of Paula's insanity. Images of her with Anthony and Hannah Mills came to him like a badly edited movie, scenes jumping back and forth in time—one moment the blood flowing from Hannah's wrists as she struggled with consciousness, the next moment her innocent face smiling, unaware of the fate she was to meet. And then more blood appeared, this time from her head, dripping down her neck as Paula stood behind her, glassy eyed and calm—Anthony, her onetime lover, looking on.

Alan turned onto Georgina Avenue, his window down to soak up the ocean breeze, the shimmer of perspiration on his skin quickly evaporating. He was pleased to see the news vans were gone from his street. But hidden from view, a few more vultures silently circled, waiting to swoop down. As he approached his driveway, Alan was startled by three men who leapt from behind parked cars. Their faces were hidden by cameras that rapidly clicked away, the shutters sounding like cockroaches scurrying across a tile floor.

The same paparazzi that stalked The Little Delicious whenever the occasional celebrity popped in were now stalking him.

Was he a celebrity now? Would his picture actually be worth money because his wife killed somebody? *What the fuck is wrong with the world?*

He raised his middle finger to the three men as they fired questions like bullets, never pausing for an answer, aiming only to draw blood. "Where's your wife?" they yelled. "Did you have any idea Paula was a killer?" "Do you feel safe around your wife?" The questions continued, the shutters clicking, until the garage door lowered behind him, sealing him in.

For a long time, Alan sat in his car, excoriating himself. The picture of him insolently flipping the bird would undoubtedly be spun by the media as showing contempt for the investigation into the sad death of Hannah Mills. He had even smiled, hadn't he? Alan tried to convince himself that he hadn't, that he had, in fact, looked beaten down, accosted—that he didn't look like an asshole. He imagined his students seeing the picture, their admiration and respect for him diminished by the callous behavior so unlike the intellectually superior professor they'd once considered him to be. "An appalling lack of judgement," he heard that smug asshole, Lincoln Childress, scolding him. Unable to contain himself, Alan pounded the steering wheel with open hands, screaming like a feral animal.

When he at last entered the house, he tossed his keys onto the kitchen counter and then stopped short. He was not alone. The stillness of the house was disturbed by a faint sound of rustling, which seemed to be coming from the downstairs bedroom—Paula's bedroom. He moved into the hallway, listening. He heard the soft mewling he had, over the years, grown accustomed to. Rounding into Paula's room, he watched as his sister changed the sheets on his wife's bed, her face wet with tears.

"What the hell are you doing?" he asked.

Wendy pulled the sheet toward the end of the bed and began the precise task of tucking it tightly under the mattress. "When Paula comes home, she's going to need help," she said. "Everything should be in order."

"Oh, so you're in charge of the order of things? Jesus Christ, what makes you think she's even gonna come home at all?"

"Once she's better, she'll be home," Wendy insisted, smoothing out the sheet before crossing to the opposite side of the bed. "I saw on the news that the police haven't arrested her. She's only a person of interest. She obviously didn't do it. If they had the evidence, they would have arrested her already."

"They haven't arrested her because there's no rush for them," Alan explained, too emotionally depleted to rise above his mocking tone. "She's on a fifty-one-fifty. That gives them seventy-two hours to hold her. Once that's over, she's going to be arrested and put in jail. They're gonna hold her there for trial, where she'll be found guilty of murder. And changing her fucking sheets isn't going to make any diff—"

"Don't do that!" Wendy bolted upright, leaving half the sheet hanging free from the mattress. "She wouldn't hurt any-body! Not like that!"

Alan could have told her everything Doctor Santini and the real Doctor Horst had told him, could have blown up every last corner of the fantasy world his sister had constructed around his wife, but he was not up to having the conversation that would follow. So he left the room, leaving his sister behind to finish her goddamn therapy cleaning.

Wendy did not emerge from Paula's bedroom for nearly an hour. She had grown so quiet that Alan forgot she was there at all. He spoke briefly with Jameson Lynch, the chair of the Global Studies Administrative Committee at UCLA, to discuss his leave of absence for the remainder of the semester. At one point he considered eating lunch but couldn't muster the energy to prepare anything. He was nearly asleep in the leather club chair tucked into the corner of the den, the muted television broadcasting frantic images of unrest along the Myanmar/Thailand border, when Wendy entered the room.

"Alan," she said, her voice timid, as if afraid to further upset him.

He stirred and blinked. "Are you leaving?" he asked.

"I found something." She was holding a black book.

"What is it?" Alan sat up, turning off the television.

Wendy looked down at the journal. "It's Paula's. It was under her mattress."

Alan reached a hand out, but Wendy did not give him the journal.

"It's bad, Alan," she said, her eyes once again tearing.

Alan kept his arm outstretched. "Let me see it," he said, feeling sorry for his older sister.

Wendy handed him the journal, then sat on the couch, saying nothing more through her gathering tears.

CHAPTER SEVENTEEN

Lisa Robbins walked the two detectives to the door of her apartment. "I'm sorry I can't tell you more," she was saying. "I only met her that one time and it was so quick. I really wish I knew what Mrs. Mills and she were arguing about."

"You've been very helpful," Detective Kerr assured her, handing her a business card.

Lisa cleared the emotion from her throat. "It's so strange to realize she's dead. Just gone like that." She held up the card. "But I guess you guys are used to it."

"It's not something you ever get used to," Melendez said, opening the door.

"I guess, yeah," Lisa said, still working off the adrenaline that came with being the last person to see Paula and Hannah together. "I'll definitely never get used to the memory of her face—that woman's face—when she came running out of the studio. She was so wild looking."

"As I said, Ms. Robbins, sometimes people remember things once the stress of an event has passed. If anything at all comes up, no matter how inconsequential it might seem, be sure to contact us."

The detectives were near the end of the walkway, in the

shadow of the adjoining apartment building, when Lisa called after them. "Detectives? I don't like to say anything, because he didn't do anything in particular, but, if it were me, I'd look into Mr. Mills's brother."

"Why's that?" Detective Melendez asked.

Lisa nervously smoothed the ends of her hair through her fingers. "I mean, he's on parole and everything, and there's just something about him. He's kinda sketch, you know?"

Detective Melendez smiled. "Thank you again for all of your help," he said.

"Okay," Lisa said. "If you see Mr. Mills and his little boy, tell them I said I'm thinking of them."

*

An hour later Detectives Melendez and Kerr sat in Anthony's living room, waiting for him to make an appearance. He was in his son's bedroom trying to calm the boy down, they were told.

"He's been acting out," Violet Mills said, sitting on the couch opposite the two men, bookended on either side by her granddaughters, Kimberly and Shawna. The girls, one seven and the other eleven, stared at the men in their suits with either suspicion or boredom, it was difficult to tell. "It's so hard, so hard," Violet sighed. "That poor boy has a heavy load to carry."

"I'm sure having you here is a big help," said Detective Kerr.

Violet patted Shawna's leg. "Well, their mom's gotta get these two back up to Oakland to finish up with their school year, but I'm gonna stay a while longer."

"Are you retired?" Detective Kerr asked.

"Yes, sir. After thirty-five years working for Ralph's supermarket."

"I got sandwiches in the kitchen," Anthony's sister, Devika, said as she stepped into the room, ignoring the two policemen altogether. Her daughters, however, turned their hopeful stares from their mother back to the detectives. "What you two lookin' at?" Devika snapped her fingers. "You don't have to ask them permission. If you hungry, then come on."

The girls climbed silently from the couch and went into the kitchen.

"You seen Darius?" Devika asked her mother. "I got some for him, too."

"He's out," Violet said.

Devika's hoop earrings swayed as she shook her head and glanced at the detectives. "Must have heard who was coming," she said, and then turned and left the room.

"Don't pay that no mind," Violet said to the detectives, clearly annoyed with her youngest child. "Darius ain't trying to avoid you. He's just trying to lay low, you understand. He don't need no trouble. Lord knows having him here was another strain on Anthony and Hannah, so he ain't doing anything he's not supposed to."

The detectives glanced sideways at each other.

"Family dynamics can be hard to manage," said Detective Kerr.

"Amen," Violet agreed.

"When you say his brother's arrival has been another strain," Detective Melendez said, "what do you mean by that? Has Anthony been under some stress?"

"Oh, Anthony doesn't like to be a burden on anyone, he's always more concerned about others, so he don't talk much about his problems. I'm his mother, for goodness sake, and he ain't ever asked me for a thing since he was grown, always giving, never taking. But it's been hard on him, moving down here and having to start fresh. He and Hannah didn't always see things the same way. But that's marriage, ain't it?"

"Yes, ma'am," said Kerr, nodding.

"The move here was causing problems for Hannah and Anthony?" Melendez asked.

Violet glanced toward the hall and then lowered her voice. "Between you and me, Hannah could be very emotional, which caused some issues. That's why they hired that young nanny. I raised three kids myself, without so much as a babysitter. But I can't say nothing bad about Hannah, not now. She did the best she could."

"Did your son and his wife argue a lot?" Melendez asked.

"I'm afraid so, yes," Violet said, sadly. "He did so much for her, too."

"Sorry for the wait, detectives," Anthony said, coming into the room, his face stippled with the salt and pepper growth of two days without a shave. "Mom, can you stay with Alex for a bit?" he said.

Violet's dour expression immediately lightened at the approach of her oldest child. "Of course," she said, raising her seventy-four-year-old frame up from the couch. "It was nice chatting with you two."

"Thank you, Mrs. Mills," Detective Kerr said, he and his partner respectfully standing.

Once alone, Anthony motioned for them to sit.

"Maybe it would be better if we talked someplace a little more private," said Detective Melendez.

The three men reconvened behind the closed door of Anthony's office, and the detectives laid out the state of the investigation into Hannah's murder. "We got the report back,"

Detective Melendez began. "The knife Paula used on her hands did not match the wounds on your wife."

Anthony briefly lowered his head between his shoulders and stared at the floor. "Okay," he said, before raising back up to look at the detectives.

The detectives didn't mention that they were still operating under the "murder-suicide" theory that after killing Hannah, Paula could not find the will to kill herself. The wounds on her hands were deep, intentional, possibly done out of frustration for not having the will to cut her own wrists. But they kept those details to themselves. "Not finding a murder weapon makes things more challenging," Melendez said. "But there are still some things we're looking into."

"Like what?" Anthony asked.

Detective Melendez gestured with his hands, palms out, indicating they were about to venture into difficult territory. "In an investigation like this, we have to look at every angle. You understand?"

"Of course."

"All right Anthony, with that in mind, we'd like to talk a little bit about what happened when you were at Berkeley."

"Oh, come on," Anthony bristled.

"We understand that you were put through the wringer during the investigation into the death of Emily Jenkins. But there's some things we—"

"Forget it," Anthony said. "I accept this shit has to be covered, but I had nothing to do with Emily jumping off that roof."

Detective Melendez remained neutral in his bearing. "We aren't trying to relitigate her suicide, but in light of your wife's death, and the unusual circumstance of you having recently moved across the street from Paula—"

"It's not an unusual for two friends to live close to each other."

"No, it's not," Melendez agreed. "But for those two friends to be so closely tied to two separate deaths?"

Anthony leaned back in his seat and tapped his fist to his mouth. This was not merely an update, then, but another round of questions. He had answered so many already, had sat with these very same men less than twenty-four hours earlier, and he was still being treated like a suspect. "That is an unusual coincidence, yes," he agreed. He sucked in a mouthful of air and blew it sharply back out. "But just as I had nothing to do with Emily Jenkins's suicide, I had nothing to do with the death of my wife."

"But can you be sure that Paula didn't?"

"No, of course I can't. But I can't fathom any reason why she would do such a thing."

"Jealousy?"

"No matter how many ways you hint at it, the answer will be the same. Despite our relationship in college, Paula and I were nothing more than friends. We have a shared history that was very intense. It was a time in our lives that bonded us, that's all."

"How often did you and Paula talk before you moved here?" Detective Kerr asked.

"Only every so often. We used to email quite a bit, but not so much the past few years."

"Since you got married, you mean?"

Anthony's chest froze at the top of an inhale. "That's correct."

"And she and your wife had never communicated with each other?"

"We covered all this yesterday, didn't we? They met for the first time a few days after we moved in."

"Why did your email exchanges with Paula taper off?" Kerr

asked. "Were there any disagreements between the two of you? Any arguments?"

"No, nothing like that. There was nothing to argue over. Our talks became less frequent because I became very busy with my work, and then when Alex was born I only got busier."

Detective Kerr continued to press. "Did Paula ever express anything to you about still having feelings for you—romantically, I mean?"

"No, of course not. College was a long time ago."

"And how were you and Hannah doing? Moving to a new city can be very stressful."

"My wife and I had been going through a difficult time. We weren't always on the same page."

"That's interesting," Detective Melendez said. "Alan Hickman said the exact same thing about his wife."

"Is it really that interesting?" Anthony challenged him. "I'm gonna guess that our two marriages aren't the only ones having problems in this neighborhood."

Melendez remained undaunted. "What sort of things did you and Hannah argue about?"

"Hannah's had a hard few years since our son was born," he said, calming. "She was very successful for a long time but ran into some trouble last year."

"Trouble?" asked Detective Kerr.

Anthony steeled himself, as though dredging up his wife's past took a great effort. "She was a junior partner at her firm in Mountain View, she was a very good lawyer, contract law. But she made a mistake—a 'mistake of fact,' they called it— that caused a rather large deal to be voided, costing her firm a considerable amount of money. They later discovered that she'd been smoking pot. Trying to juggle a young son and her job was creating a lot of stress for her, so there it is. But she was indignant that those men, who all got pretty fucking loose on martinis on a nightly basis, would point to that as a pertinent issue. It was not. The entire situation was just an unfortunate mistake caused by some paperwork their client didn't disclose. But none of that mattered. They were looking for a scapegoat and they got what they wanted. In the end, it was agreed that she would step down from her position at the firm. She had a very hard time dealing with it all, and despite my encouragement, she had no interest in trying to find a new firm, or in doing much of anything for that matter. It was a bad time for us, so when I was offered a job here, we decided the change would be a good one."

"You both felt the same way about the move?" Detective Kerr asked.

Anthony collected himself. "She wasn't as interested in relocating to LA as I was."

"That must have been hard on you—stressful."

"Please stop saying the same damn thing over and over. Yes, it was stressful. Life is stressful. Look, I understand how this works. The husband is always a suspect, I got it. But the fact that my wife and I argued over her generally crappy outlook doesn't mean that I had anything to do with her death."

"Nobody's saying you did," Detective Melendez said. "We're only trying to get a clear understanding of the situation leading up to the other night."

"Mm-hmm," said Anthony.

The three men sat pondering where they could go from there and whether or not they'd all be going in the same direction. Detective Kerr spoke next, making it clear they wouldn't be. "Where's your brother?" he asked.

Anthony's jaw clenched. "Running errands."

"Do you know where he was, night before last?"

"At home. With me."

"You were with him the whole time? As I recall, yesterday you told us you fell asleep around ten. I'm gonna guess you and your brother no longer share a room?"

"Darius didn't kill Hannah. He had nothing to do with this."

"Like he had nothing to do with the death of Emily Jenkins?" said Detective Kerr.

Anthony looked hard at the detective. "Man, fuck you."

Kerr looked surprised by Anthony's anger. "I wasn't trying to offend you, Mr. Mills."

"It's hard to tell," Anthony said. "Because I'm pretty sure you would've said the same thing if you *had* been."

Detective Melendez gave his partner a look, and that was that. Kerr took his foot off the gas and, after a strained effort to ease their combative exchange, thanked Anthony for his time. "If you could just have your brother give us a call when he gets back?"

Anthony took the request like a drop of foul-tasting medicine. "Sure," he answered.

The detectives walked to the door of the office and then Kerr turned back. "Oh, and one more thing," he said. "If you could supply us with those emails between you and Paula, that would be great."

*

Once alone, Anthony checked in on his son, who had fallen asleep in the loving arms of his grandma, and then returned to his office. He called his brother but left no message when it went to voicemail. He then logged onto his secured internet account. He had learned so much while working for HSH up in Mountain View. How to fake his computer's IP address, how to use email spoofing to gain access to another comuter, how to erase all of his digital footprints.

After a few keystrokes, Anthony stared at the Facebook account registered to the phantom person he had named Brice Lawford. His profile photo was a picture of Snoopy sleeping on his doghouse. He then went to the depression support group he'd been a member of for the last four years. There were over forty-seven thousand members of the group, but he had joined solely because of one.

Anthony read for a while, scrolling though the archives of all the discussions Brice had with Jill Carlson, the lonely redhead who lived out in Los Angeles, whose husband was deployed overseas. Brice and Jill got along so well, always had, right from the beginning. They often talked about the difficulties of raising children without a present spouse. It was a secret pleasure for Anthony to be with her as Brice, to share all of his deepest concerns, to be so open and honest with her about the state of his failing marriage. He was never lonely, never unsure, when talking with Jill.

Anthony's hands tightened as he drew them away from the keyboard. He sat silently for a few moments. He tried—for the second time in as many days—to write her a new message, if only to retrieve some of the comfort he'd found in the fantasy of their relationship, but he could not bring himself to type the words.

It didn't matter anyway. Jill Carlson was no longer there.

CHAPTER EIGHTEEN

WHEN AN ORDERLY found Paula sitting up on the corner of her bed, she spoke her first words since being brought to the Resnick Neuropsychiatric Hospital twenty-four hours earlier. "Can I go outside?" she asked.

The orderly shrugged and said he'd go find a doctor. As Paula sat and waited, the reality of Hannah being dead bored through her. Emotion swirled in her gut like burning leaves caught in a breeze—she could not hold onto any one thought long enough to tamp it down. Fleeting stabs of pain cycled through, echoes from a lost memory.

Hannah. What did I do to you?

"Hello Paula," Doctor Santini said, suddenly standing before her. "Do you remember who I am?"

Paula nodded. "You're the Easter Bunny. No wait, Benjamin Franklin." Doctor Santini smiled. Paula liked his smile; it made her feel normal, whatever that meant. "Can I go outside, please?" she asked.

Doctor Santini led her down the hallway. The floor was buffed to a high shine, and Paula found a silent pleasure in sliding along in her slippers. They passed the day room, where several men and women sat, dressed in casual clothing, looking more like they were waiting for a table at Applebee's than sitting in a psych ward. Averting her eyes, Paula continued on, past a man in a black hoodie and an LA Dodgers cap walking gingerly up the hall as though the soles of his feet had been burned. He gave a friendly wave. Paula pressed together the thick gauze dressings on her hands, suddenly conscious of the blue smock draped loosely around her. "Can I get my regular clothes back?" she asked.

"Of course," said Doctor Santini, taking a manila file handed to him by a passing nurse.

They found their way onto an outdoor patient terrace, where Paula eyed the pink underbellies of the high-hanging clouds. "What time is it?" she asked.

"Ten minutes to seven," Doctor Santini said.

Paula traced a flock of seagulls soaring toward the ocean, chasing the last light of day. "How long am I going to be here?" she asked, keeping her eyes on the birds until they were blocked by one of the tall building surrounding the hospital.

"A couple more days, at least. First we have to make sure you're stabilized and processing things clearly."

"Processing what things clearly?" Paula asked, turning to face him.

"Let's start with how much of the past few days you remember?"

She blew out a slow breath. "Enough to know that I'm a suspect in the murder of Hannah Mills."

"What do you think about that?"

"I think it's not good," she said.

Doctor Santini motioned to a wooden bench and they sat down next to each other. "Let's talk about what happened that night," he said.

She stared off. "Won't be much of a conversation, I don't have any memory of anything that happened. I'm totally lost."

Doctor Santini leaned forward to catch her eye. "It's okay to be lost, we're going to help get you back. I promise, you're doing great."

"That's odd, because I feel like shit."

"You've had a very intense couple of days," he said, patting the folder resting on his lap. "I'd like to go over with you some of the things we found in your system."

"You sound like a dad who caught his daughter smoking weed behind the garage."

"And have you been smoking weed behind the garage?"

"As all busted kids say, 'Just that one time, I swear.'"

"I believe you. But why was that? After so many years?"

"I wanted to be numb."

"And you got it from your husband?"

"I took it from him, yes."

"Did you take anything else from him?"

"What does that mean?"

Doctor Santini pulled a medical report from the folder and handed it to her. "These are your toxicology results. I'd like you to see for yourself what I'm seeing."

Paula scanned the report. She saw her name on the paper, and her birth date. There were many narrow rows and tiny boxes—some empty, others filled with words and numbers she didn't understand. "What am I looking for?" she asked.

Doctor Santini pointed to three rows. "You can see here that there were several different medications found in your system: benzodiazepine, phenobarbital, and, here, slight traces of beta-adrenergic blockers. That's quite a combination."

"It doesn't make any sense," Paula said.

"You have no recollection of taking any of these?"

She shook her head.

"Were any of these medications in your home? Maybe in your husband's room?"

"I don't know what he takes, but nothing like this, I'm sure."

"And no recollection of being with Hannah last night?"

Paula's stomach lightened, as though she had crested a wave and was dropping at a fantastic speed. "I don't remember leaving my house. I fell asleep at some point and then woke up in the morning when I heard voices outside my bedroom. When I looked at my phone to see what time it was, there was a text message from Hannah asking to talk with me, but I hadn't responded. And then the police were there, pointing their guns at me. It was like I was still in a dream."

Doctor Santini considered her. "When blackouts occur, they're usually accompanied with short-term memory loss. It's not necessarily a surprise that you experienced one, especially if you hadn't been exposed to alcohol and THC and then consumed so much, along with these other medications. Did you have any nausea? Any vomiting?"

"No, I didn't get sick at all."

Doctor Santini took back the file. "How about we talk about Doctor Horst?"

Paula's emotions slipped ever faster. "If you mean the woman from yesterday, that's not the Doctor Horst I know. There's another Claire Horst. She has an office in Pasadena."

"And if I showed you a list of every doctor licensed to practice in the state of California and there was only one doctor listed with that name, how would it make you feel?"

Paula steeled herself. "Disoriented," she said.

"Another appropriate response."

"That's what Doctor Horst used to say to me—*appropriate response*. But being full of appropriate responses to one's insanity is not as comforting as you may think it is."

"You're not insane, Paula. But you are living a specific experience, unique to yourself."

"A specific experience, unique to myself? That's a hell of a long way to go to avoid calling me crazy, but I appreciate the effort."

"You're very self-aware," said Doctor Santini.

"Also noted by Doctor Horst. You guys all follow the same playbook." She shook her head. "I'm guessing that's probably another appropriate response."

"Yes, it is. Though it's our belief that what you're responding to is the anxiety that comes with depression. Unfortunately, depression isn't some mass that can be cut out and thrown away, solving all the problems. It's a chemical imbalance in your brain, one that has been made worse by your efforts to treat yourself."

"Treat myself?"

"It appears to me that, over time, you've created a fantasy life for yourself, one that you've been relying on to help you cope with your anxieties."

"None of this is a fantasy," she insisted.

Doctor Santini took out a black and white photograph from the file, clipped from that morning's LA Times. "Do you recognize who this is?" he asked.

Paula stared at the photo. "That's Hannah," she said, finally.

"Yes, it is. But according to your husband, you've been convinced that Hannah Mills was physically identical to you."

Her heartbeat pulsed in her neck. "Not anymore," she said.

"Why not?"

She shook her head, fighting to keep her emotions from spilling out. "It was that day in Hannah's studio, the day before she died. She was upset because she found out that Anthony and I had once loved each other and that some bad things had happened when we were together. She was very angry with me. She was yelling and her face changed, she—" Her tears momentarily overwhelmed her and it took a moment to regain control. "She looked different, no longer identical to me."

"So, after she saw the real you, you saw the real her."

Paula squeezed her eyes closed.

"And now that you've met the real Doctor Horst," Doctor Santini went on. "Perhaps you'll no longer see the phantom woman you believed to be her."

"I don't understand any of this," Paula cried.

"I know you don't, Paula," Doctor Santini said, placing a consoling hand on her shoulder. "But there are explanations—"

"It was a delusion," Paula interrupted, wiping tears from her face. "Part of something called the Syndrome of Subjective Doubles."

Doctor Santini looked surprised, though pleased. "That's exactly right. You've been doing some research."

"No," Paula said, looking intently at him. "Doctor Horst told me all about it."

Doctor Santini angled his body toward her. "Or did you maybe read about it after creating a soothing presence in your mind, someone you could trust and who would help you cope with the reality of Anthony Mills coming back into your life? Perhaps in the same way you created an image of Hannah Mills that looked exactly like yourself?"

Paula blinked through fresh tears and then buried her face in her hands.

CHAPTER NINETEEN

IT WAS DARK when Jacob Russo and Lincoln Childress arrived at the Hickman home. There were four police cars idling in front, their blue and red lights drawing neighbors from their homes like moths, unable to resist the excitement. Lincoln parked the BMW he'd borrowed from Heather and he and Jacob stepped toward the uniformed officer stationed at the curb.

"I need you to stop right here," the officer said, holding up his hand.

"I'm afraid need and want are two separate desires," Lincoln said. "Though neither of them have any influence on us going inside."

"Excuse me?" the officer said, repositioning his wide frame.

"Must you be this way all the time?" Jacob said to Lincoln, shaking his head.

Ignoring the question, Lincoln pointed toward the home. "I'm assuming Detective Danny Melendez is the one serving the warrant? Please inform him that Lincoln Childress is here to see his client."

The officer kept his eyes trained on the impertinent lawyer and spoke into the radio attached to his shoulder. A few seconds later a voice came back and, reluctantly, he stepped aside.

Alan stood helplessly in the foyer when Lincoln and Jacob entered.

"Relax," said Lincoln. "It means they didn't find anything that matched the wounds on Hannah Mills—otherwise they'd be serving an arrest warrant, not another search warrant. Let me take a look at it."

"I don't have it," Alan told him. "I didn't even read it."

Lincoln hooded his eyes into another condescending critique, but said only, "Get some fresh air and I'll take care of it." Jacob and Alan moved toward the front porch but were stopped short by Lincoln's sharp reproach. "The *backyard*, gentlemen," he said.

Alan and Jacob peered through the open front door at the gathering of neighbors in the street, most of whom had their phone cameras held up, and sheepishly crossed toward the rear of the house.

There were six officers idling inside, one of whom was able to locate the misplaced search warrant on the kitchen counter. "Electronic communications?" Lincoln said to Danny Melendez as the detective entered the kitchen from Paula's bedroom. He dismissively tossed the warrant back onto the counter. "On what grounds? Death by lethal email?"

"Take it up with the judge who granted it," Melendez said.

A police officer walked through with an evidence bag containing Paula's laptop. "They recovered the second iPad in the upstairs bedroom," he said to Melendez. "We're all finished."

Melendez nodded, then turned back to Lincoln. "We'd like to look at Alan Hickman's phone too."

"No," Lincoln said.

Melendez smiled. "Yeah, the judge said the same thing."

"That's because he knows you're grasping at straws."

"We'll see," Melendez said. "And by the way. The judge isn't a *he*. You should probably stop the patriarchal assumptions. It might be keeping you from realizing that women are just as capable as men to do extraordinary things."

He tossed an unused prescription pad on the counter, next to the dropped warrant. Lincoln did not pick it up. "We found it in Paula's desk while looking for her laptop," said Detective Melendez.

Lincoln shrugged off the discovery. "Not covered by the warrant and not discovered in plain sight," he said.

"You wanna explain it anyway? Forging scripts is a felony."

"It's not hers. She has no idea how it got there. She found it on the sidewalk. The police planted it. It's the maid's. Would you like some more or do you wanna take your pick now?"

"Like I said," Detective Melendez grinned as he walked off. "Extraordinary things."

Within thirty minutes, the storm of activity had passed—leaving an eerie silence in its wake. Alan remained with Jacob on the back porch, despite the night chill. The house seemed too foreign to him now, devoid of any of the warmth it once held. When Lincoln finally came out to join them, he wasted no energy on reassuring small talk. Using the tone of a prosecutor in a courtroom, he relayed the information about the discovered prescription pad and zeroed in on Alan.

"Where could the pad have come from?" he asked.

"I have no idea."

"Your wife was smoking weed, using heavy barbiturates and tranquilizers, and yet you keep saying that you had no indication of anything at all."

Alan sat forward in his seat. "Is that supposed to imply I was somehow involved in getting her those things?"

"In point of fact, you're the one who's suggesting that."

"Lincoln, that's enough," Jacob said. "We all need to be pulling in the same direction, not placing blame where none is to be found."

Alan leaned back in his chair. "Maybe I am to blame. She was so lost in her delusion about Hannah, and I just let her be, trusting that the doctor she was seeing was helping her."

"The doctor who was also a delusion," Lincoln said.

"That's right," Alan said, sounding defensive, despite his best efforts. "She stayed in her room all the time, avoiding me, building up some fantasy life outside of her ever-shrinking reality. After a while, whatever it was she conjured became more real to her than I was."

"You could have called me," Jacob said.

"Thank you for saying *could* have, instead of *should* have."

Lincoln stared intently at him and Alan could not break the code behind his eyes. *Does he believe anything I say? Am I acting appropriately, in his fucking privileged estimation?* "Is there something on your mind, Lincoln?" he asked.

"I'm in line with Jacob that we should be pulling in the same direction," he said. "Do you agree with that assessment?"

"Of course."

"Then I'll assume that you'll not be giving the finger to any more photographers?"

Alan's heart fluttered.

"What're you talking about?" Jacob asked. But his questions were ignored as Lincoln continued to hold Alan in his piercing gaze.

"It was a mistake," Alan said. "Those bastards wouldn't leave me alone and my emotions got the better of me."

"What bastards?" asked Jacob.

"And now your picture is all over the internet."

"What picture?" Jacob sputtered.

"Are we on the same page here, Alan?" Lincoln asked.

Everything in Alan's life was so unsettled it felt as if he would never be comfortable again. If the journal hidden on the top shelf of his closet were found, if the often-violent obsession it chronicled was revealed to the world, it would undoubtedly lead to his wife's immediate arrest for the murder of Hannah Mills. He would not allow that to happen. "We are," he said.

"Good," said Lincoln. "So tell me, what are the police going to find on Paula's computer?"

Alan met Lincoln's stare head on. "Trouble."

CHAPTER TWENTY

Darius sat on a metal chair, tucked into the corner of a small office inside the Santa Monica Police Station, facing the two detectives, unable to find anything resembling comfort. He was on his third can of Coke, but he licked his lips as though his mouth held no moisture at all.

"There's still something about all this that isn't sounding right," Detective Kerr said. "Tell us again what time it was when you went into the backyard?"

"I couldn't say, not exactly," Darius said, trying hard to remember. "But I guess it was after midnight, cause I was watching a rerun of *The Game* and that didn't even come on till eleven-thirty."

"What game was that?" asked Detective Kerr.

"No, man, *The Game* is a TV show. It was on BET for, like, ten years."

"Never heard of it," said Detective Kerr.

"You need to stop watching reruns of *Seinfeld* and shit," Darius said, taking another sip of Coke.

"The problem I'm having here is that it seems like an odd thing to do, going outside at that hour for no reason," Detective Kerr said.

"I'm always up late. I get insomnia."

"That's not what I'm talking about, Darius."

"For real, I was getting air is all."

The detectives were quiet, remaining as calm as if the three of them were sitting over coffee, reminiscing about some inconsequential event, not an unsolved murder. "Were you smoking weed?" Kerr asked him, a dart meant to startle him.

Darius shifted in his chair. "No, sir."

"We can do this all day, Darius," Kerr said. "We already know that Hannah smoked a little. She had it in her system when she died. Maybe you were out there smoking with her?"

"No, man," Darius insisted. "I ain't doing that no more."

"You do understand that random drug testing is a part of your parole," Detective Melendez said. "If we tested you today, would we find anything?"

Darius took another swallow of Coke and then licked his lips again, his tongue darting in and out of his mouth. "Come on, man, I'm trying to help you guys out here, why you playin' me?"

"We don't want your *help*, Darius," said Detective Melendez. "We want the truth."

Darius leaned back in his chair and rubbed his eyes, readjusted his feet. "Shit, man," he said, before asking, tentatively, "What would happen if I was smoking a little?"

The detectives shared a look and Melendez said, "We're not interested in jamming you up on a small parole violation. Tell us the truth about what happened and we'll let it slide."

Darius rocked back and forth in his seat before steadying himself. "All right, man," he said. "I got a little bit from Hannah."

"She gave it to you, or you took it from her?"

"She gave it to me."

"You two smoked together?" asked Kerr.

"No. She gave it to me as, like, a peace offering or something. We didn't get along so good, you know what I'm saying? She wasn't happy with me being there and all. Hell, maybe she was tryin' to get me in trouble, but I took it anyways."

"She give any weed to Paula Hickman?"

"How would I know that?"

"You said that you had talked to Paula in the driveway a few days before. Did you give her any weed?"

"Hell no, man. I didn't have any when she and I talked. Hannah didn't give it to me yet, for real."

"Okay," Detective Kerr said. "So Hannah gives you this one joint and then what?"

"So I had this joint and, like I said, I couldn't sleep, so I went into the backyard. She didn't even know I was there when she came out the house."

"What was she doing going outside at that hour?"

"She and Anthony had another argument, yelling at each other and shit. She probably didn't want to be around him, or something. He was already in bed, so she couldn't go there. Even with him asleep it was still fucking tense in the house, so—"

"What were they arguing about?" asked Melendez.

"Hannah was pissed because I had let it out about Anthony and Paula being together back in the day, and then that led to all that shit about Bunny."

"Why'd you tell her if you knew it was a secret?"

Darius shook his head, looked at the floor. "'Cause I was a little fucked up, and it slipped out."

"Fucked up on what, Darius?"

Darius hesitated, then raised his eyes to meet the detective's. "On the shit she gave me."

Melendez fixed his stare. "I thought you said you two didn't smoke together?"

"We didn't," he said, taking another sip of Coke.

"But you said she only gave you that one joint, the one that you still had?"

Darius's eyes darted between the two detectives. He licked his lips.

Melendez's tone shifted. "If you're not honest with us, then we can't help you with your parole, Darius. So, let's cut the bullshit. Were you and Hannah getting high together when you told her about the relationship between Paula and your brother?"

"Man, come on. Maybe we were, all right? But it don't mean nothing. It was only one time, for real. She was out in the art studio they got and I walked in on her that afternoon when she was smoking a J, so we shared it. That's it."

"Why'd you lie about it?" Melendez asked.

"'Cause I didn't want Anthony finding out. He was already angry enough that I had said something about Paula, with Hannah yelling at him and shit when he got home."

"How bad was it between them?" Melendez asked. "Did it get violent?"

"No, Anthony ain't about that."

"So, were you also smoking weed with Hannah in the backyard the night she died?"

"No."

"Don't lie to us, Darius."

"I swear, man. I wasn't with her. I was already outside, like

I said, and she came out, talked to the dog for a second, like petting him and shit, and then she took off."

"Without seeing you?"

"She came out the side-yard door, off the kitchen, and I heard the door slam. She didn't even look over to where I was in the yard, and she went out the back gate to the front of the house. And then that's when I heard her calling out, all right?"

"Calling out what?" asked Detective Kerr.

Darius took a breath, sucked on his lips. "Man, I heard her call out to Paula."

"Hold up," said Detective Melendez, leaning forward in his chair. "You're saying Paula Mills was with her?"

"No, man. She was, like, calling out to her," Darius said. "She said it twice. It was like, 'Paula! Paula!'"

"Did it sound as if she was afraid?"

"No, not like that. Like she was letting her know she was there."

Detective Kerr nodded. "And then what?"

"And then nothing."

"What do you mean, nothing?"

"That's it, man. I didn't hear nothing after that. I was out there a couple more minutes and then I went back into the house and went to bed."

Darius drank the last of his Coke and put the empty can on the table beside him. "It's all fucked up, huh?" he said.

"Yeah, Darius," said Detective Melendez. "It is."

The detectives had him go over the account another three times, coming at him from different angles each time, but the story didn't change. They talked a bit more about the tension filling the house, learning nothing new, even when the conversation again hit upon the death of Emily Jenkins. Darius retold the same story Melendez and Kerr had heard from the (now retired) detective up in Berkeley, with no variation from what they'd been told by Anthony. Emily was Darius's girlfriend, she was unstable, she'd scratched Anthony's face during an argument after she accused him of raping her, and then she jumped off the roof of a building a few blocks from campus while he and Anthony were driving home to Oakland.

"Fuck all them people who say Anthony had somethin' to do with it," were Darius's last words on the matter.

Two hours after he arrived at the police station, Darius left.

"Do you believe him?" Detective Kerr asked his partner, once they were alone.

"Hard to tell. He's got a history with the police. He knows how to handle himself."

"Maybe we threaten him with the parole violation if he doesn't give us something more?"

"Not worth it. Anything he gives us will be easy to disregard as coercion to get him to say what he thinks we wanna hear."

"Well, something doesn't smell right. I get the sense he's trying to protect his brother."

"Or throw the scent off himself," said Melendez.

"I'd expect nothing less from any ex-con that was worth a damn, even if he had nothing to do with it. Paranoid little prick."

"How questionable do you see Anthony being on this?"

"He's the husband, isn't he? They were clearly unhappy in their marriage. But, shit, Paula's as tied into all that as he is."

Detective Melendez looked seriously at his partner and voiced a theory he was sure Kerr, too, had under consideration. "Maybe they did this together?"

"Maybe," Kerr nodded. "Or maybe they're all telling the

honest-to-God truth. Maybe Darius really did hear Hannah calling after Paula—she did text her, after all. And maybe Paula is as crazy as she appears."

Melendez checked his phone for an incoming text. "Well, it looks like we might find out if that's the case. They've got something for us from her computer."

CHAPTER TWENTY-ONE

Jacob Russo walked along Abbot Kinney Avenue in Venice, heading for The Patio Bar. The mile-long street was lined with an eclectic mix of scruffy hipster vibes and upscale sophistication, courtesy of the tech boom that had upended the city. It was not the most convenient of places to meet—the sidewalk was crowded with tourists and locals alike, with limited parking—but it was only a few blocks from RuskTech, the medical technology company whose recently hired executive he was to meet.

As he approached the small bar, his phone rang. He stopped to check the display and then ignored it, tucking the phone back into his coat pocket. Once inside, he spotted Anthony sitting at a corner table, away from the windows facing the street. Anthony stood as Jacob approached. It had been eleven years since the two of them had been together, at Paula and Alan's wedding, and Jacob was unsure how to begin. He cleared his throat and extended his hand. "Thanks for agreeing to meet me. This must all be extremely difficult. I'm so sorry, Anthony."

"Thank you, Jacob. I appreciate it," Anthony said.

"How's your son doing?" asked Jacob, bringing his left hand to Anthony's elbow as the handshake continued.

"It's been hard. He can't accept what's happened. He still hasn't quite fully realized that his mother's not coming back."

The two men sat opposite each other.

"And how are you?" Jacob said.

"I'm swimming in it."

A waitress interrupted and Jacob ordered a screwdriver. Anthony stuck with the cup of coffee he'd been nursing. "I have to get back to work," he explained, needlessly.

"Strange how life doesn't stop," said Jacob.

Anthony sipped his coffee. "Hannah's funeral is in three days and two days later I'm supposed to deliver a presentation to some major Chinese investors concerning force-feedback in virtual-reality surgery systems. I'd say life not only doesn't stop, it picks up speed."

Jacob could not help feeling proud of him. "You've become a very impressive businessman," he said.

Anthony pushed his coffee to the side. "You mean I'm no longer the same young nigger from Oakland who needs your money."

Jacob's faced paled, the lines on his forehead becoming even more pronounced as he frowned. "That's not what I meant at all. I never felt that way about you."

"You know, I never even told my mom about the money. She probably still thinks I have outstanding student loans."

"My only desire was to help you."

"You trying to bullshit me or yourself? You wanted my silence and you got it. I never told a goddamn soul about Paula being Allyson, including my wife, and Sullivan Manufacturing continued on without a blip. Now what do you want from me?"

The waitress returned with the screwdriver and Jacob gladly

took a sip. It was clear Anthony wasn't interested in talking about the past, nor was he looking to be consoled. Jacob, though, still wasn't sure how to proceed. "I don't believe Paula killed your wife," he said, finding his voice.

Anthony's expression didn't change. "You could have told me that over the phone."

"And you could have declined my offer to meet in person."

Anthony nodded. "Twenty-five years later," he said. "And here we are again. Why're you so sure Paula didn't do it?"

"For the same reason I never believed you killed Emily Jenkins."

Anthony angled his head at a disbelieving angle. "Sure you did."

Jacob took another sip of his drink, unable to hide his discomfort. "You're not gonna give me an inch here, are you?"

Anthony looked exhausted. "We all have our psychological burdens to bear."

"Speaking of that, the psychiatric hold on Paula is over tomorrow," Jacob said. "There's been some discussion of what should be done next. I could argue that she remain there for treatment and that would undoubtedly carry some weight. She does have her issues, after all. But I'm not going to do that. I owed it to you to say why in person. She needs care, there's no denying that, but the best place for her now is somewhere she can feel safe."

"Where *she* can feel safe?"

"It's not going to be easy on your family to have her across the street," Jacob said. "I'm going to do what I can to see to it that she and her husband stay elsewhere, at least temporarily."

Anthony studied him. "Your hubris is extraordinary."

"I'm sorry?"

"You've spent so much of your life trying to control her, it's never occurred to you that it isn't up to you what Paula does or doesn't do." He leaned forward and lowered his voice. "If it were, neither of us would be sitting here right now."

"I truly am sorry, Anthony."

"So am I. For a lot of things." He stood. "I understand your impulse to reach out, Jacob. And I came here to show that I respect you. But I don't need you to protect me." He dropped a ten-dollar bill on the table, defiant. "Drinks are on me."

And then he walked away, leaving his old benefactor behind.

Jacob sat in silence, finishing his drink, and then he walked out into the sunlight of Abbot Kinney. Stepping onto the sidewalk, he was unaware of the black BMW idling in the red zone across the street. Nor did he notice the brunette woman inside, watching him. But a moment later his phone rang again. It was Lincoln Childress calling for the second time.

*

"Heather wasn't following you," Lincoln said evenly, though he was clearly annoyed. "She was following Anthony. She's been surveilling Mr. Mills and his brother since we arrived."

Having just walked back into his Ritz Carlton suite in Marina Del Rey, Jacob was heavily perspiring. It was not only the temperature outside getting to him, but the heat applied by his lawyer. He draped his jacket over the back of a chair and rolled up his shirt sleeves. "Why?" he asked.

"Gathering information," Lincoln said, still standing right inside the door, not sweating at all. "If he's having an affair, I need to know about it. If he has a gambling problem, I need to know about it. If he—"

"I got it," Jacob said, sitting. "I hope you're paying your assistant well."

Lincoln crossed to the mini-bar and began filling two glasses with ice. "Heather is a retired intelligence specialist for the US Navy," he said, "not an *assistant*. She's an associate, with specific skills that are quite useful."

"Vodka," Jacob said. "Not scotch."

"I remember," Lincoln said, continuing to make the drinks.

"Has she discovered anything of value?"

"So far the Mills brothers have proven to be quite the self-contained pair. Nothing out of the ordinary. Darius works part-time for Anthony's company, but otherwise rarely leaves the house—though he did spend one rather pathetic afternoon inside the 4Play strip club over on Cotner, while his brother was being questioned by the police."

Lincoln set a can of honey-roasted peanuts from the mini-fridge on the table and then handed Jacob a vodka and tonic, before sitting opposite him with a glass of Dewar's.

"Second drink of the day and it's not yet noon," Jacob said, taking a sip of booze. "What do you say we cut the lawyer bullshit for a second and you tell me if you think one of them killed Hannah?"

"Any number of people could have killed Hannah, including Paula. Which brings me to my point. If the police, or, God forbid, the media, discover that you paid Anthony's tuition, it will undoubtedly be construed that it was to buy his silence. And if you're seen with him, it will be just as easily construed that you're attempting the same arrangement to protect her once again."

"That's ridiculous."

Lincoln tossed a few peanuts into his mouth and stared at him.

"Well, it's wrong, anyway," Jacob softened.

"Be that as it may, no more meetings."

Jacob waved his hand as though it were a flag of surrender.

Lincoln sipped his scotch. "And here I thought containing Alan's behavior would be the difficult task."

"So, then, I assume you include him in your web of suspicions?"

Lincoln smiled for the first time since arriving. "Don't you?"

"No. But you said 'any number of people.'"

"That I did." Lincoln nodded. "Heather confirmed that Alan was in his class at UCLA until ten-thirty the night Hannah was murdered, and then was surrounded by drunk students at Barney's Beanery until after one-thirty in the morning. She tracked down the Uber driver who drove him home at two, recalling that he was indeed as drunk as he has professed."

"She's very thorough."

Lincoln sipped his drink, then said, "It's time we discuss the financial ramifications in relation to Alan, if Paula does go to prison. He's still a young man, there would be no reason for him to remain married, and the prenup between them is a complicated animal, to say the least. It could get very messy if he decides to fight it."

"We'll cross that bridge if and when we come to it," Jacob said with a flash of annoyance. "For now, your focus should be on keeping Paula *out* of prison, not on what will happen to her money if you can't."

"I assure you that I'm being as thorough on my end as Heather is on hers. With that in mind, I hope you're able to look at the entirety of the situation with clear eyes."

"Meaning what?"

"Meaning you have a blind spot when it comes to Paula."

"Perhaps."

"I've run their credit cards for the past few months," Lincoln said. "And I discovered something a bit disconcerting."

Jacob set down his glass, which was already empty.

"A few days after Anthony Mills moved to Santa Monica, Paula used a credit card to park at a meter outside his office in Venice for five hours."

"Is that right?" said Jacob, clearly trying to sound casual.

"Why do you suppose she would have done that?"

"I'm sure you have plenty of ideas."

"Ideas, yes. But no answers. Did they spend that day together? Or was she stalking him? Whatever the case, when the police find out about it—and if I did, they will as well—they'll start drawing their own conclusions, and as that happens, Paula's odds of staying out of prison will fall precipitously."

Jacob got up to make another drink. "Let's be honest," he said, no longer trying to sound casual. "The odds aren't so good now, are they?"

"No," Lincoln told him. "I'm afraid they're not."

CHAPTER TWENTY-TWO

PAULA WAITED IN the ward community room among a few other patients, all of whom ignored her as intently as she ignored them. She hadn't participated in any group sessions over the past three days, had not learned a single one of their names, and was certain nobody there could remember hers. She'd been sitting there for an hour, ever since completing the exit evaluation with Doctor Santini. During their discussion, he'd been very kind, Paula thought. But also patronizing. "You're so sweet," his smile said, "but this is all too much for you to understand." It was clear that his opinion was for her to stay and be treated more thoroughly. But the seventy-two-hour hold was over and she insisted on getting out.

She wondered what Alan, Jacob, and Lincoln were saying to Doctor Santini right then. Would they fight her desire to leave, and if so, did she truly have any say in the matter? It was as though her chair rested on a trap door, threatening to open and drop her through the floor and back into her isolated room.

Hearing voices approach from down the hall, she looked up as Doctor Santini rounded into the room, followed by Alan.

"Hi sweetheart," Alan said.

Paula did not stand. A ball of emotion caught in her throat, making it difficult to swallow. Alan looked so drained, so weary, so unlike the man she'd loved for so long.

"You ready to go home?" he asked.

Paula leapt to her feet and threw herself into his arms.

Alan held her hand as Doctor Santini walked with them to the elevator, where Lincoln and Jacob stood waiting. The doctor had pronounced her free from any immediate danger—to herself or anyone else—declaring she was "displaying the appropriate sadness." As he went on now, talking of emotional triggers and warning signs of "relapses," Doctor Santini's words barely penetrated. The doctor handed Lincoln some mysterious paperwork, and Paula's familiar sadness returned. Or was it fear? So many emotions, so difficult to tell apart.

"Good luck, Paula," she heard Doctor Santini say.

"Thank you," she said, looking at her shoes and trying not to cry.

Riding down in the elevator, she continued to clutch Alan's hand. To her great relief, he held on to her as tightly as she did to him. His flesh was warm, grounding the troubled current running through her. Nobody spoke until the ding announced the bottom floor. "You can wait in the lobby," Lincoln said. "I'll bring the car around."

Paula's heart lightened as she stepped off the elevator into the bustling lobby. After having so much attention focused on her in the last seventy-two hours, it was a relief to be anonymous in a crowd. She became aware of being hungry. She rejoiced in the simple notion of being able to eat whatever she desired. And then there was a commotion and her chest seized. "Shit," she heard Jacob say—swearing was so unlike him.

"Paula Hickman?" a voice cut through the din.

She looked up to see the detective she'd last spoken with at the police station, the one who had mentioned that he loved the chocolate eclairs from The Little Delicious.

"Hello," she said, politely, surprised but not shocked at his unexpected appearance.

Detective Melendez stepped close to her. "We have a warrant for your arrest," he said, "for the murder of Hannah Mills."

Paula gasped as Alan's hand slipped from hers.

"Hold on," Alan said, stepping past her in an effort to cut the detective off.

"Sir," another voice sounded. "Step back, or we'll arrest you too."

Other voices mingled, lost in a jumble of agitation.

"Lincoln!" she heard Jacob shout.

Detective Melendez grabbed her arm and pulled her forward, into a crush of people. She turned her head to find Alan but saw only the determined face of the detective.

"You don't have to do this here," Jacob said, from somewhere to her left.

Paula instinctively tried to pull away but could not. Detective Melendez spoke close to her ear. "If you resist, I'm going to place you in handcuffs, do you understand? I'd rather not do that."

Tears blurred Paula's vision as Detective Melendez led her toward the sliding doors across the lobby. People gawked and whispered, many of them with phones raised, recording the action as if it were all street theater performed for their enjoyment. Her knees buckled, Detective Melendez's strong grip the only thing holding her up.

*

Jacob sat with Alan in his Mercedes, their eyes on the reporters gathered in front of the Santa Monica Police Station. Having spotted a second crush of reporters staking out positions at his home, Alan had driven them to the station without Jacob's consent—as if he needed to see for himself to believe it was all truly happening. One reporter after another stood in front of yet another camera and talked with yet another anchor in yet another studio far away, recounting the arrest of local business owner Paula Hickman. It was likely the viewers at home knew more about the arrest of Paula than did both men inside the Mercedes. Since Lincoln had not answered any of the phone calls from Jacob, they'd had to turn to KNX news radio to learn that, despite her lawyer's efforts, Paula's arraignment would not be until morning.

A text dinged on Jacob's phone.

"Is it him?" Alan asked.

Jacob held the phone at arm's length to see more clearly. "No, it's Heather. She gathered your personal effects from the house and is back at the hotel, wondering where we are."

"It's ridiculous for me not to go home," Alan said.

"It's Lincoln's game now," Jacob said, putting the phone back in his coat pocket. "Play along and you'll be back home tomorrow, *with Paula*."

"I've no doubt that Lincoln is a fantastic lawyer, but you know as well as I do that not even he can guarantee she'll be granted bail."

"No, I don't suppose he can," Jacob said, staring out the window. "Especially not now that they think she's a flight risk." The radio station had just reported a rumor that Paula had a private jet waiting to take her to some island off of Venezuela that had a processing plant that did business with Sullivan Enterprises. "They report it and it becomes fact."

"They have enough facts," Alan sighed. "They don't even need to make up any more." His jaw tightened. "Those fucking Facebook posts."

"Were you aware she was using a fake persona?"

"No. I knew she was posting, of course—she spent so much time doing it. I figured it was one of the only things that made her happy, or *content*, anyway, so I never questioned it."

Jacob eyed the distant reporters. "We'll, they're questioning it now."

They were silent for a while.

"You ever hear of a video game called The Sims?" Alan asked, eventually.

"I stopped paying attention after Pac-Man."

"It's a life-simulation game. You create these virtual people and give them lives and moods and take care of them as if they were real. They've sold something like two hundred million copies. Are all of those people crazy? I mean, that's all Paula was doing with that fucking Jill Carlson persona. She was just playing her own version of The Sims." He sighed. "Of course, couple that with her delusion of Hannah—and let's not forget the late, great Allyson Clemens up in Berkeley—and it does makes her look like a goddamn crazy woman."

"Do you believe she is?"

"I don't know anymore. I truly don't. But I do know that Paula's not the only one who fantasizes about having more than one life to lead. Everyone wishes for that."

Jacob now eyed him closely. "Do you wish for that, Alan?"

Alan turned to face him. "Would you blame me if I did?"

"No," Jacob said. "I wouldn't." His phone rang.

"Tell her we went to In-N-Out, so she can stop worrying," Alan said.

"It's Lincoln."

Without saying a word, Alan nodded, then turned over the engine and put the car in gear.

*

That night Alan was unable to fall asleep, and it came as a welcome distraction when Wendy called. He spoke to his sister for close to an hour, allowing her the space to vent, but he never quite succeeded in calming her down. Though annoyed by her histrionics, he was quietly appreciative that she'd at least remained a presence. Calls of support from friends and colleagues had all but ceased. After the announcement of Paula's arrest that afternoon, only Jameson Lynch, the head of his department, and one fellow teacher at UCLA had reached out at all. He'd spoken, too, with Jeffrey Williams, the manager of The Little Delicious, deciding it was best if they shut down for the time being. There were far more reporters than customers coming in these days anyway. Jeffrey was nearly as upset as Wendy, but he calmed down considerably once Alan told him he'd continue to pay everyone's wages until a long-term plan was put in place.

After dispatching his sister, Alan lay in bed, contemplating what would come next if Lincoln was unsuccessful at the hearing in the morning. What if Paula were to be denied bail and left in jail? Jesus. What if, despite the empty assurances he'd spent the past hour offering Wendy, Paula never came home again? He tried to imagine her at that moment, in her cell, reaching out for him, begging for him to comfort her. Despite everything, they were still connected. They always would be. She would always need him.

As he mulled over Jacob's question about wishing for another life to live, he accepted that, despite his exhaustion, he would not sleep at all that night.

CHAPTER TWENTY-THREE

A DEPUTY STOOD at the cell-door. "You all right?" he asked.

Paula had developed a rash that had spread down the left side of her neck and onto her chest. "I woke up like this," she said, tapping the patch of blotchy skin below her jaw.

"Probably nerves. Come on out."

"Is Lincoln Childress here?" she asked.

"I have no idea, Ma'am," the deputy said, waving her forward. "Step out of the cell, please."

Paula hesitated, and then walked onto the grey cement floor.

She had slept only fitfully, her mind never winding down long enough to keep her body quiet. Her hair was dirty, darkened with sweat, and felt brittle in her fingers when she tucked it behind her ears. Her throat was swollen by the effort to remain silent during the long night, afraid to make any noise as she sobbed. The Santa Monica jail held up to ninety-two inmates, but it was impossible for her to know how many cells were occupied. As it was, only three or four women in the adjoining holding cells had taken any real interest in her, though they were more than enough. They'd kept at her throughout the night, calling her names, calling her a murderer, threatening to fuck her and to stick a knife into her. Other voices had called out from behind the heavy white doors of the modular cells, warning them to shut the fuck up, but none of them did.

Now, as Paula was led away, one of the faceless women again twisted her voice into a sneer. "Good luck, baby," she said.

"Ain't no luck gonna help that bitch," a final monotone voice trailed after them.

Metal doors clanged open and closed and Paula was put into a line of seven women, all scheduled for court that morning. None of them would be returning to the jail in Santa Monica; they'd either be released, post bail, or be remanded to the regional detention center, twenty miles away in South Central Los Angeles. Lincoln had assured Paula that he would do everything within his considerable powers to have her granted bail, but as she stared, dead-eyed, at the wide back of the grunting woman in front of her, and heard the wet coughing of the wretched drug-addict behind her, she held little hope that she would be delivered anywhere but hell itself.

A deputy walked beside them, and the line of broken-down women started moving. Paula shut her eyes and put one foot in front of the other all the way out to the police van waiting to drive them to the Los Angeles Superior Court near LAX. A premonition struck her, as she took that final step up into the van: she would never set foot in Santa Monica again. Her tears returned, again choking her in silence.

*

The courtroom was on the seventh floor of a ten-story building. It was small, with two brown desks facing the judge and the benches behind them lined up like church pews filled with a packed menagerie of interested parties: reporters, lawyers, other prisoners, and gawkers. Paula stood next to Lincoln as he waived the formal reading of the charges. There was a numbing order to the proceedings. Nobody raised their voice, everyone was professional, polite even, talking in measured tones. A clerk handed Lincoln a copy of the complaint and then Paula heard the judge, a black woman with grey hair pulled back from her face.

As she listened, the buzzing in her head grew louder.

"Do you understand the charges against you, Mrs. Hickman?" the judge asked, looking up from the papers laid out before her.

Lincoln's hand landed on Paula's shoulder, shaking the answer loose. "Yes," she said.

"And have you discussed the complaint brought against you with your lawyer?"

"Yes," she repeated.

"At this time do you wish to enter a plea, guilty or not guilty?"

Paula's knees locked. Her skin itched where her rash had spread across her cheeks. "Not guilty," she said.

Lincoln's fingers squeezed her shoulder, as if to say, "Good job," and then he drew his hand away. Paula's vision clouded. Words swirled around her, but she could not follow the thread of what was being said. Lincoln said something about a preliminary hearing to be scheduled as soon as possible, and then there was more back and forth between the judge, Lincoln, and the assistant deputy attorney who stood at the adjacent desk. Paula swayed, her knees now locking and unlocking, as she listened to the muffled voices.

"...circumstantial evidence..." Lincoln's voice wafted through the thickening haze. "Longstanding ties to the community...The Little Delicious...Doctor Marcus Santini at

Resnick Neuropsychiatric Hospital…not a danger…no criminal record…"

*Hannah. I'm sorry this is happening. I'm sorry for Anthony,
for everything.*

The voice of the assistant D.A. cut through, high-pitched
and annoyed, the first sign of acrimony. Paula focused on her
breathing: in and out, in and out. Lincoln was speaking now.
Despite the enmity coming from the opposing council, Lincoln's voice remained unburdened, as though this were a simple
disagreement between friends and nothing to get excited about.

"Paula," Lincoln's voice suddenly bounced into her ear,
startling her, as his hand again found her shoulder. It was
heavier this time, more insistent.

A chattering commotion in the gallery distracted her.
Something had upset them.

"I'm sorry," she said. "What's happening?"

Lincoln smiled. "You're going home."

*

Jacob pushed for them to return to the hotel but ultimately
accepted the argument that the hotel wouldn't want them.
Besides, getting Paula and Alan home was part of Lincoln's
media campaign. "Public opinion affects public prosecutors,"
he said. "Before people become jurors, they're spectators. Paula
and Alan need to be seen together, going home. That's where
innocent people go. They don't hide."

So, not long after forfeiting Paula's passport and handing
over a cashier's check for the bail amount of one and a half
million dollars, Alan and Paula were back on their street in the
lawyer's car with Lincoln and Jacob. Lincoln directed them
to hold hands as they walked into the house. "Don't smile,"

he instructed. "Alan, open the door for her, and Paula, look at the cameras before you go in. Don't avert your eyes. Walk with purpose, but not too quickly. You don't want to look like you're rushing. I'll be in momentarily."

The car came to a stop in the driveway. Alan climbed out first and held his hand out for Paula, who took it and looked as instructed toward the crush of reporters filling the street behind them. With questions shouted at them, they walked together into the house, Jacob beside them, looking like everyone's favorite grandfather.

Lincoln strode to the sidewalk and stood in front of the bank of cameras, where he was immediately assaulted with overlapping questions. When the reporters' eagerness abated to his satisfaction, Lincoln said, "As you can imagine, this continues to be a difficult time for Paula and Alan. Their hearts remain broken by the death of Hannah Mills, and their prayers are for her and her family. When the police originally made it clear that they saw Paula as a suspect in this truly heinous crime, she was brought to an emotional crisis. That alone was the reason for her recent stay at the UCLA medical center. It was for her own emotional protection." He paused. "I would like to remind all of you that there is no direct evidence against Paula Hickman. Her arrest is solely the result of the police rushing their investigation. We maintain that they arrested her not because they believe she is guilty, but because they were afraid she would be a flight risk. Fair enough. That is why I stand here today with the guarantee that Paula has no intention of running away, that she will face these unfounded accusations head on. The city of Santa Monica has been rocked, and, understandably, the public seeks not only justice for Hannah, but the safety of the community. That is something the Hickmans are in full agreement with. Though she asked to, I insisted Paula not make any public statements, as the police investigation is still ongoing, despite their rush to press charges. I request that you give the Hickmans the privacy they deserve and the respect they have earned as longstanding residents and contributors to this great city. Thank you."

Lincoln turned and walked away from the reporters, ignoring the chaotic frenzy of questions launched at him.

*

Inside the house, Alan brought Jacob a drink. They'd been silently watching Wendy's strained effort to comfort Paula.

"I understand how exhausted you must be," Wendy was saying as her brother sat opposite them on the couch. "I was arrested a few years ago as part of a protest group at the nuclear plant in San Onofre and ended up spending six hours in jail. Of course I wasn't by myself, there were thirty of us. I can only imagine how difficult it must've been for you last night, all alone."

Paula did not look at her sister-in-law. She turned only toward Lincoln when he entered.

"How did it go?" Alan asked.

"Fine."

"They're such vultures," Wendy sighed.

"It's a living," Lincoln said. "And I hope it goes without saying, we don't need any statements to the press, off-handed or otherwise, from anybody else."

"Is that directed at me?" Wendy asked.

"Yes," Lincoln answered.

"I'm not a child, Mr. Childress."

"Just do what he says, Wendy," Alan instructed his sister.

"Paula," Jacob said, his focus having never left her. "Why don't you go have a shower and we'll talk about what we want to do for food. We're certainly not going to be going out."

"I made a vegetarian lasagna," Wendy announced. "It's in the fridge. I can heat that up for everyone. I also bought some French bread."

"No," Paula said, her first word since arriving. "I don't want anything from you."

"Paula," Alan said sharply.

"Why are you upset with me?" asked Wendy.

All eyes were on Paula, who was not sure if she had the emotional capacity to give voice to her disturbing revelation. The notion had not been there until the moment she came home to discover her sister-in-law standing in her living room, waiting to receive her with a suffocating hug. It was only then, with Wendy's consoling arms pulling her close, that it arrived like a flash of lightning. Up until that moment, Paula's mind had been preoccupied primarily with physical needs—what to eat and how good a shower would feel. But now her attention was focused only upon the unfathomable evil that had been perpetrated against her. She walked quickly from the room, leaving a disturbed wake.

"It's all too much for her," Wendy suggested. "She's not in her right mind."

"And which mind would that be?" asked Lincoln.

Paula returned in a barely contained panic. "Where are the pills?"

"What pills?" asked Jacob.

"The pills!" she yelled at Wendy.

Jacob held up his hands. "Paula, what pills are you talking about?"

"The supplements, Wendy. Where did you put them?"

"They're in the pantry. When you were in the hospital, I came by to straighten up and to look in on Alan."

Paula bolted from the room, this time into the kitchen. She tore open the pantry door and found the cardboard box containing the Nature's Affinity supplements on the bottom shelf. They were all sealed shut, save for one. She grabbed the opened bottle and returned to the living room.

"You poisoned me!" she yelled, holding up the evidence for all to see.

"What the hell are you talking about?" Alan said.

Paula moved aggressively toward Wendy, and Lincoln stepped between them. "No!" he warned, grabbing her arms. "Calm down."

"You insisted on me taking these!" she ranted. "You put something in them, didn't you? All that shit they said was in my system came from you! You did this!"

Wendy was in tears. "No, I would never do something like that."

Paula threw the bottle, striking her in the chest.

"Enough!" Alan yelled.

"Check the pills!" Paula screamed, kicking her feet wildly, trying to break free from Lincoln's hold. "What else did you do, Wendy? What did you do?"

*

It was dark outside when Paula woke. She rolled onto her side and stared at her bedroom window, listening for voices or any sign at all that the others were still there. But there was only silence. She rolled over and looked at the bedside clock: one-thirty in the morning. No wonder it was so quiet. Despite her exhaustion after the night spent in jail, she'd slept for only six hours.

She went to the bathroom and splashed water on her face. Seeing herself in the mirror—pale skin streaked from the mattress, dark circles under her eyes, hair dirty and tangled—handed her a twinge of pain. She looked like a mad woman. And she had gone mad. Every internal structure designed to support self-control had collapsed. She had lashed out at Wendy, a spectacle that undoubtedly made her look even more unstable. She was unable to stomach her unpleasant reflection and shut off the light. She went to the kitchen for a drink, but the cold water made her nauseous and she dumped half the glass down the drain.

Through the window over the sink she saw a shadow cross the backyard lawn. At first Paula thought it was an intruder, a reporter perhaps. She ducked to the side of the window, wishing she had her phone to call 911. But then the dark figure came closer and Paula saw that it was her husband. He had walked in from the music studio behind the pool house, where he had undoubtedly been beating the hell out of his beloved drums; anything to get his frustrations out. Reaching the patio, he staggered slightly, his left foot hopping twice to keep him upright.

"You're up," Alan said as he entered through the side door. "Feeling better?"

Paula did not turn to face him. "Not particularly."

"Neither is my sister."

"I can't help that," she said, shutting her eyes.

"Lincoln said your outburst of paranoid behavior was perhaps another one of your manic episodes. Is he right?"

Paula opened her eyes and turned to face him. "What difference does it make?"

Alan was still wearing the same clothes he'd had on all day. "They're gonna test the supplements," he said, slurring slightly. "Wendy insisted."

"Good."

"No, not good," Alan said, teetering slightly as he stepped forward. "All it's going to show is that you're fucking insane for insisting there's anything in them other than all that homeopathic bullshit."

"I don't want to talk with you anymore tonight," Paula said.

"You killed Hannah Mills, didn't you?"

She clenched her jaw to keep from shaking.

"Don't worry," Alan said. "They're all gone. Nobody can hear us. You can tell me the truth."

Paula smelled the sweet scent of booze coming from her husband. What could she possibly say? She couldn't defend herself, so she remained silent.

"*Cum tacent, clamant*," Alan said, his eyes dark. "When they are silent, they shout out."

"Is that what you think of me?" she asked. "That I'm crying out to admit I killed her?"

"I didn't want to believe it, Paula. I worked so hard to convince myself you couldn't have done it, that you were only capable of hurting yourself. But then I realized you *saw* Hannah as yourself."

He reached for something tucked into his belt at his lower back. Bringing his hand forward, he tossed the black journal onto the island. It landed with a solid thwap, and Paula flinched. Staring at the notebook, her nausea returned, nearly overwhelming her.

"I was going to give this to Lincoln," Alan said. "*Wendy's* the one who said I should keep it hidden—to protect you. It's all in there, Paula. All the anger, the desire to lash out. *Maybe I can finally find peace. Hannah is gone.* That's that last entry. That's what you wrote. You did this, Paula. And I have no idea what I'm supposed to do about it."

Paula's jaw loosened. "There's nothing to be done," she whispered. "Nothing anyone can do."

Alan nodded, and then he turned and walked out of the kitchen.

CHAPTER TWENTY-FOUR

"**There are no** phone records."

"I never called her," Paula said from the back seat of Lincoln's newly rented Mercedes. "I always made my next appointment in person."

"How did you get her address?" Lincoln asked, glancing up into the rearview mirror to gauge her expression.

Paula honestly could not remember. "Alan must have given it to me."

"He did, yes. But it was to an office in Santa Monica, not Pasadena. And there are no records of any payments made."

Paula looked down at the wounds on her hands. It seemed so much longer than six days since she'd cut herself the night Hannah was killed. She tried to retrace all the steps behind her, but moments jumbled together. She was confused by her memories—nothing seemed real. She grasped for recollections that slipped free, as if they had never truly happened.

"Paula?"

She said quickly, "She never asked me for money."

Lincoln eased back. "Doctor Santini suggested that your memory of Doctor Horst is a part of the delusion you manifested surrounding Hannah."

Paula stared at her hands. The pain was real. That she remembered.

"It's okay, Paula," Lincoln said.

She shook her head. "No," she said. "It's not."

"You sure you're up to this?" Jacob asked, turning to look over his shoulder.

Paula stared out the window. The city washed by, a blur of life she had no connection to. "Yes," she said.

Jacob looked to Lincoln, who glanced back only briefly before returning his eyes to the road. The rest of the ride to Pasadena passed in silence.

No comment had been made regarding Alan's refusal to join them. "A trip to nowhere," he'd called it. His hangover that morning was surely noticed as he voiced his disdain, but he said nothing to the others about the journal.

Paula was surprised that he hadn't, though a part of her believed it might be better if everything was brought out into the open. That was why she was happy to go to Pasadena. To find Doctor Horst. To prove to Alan (and herself) that she wasn't crazy. Doctor Horst could explain that those horrible words scrawled across the page were done as therapy, that they were not meant to be taken literally. She tried to imagine Doctor Horst in her tiny office, confused by the misunderstanding, so worried about the arrest of her patient. But conjuring the doctor in her mind's eye, capturing the sound of her voice, was like trying to rejoin a dream after waking.

After another half hour on the packed 110 Freeway into Pasadena, Lincoln found a parking space a block away from the small brick building on South Fair Oaks. Paula walked between him and Jacob, leading the way up the sidewalk. It was like returning to a childhood home that was now so much smaller, less welcoming, so utterly different than it had been in memory. She put on a facade, acting as though she were not frightened by the reality that there was no more middle ground to carve out. Either she would be vindicated or she would be devoured by the emotional black hole, an abyss that had expanded that much more with her husband's harsh prosecution the night before.

They passed the Starbucks and Paula walked faster, keeping pace with her beating heart. Lincoln and Jacob stood directly behind her as they reached the brick building and huddled together at the door.

"Which number is it?" Jacob asked, squinting over her shoulder. "It's impossible to make out any of the names."

"Three-one-zero," Paula said, looking at the scratched and cloudy glass shell covering the security door intercom. "It was easy to remember because it's the same as…"

"The same as what?" Jacob asked when she faltered.

She swallowed her rising apprehension. "The same as our area code."

The coincidence, which once had seemed inconsequential, now seemed odd—too convenient.

"Go ahead and punch it in, Paula," Lincoln said.

"The buzzer doesn't work," she told him.

She turned back to see the two men exchange a wary glance, and her heart sank further.

"How did you get in?" Jacob asked.

"There was a man, the first time. He came out of the building and I went in. The other times, I guess she left it unlocked for me. It was propped open, anyway."

Jacob tried the door. "It's not open now," he said, giving it a useless pull.

"Wait here," Lincoln said. They watched him walk up the sidewalk and disappear around the corner.

"Where's he going?" Paula asked.

Jacob said he didn't know as he sought shade along the cool brick wall of the building, using a handkerchief to wipe perspiration from his forehead.

"Are you okay?" she asked.

"I'm fine," he said, tucking the handkerchief back into his pocket. "Just old."

Paula leaned beside him on the wall. "You'll never be old, Jacob," she said.

She resisted the urge to hug him, to be held by him as she'd been as a child. If she did, she would cry, and she did not want that. "You know," she said. "This is the first time we've been alone together since you arrived."

He took her hand. "I should have been here more often."

"I'm sorry for all of this, Jacob. I didn't mean to let you down."

He squeezed her hand tighter. "You stole my line," he said, winking once.

They didn't say anything more. His hand in hers said enough.

The door to the building swung open and Lincoln stepped out.

"How'd you get inside?" Paula asked.

"Come on in," was all Lincoln said.

Paula and Jacob entered the small lobby to find Lincoln was not alone. A compact man in his sixties, with tired, baggy eyes and a dusting of brown hair as wispy as cotton candy, waited for them by the elevator. "This is Mr. Keller," Lincoln said, introducing him.

"You can call me Ray," the man said. "Sorry about the front door. The tenants have been complaining about it for weeks. I've got a guy coming to replace it."

"Not a problem," Lincoln assured him. "Do you mind taking us up now?"

"Of course," Ray said, pressing the elevator call button. "But like I explained the other day, I can't let you inside. Only a look, right? I can get fired for trespassing."

"You've been here before?" Jacob asked.

Lincoln shook his head. "Heather found it. Doctor Santini at UCLA gave us the description Paula had given him. There's only one brick building with a busted security buzzer on South Fair Oaks."

"Who's Heather?" Paula asked.

Jacob rested his hand on her back. "She's an associate of Lincoln's."

Paula looked at the men surrounding her, who all were considering her cautiously. "Jacob, what's going on here?" she asked the one man she knew wouldn't lie.

"Let's go upstairs, sweetheart," he said, his worried eyes narrowing.

Paula walked slowly into the elevator, followed by Jacob and Lincoln. The three of them rode up to the third floor with the curious building manager, who reiterated that he would only let them look inside the office, but not go in. "I could get fired, you understand?" he repeated. Paula's mind raced. Her body shook. When the elevator door dinged open, it took a gentle hand from Jacob to move her forward. They walked to suite 310, and Ray unlocked the door, using a master key, before pushing it open and moving aside.

It took only a quick glance inside for Paula's body to convulse with shock. She made no sound, other than a panicked exhalation of air as she stumbled backward into Jacob, almost knocking him over. Steadying herself, she wheeled and walked back up the hallway, tears blurring her vision. She managed only four or five halting steps before falling to her knees and retching.

Jacob kneeled next to her as she wept, placing his hands gently on her shoulders. "I love you, my girl," he whispered. "I promise I'll do everything within my power to help you."

Paula continued to sob and Jacob's tears mingled with hers.

Lincoln turned away, looking back into suite 310. A drafting table rested in the center of the room, with a long folding table along one wall, on which sat three industrial sewing machines. A metal shelving unit in the corner held stacked and rolled bolts of all manner of colorful fabrics.

"Are you all finished?" Ray asked, wide-eyed.

"Yes," Lincoln nodded. "We're done here."

*

The office had been leased for several years to a medical transcription company and then recently sublet to a Russian man named Vadim Boyarov, for his daughter, Natalya.

"Heather met her yesterday," Lincoln explained to Jacob as they drove back through Pasadena to the freeway. "She's evidently a spoiled rich kid who was upset they moved to America in the first place. Dreams of starting her own fashion line. According to some of the other tenants, she'd spend a few hours there every day, generally blaring music, which a few of them complained about. All reports are that she was friendly enough. She'd always apologize and turn it down, until the next time. There were a few workers hanging around, mostly

Latinos, according to Mr. Keller. He said they'd carry up the fabric bolts because of Natalya's nails and she also needed help with the sewing. Heather got the feeling it had more to do with lack of skill and the availability of cheap labor."

"Nobody ever saw Paula?" asked Jacob.

"Heather showed her picture around and only one tenant had a vague memory of seeing her. He did say if she only came on the weekends, that it was generally pretty quiet in the building."

Paula lay down in the back seat of the car, curled into herself like a child.

"You should have told her instead of bringing her back," Jacob said, lowering his voice.

"She wouldn't have believed me. She had to see for herself."

Jacob stared out the window. "Pasadena," he said. "Of course she came here."

Lincoln looked sideways at Jacob, who continued to look away.

"You're right," Paula said softly from the back seat.

Lincoln's confused stare came off Jacob and briefly landed on Paula. "Why is that?" he asked.

"My dad called it an escape to something magical," Paula said, her hands tucked under her cheek. "A parade of roses that made its way right down the middle of the street on New Year's Day."

Jacob looked back at her. "I remember, sweetheart."

Paula was six years old again. Her face pressed to the car window, the world outside a diffused memory—seen only in drowsy glimpses of red, green, and blue Christmas lights twinkling from the eaves of silent houses. Allyson next to her, singing along with a song on the radio that Paula could not quite remember. They passed a family of deer, their bodies a jumble of white lights, grazing on the front lawn of a house. Paula smiled. Her father made a joke as he honked the horn at a brightly glowing inflatable snowman and her mother laughed. Paula remembered the sound of her mother's laugh. Outside, the world was crisp and clear and Paula felt her place within it. She was as safe and as happy as she would ever be again.

Jacob's expression slackened as he stared down at Paula. It had been forty years since the accident that took the life of his best friend's wife and one of their two precious little girls.

"My dad told me I was on a special path," Paula said, slipping further and further away. "And that with every step I took, I carried with me a little bit of the dust kicked up by the steps my mother and sister took before me."

Jacob watched Paula as her eyes closed. It seemed that her life could not spin any further out of control. Then Lincoln's phone rang and that's exactly what happened.

CHAPTER TWENTY-FIVE

As NIGHT SET in, the local news channels were joined by not only CNN and Fox, but also by crews from network affiliates all across the country. There was even a reporter from the *Wall Street Journal* camped out on Georgina Avenue; after all, Sullivan Manufacturing had a market capitalization of four and a half billion dollars, and when an anonymous source reveals that the sole heir of the family fortune is the ex-lover of a murder victim's husband, not only do newsrooms get giddy, but investors get jittery. Throw in the added leaked bombshell that the ex-lovers had once been involved in the suspicious death of a coed, and it's pandemonium.

Lincoln stood in Jacob's suite at the Ritz Carlton, watching the story unfold on television as a reporter gave a standup report in front of Alan and Paula's house. "…the past relationship between Paula Hickman and Anthony Mills is only the latest twist in this increasingly complicated saga," he gravely intoned. "There's been no comment from the district attorney's office about today's startling revelations, but news of Paula Hickman's sordid past certainly shines a bright light on the already controversial decision to grant her bail. So far this evening, neither Paula Hickman nor Anthony Mills has made an appearance, leading to a rising cacophony of concern that the accused murderer of Hannah Mills—with apparent access to an unlimited amount of money—remains a flight risk."

Lincoln shook his head. "*Cacophony of concern*," he said. "Fuck you."

"I don't think the overuse of alliteration is our primary issue here," Heather said, without looking up from the flood of emails on her laptop.

"Does the board of directors at Sullivan have a game-plan in place to deal with this?" Lincoln asked Jacob.

"Yes," Jacob said, pouring himself a drink. "But that's not our primary issue either, is it?"

Lincoln turned off the television. "How's she doing?" he asked.

"Finally asleep, but the last thing she asked me was to take her home."

"That's not going to happen," Lincoln said. "At least, not tonight. First, we need a game plan ourselves. It's going to be very difficult for her to be in public from here on out."

"What if a chatty bellhop saw us bring her in here?" asked Heather.

"The locusts would have swarmed by now."

"You making a statement tonight?" Jacob asked.

"No," Lincoln said, glancing at his vintage Girard-Perregaux watch. "Let 'em twist in the wind for a while. I have to get back to my room to do some work on the preliminary hearing. Not to mention figuring out what the hell I'm going to do if the press learns of your payment to Anthony at Berkeley."

Jacob looked to Heather, but it was clear she already knew.

"With so much shit hitting the fan," Jacob said, "I suppose it's only a matter of time before some of it gets on me."

"Anybody hear from Alan yet?" Lincoln asked.

Jacob and Heather exchanged looks. Evidently, neither had.

"Those two aren't going to make it easy on me," Lincoln sighed irritably. "Call me when you do, and we'll get them together in front of the cameras as soon as possible."

"So who's the unnamed source?" Jacob asked, sitting at the bar, sipping his vodka tonic.

Lincoln raised an eyebrow at Heather.

"I don't know yet," she said.

"Keep digging."

"The police?" Jacob suggested.

"That's my guess," said Heather, closing her computer. "Trying to rattle us."

Jacob rubbed his forehead. "Mission accomplished."

"Though it could be Wendy Hickman," Heather added.

"Why the hell would she do something like this?"

"Retaliation. Paula did accuse her, after all."

"My vote's the D.A's office," Lincoln said. "They've been losing the PR battle, which is certainly added pressure they don't need."

"But why throw Anthony under the bus like that?" asked Jacob.

"Hopefully they also see him as a suspect," Heather said.

"That's absurd." Jacob shook his head.

"You think one of our major defense strategies is absurd?" Lincoln asked, pulling on his suit jacket.

Jacob sat straighter. "You're gonna go after Anthony? There's no evidence! Do you truly think he killed his wife?"

"Again, what I think is irrelevant. What isn't irrelevant, however, is the shadow of doubt. And the further that shadow reaches into the minds of a jury, the better for Paula. All we have to do is convince one of them that Anthony might have done it, and we're home free."

"For the love of Christ," Jacob said, placing his drink on the bar. "Your plan is to ruin his life, too? Why? They don't even need him! With Paula's mental breakdown, all this crap about Doctor Horst and Hannah, mixed with everything they already have on her, it won't be too difficult for them to spin it as her being a crazy, jealous ex-lover and the goddamn jury will send her straight to the—"

Jacob froze as he caught sight of Paula in the doorway to the bedroom.

Her lips were dry and cracked, her eyes vacant.

"I'm sorry, Paula," Jacob said, standing. "I've had too much to drink and I'm—"

"I need a change of clothes," she said, unblinking.

"Yes, we'll get them for you," said Jacob.

"Would you like to talk about anything, Paula?" Lincoln asked, his tone as cool as ever.

But Paula only turned and walked back into the bedroom, closing the door without word.

"Goddammit," Jacob said, hanging his head.

*

Jacob woke late the next morning but did not rise immediately. He shifted onto his back and stared at the ceiling. He'd slept surprisingly well, considering he'd spent the night on the couch. He had considered calling downstairs to request a rollaway bed, but surely the employees of the Ritz had seen the news over the past few days and would certainly recognize who he was. It wouldn't take much to spark their imagination as to why he was not sleeping in the bed he was paying five hundred dollars a night for. That was also why he didn't consider heading downstairs for breakfast; hiding the infamous Paula Hickman in his room had afforded him a surprisingly healthy dose of paranoia.

He got up, walked heavily to the sliding glass door, and stepped outside. The balcony had a one-hundred-eighty-degree view of the marina. Sunlight bounced off the glassy water, reflecting shimmering patches on the multitude of boats filling hundreds of narrow slips. It was close to ten, he figured. Going back inside, he noticed the double doors leading to the bedroom were slightly ajar. He imagined Paula coming out that morning, seeing him asleep on the sofa. He hoped she had forgiven him for his unfortunate choice of words the night before. If not, he would gladly accept her anger if it meant that she was still speaking to him at all.

Jacob couldn't imagine the mental dissonance she was experiencing with the realization that her ideal therapist had only been ideal because she had been created out of whole cloth. To what depths of isolation had she plunged to create such a fantasy? What void did the phantom version of Doctor Horst fill within her?

Trying to reconcile the little girl Paula once was with the lost woman she'd become, he chastised himself for looking the other way, for being so hesitant to confront the reality of her depression. Perhaps he'd been too lenient, too forgiving of the youthful wild streak that once led to her creation of Allyson Clemens and all of the trouble at Berkeley. Even after her stay at Newberry, he had not fully faced her problems.

Would I have been as passive with her treatment if she'd had cancer? Or MS? Or asthma? Or any other goddamn disease?

He could not reconcile why her mental disorder had always

stayed the monster hiding under the bed, why he'd been so afraid of that which he could not see.

He pushed gently on the open bedroom door.

"Paula?" he said.

There was no response as he poked his head inside. The bed was empty.

"Paula?" he called out, looking to the ensuite bathroom.

But she was gone.

*

Paula pulled her hat lower, until the brim touched the sunglasses Heather had lent her the day before. The accessories had been provided in order to sneak her unnoticed into the Ritz, and she had deployed them just as effectively to make her exit. Nobody gave her a second glance as she strode through the lobby and out to the front driveway where the taxi she'd requested was waiting.

The drive to Santa Monica was quick, and it passed in a mental cloud. She stared out the window, not sure what she was going to do when she arrived at the church. Going at all had been an impulse upon waking, an answer to a siren's call. She instructed the driver to drop her a block away from the address she'd given him. Climbing from the cab, she walked up the sidewalk, past the brightly-painted logos of the news vans lining the curb.

The First United Methodist Church, which had drawn the reporters as well as Paula, was small, but there was no need for a larger space. Hannah Mills hadn't any friends or extended family in Santa Monica, after all. Paula stood across the street, amongst a growing crowd of curious onlookers, watching the somber-looking guests stream in past the news cameras. She assumed them to be Anthony's co-workers from RuskTech, there in support of him, having barely known his lovely wife. Perhaps some were from Alex's school. Thinking of the little boy, Paula shivered.

She heard the voices around her, sibilant and excited, as someone pointed out the older black woman, who, they surmised, was Anthony's mother. *Violet*, Paula marveled. She looked frailer than she would have imagined. Twenty-five years ago, Anthony's mother had seemed so solid, so impervious to erosion. The impossibly old Violet was waiting patiently for her daughter, who, in turn, was waiting impatiently for Darius as he stopped to listen to a reporter's question. Devika had been a teenager the last time Paula had seen her, and she was rocked by the image of the grown woman before her. Devika yanked her brother away, leading him by the arm up the church steps before he had the chance to answer the reporter's question.

There was no sign of Anthony or Alex, and soon after Paula arrived, the church doors were closed. She wept behind her sunglasses as the knife wounds on her palms throbbed.

She had come to the funeral because of a Bible given to her by Jacob Russo when she was twelve years old. He had been holding on to it since being named executor of the Sullivan estate and had at last decided Paula was old enough to find it useful. It had belonged to Paula's grandmother, Katherine, when she was a child, and Katherine had given it to Paula's mother. When Jacob gave it to her, young Paula imagined a straight line running from the grandmother she'd never met, through the mother she could barely remember, directly to herself. The book bound her to an alternate reality that should have been hers, a parallel life, full of magical possibilities.

She read it obsessively, liking how the pages crinkled when

she turned them; their very fragility a call to her nurturing heart. For months she searched the verses for hidden messages, believing that God must have had reasons for doing what he'd done to her family, and that written somewhere between the Book of Genesis and the Book of Revelation, the answers would be found. But no matter how much she read, or how much she prayed, the harder she tried to connect with what the words were trying to say, the more distant she felt.

So, six months after Jacob gave it to her, Paula burned it. She went into the yard with a can of lighter fluid and burned her grandmother's Bible. The crinkly pages, the way they smelled as the flames engulfed them, the smoke rising up, gave her a beguiling sense of calm. Finally, here was something tangible, proving that she was real, that life was real—in the same way a handwritten letter is real but an email isn't—as if nothing truly existed if you couldn't burn it and see the ashes. Looking back on it years later, Paula realized she hadn't been ready to burn herself up yet, so it was the Bible that had to go. Whatever the reason, turning her family Bible to ashes gave her the sense that she had some control, some power.

And now, standing in front of the First United Methodist Church, Paula looked down at the scars crossing her wrists and realized she'd done the same thing with Hannah Mills.

In less than an hour, the doors to the church reopened and the crowds poured out. Paula searched for Anthony amongst the many white faces, but saw only Devika and Darius. They walked to a waiting car, nobody saying anything to them as they passed. Violet followed, holding the hand of Alex. He clung to his grandmother as they were approached by a balding man, who crouched down to one knee to talk to him, intent on sharing some words with the little boy. Alex nodded at whatever he was told and the man gave him a hug. Alex, who looked more confused than sad, continued on with Violet as the man walked quickly away, wiping tears from his eyes. Violet and Alex continued on, joining Devika and Darius in the waiting car. A moment later, Anthony emerged from the church. His steps were slow; he looked emotionally drained. He shook hands with a few men as he waded through the crowd and collected several hugs from women dressed in black.

At last he came to stand before the assembled reporters. From across the street, Paula could not hear what he said, though he seemed to have a difficult time saying it. The reporters asked only a few questions before the impromptu press briefing came to an end. Anthony walked to the waiting car, climbed inside, and was driven away.

Watching the car disappear up the street, a devastating notion tickled the back of Paula's mind. But it was so distant, so vague, it did not completely register. Before the notion had the chance to embed itself, Paula shook it free and pushed her way back through the crowd.

It took her over an hour to walk home, meandering like a ghost as she went. When she at last arrived back on Georgina Avenue, she was greeted by a throng of reporters who had gathered there hoping to get a shot of Anthony returning from the funeral, but quite pleased to see her instead. They had grown impatient with the chum of rumor and suddenly had a full meal in their midst. Their questions grew louder and more agitated as they swarmed around her.

"Have you spoken with Anthony Mills?" one yelled. "Are you still in love with Anthony?" yelled another. "What is the nature of your relationship?" "What happened between you and your college roommate?" "Did the two of you have anything to do with your roommate's death?" And, of course, too many times to count: "Did you kill Hannah Mills?"

Paula's focus remained straight ahead, and she said nothing in return. The reporters' voices were merely more buzzing, more bees collecting. When she was halfway up the walkway to her house, the front door opened and Alan stepped out onto the porch. He, too, said nothing. He merely stood there, waiting. Paula walked past him, into the house. The door closed behind her, sealing off the harsh calls of the reporters. But the voices in her head continued to buzz.

*

"No," Alan said into the phone. "There's no reason for that. I'm not going anywhere the rest of the day. I'll stay with her."

"All right, fine. Then we'll see you tomorrow evening," Jacob said. "Lincoln and I have an interview in the morning with a reporter from NBC about the preliminary hearing, then he and I have to meet with some board members to iron out some things involving the Sullivan estate."

Alan hated the way he always referred to it as the *Sullivan* estate, as if to constantly remind him that the money was Paula's, not his. "What things might those be?" he asked, unable to restrain himself.

"I'll explain later."

"Lincoln's pressing for clarification to the prenuptial agreement again, isn't he?"

"Lincoln is pressing for clarification on many things, because that's what he does. Let me deal with him. Your only concern right now should be taking care of Paula."

"That's what I've been trying to do," Alan barked, frustration boiling over.

"I know, Alan. And I know it's been difficult. I was going to wait to tell her myself, but if it will help you today—we got the results back from those supplement pills your sister gave her."

Alan listened to Jacob, unable to summon the energy to feign much concern over how the news would affect his wife. It was merely another goddamn scent leading him like a conditioned rat through the maze of his marriage. There was no end to it; he remained as lost as ever.

Once the conversation ended, it took a few minutes for him to enter the kitchen where Paula sat, hovering over a bowl of Cheerios she'd poured herself. She hadn't eaten in over twenty-four hours, but the food did not go down easily.

"You're instructed to stay put," Alan said. "Your little disappearing act didn't go over so well. Where the hell did you go, anyway?"

Paula forced down a spoonful of cereal. She chewed slowly and swallowed. "Hannah's funeral was today."

"Are you kidding me? You went to her goddamn funeral?"

"Please stop swearing at me."

Alan stared at her. His voice had softened when he spoke again. "What were you thinking, Paula? Did anyone see you?"

"No, nobody sees me anymore. I've become invisible. Not even I see myself anymore. I'm no longer a person—no longer Paula, if she ever truly existed at all. And I'm certainly not a wife anymore. You can't deny that."

"Then what are you?" Alan asked, leaning in toward her.

She spoke matter-of-factly, without undue emotion. "I'm a burden. An unpleasant ache you have to stomach, wishing it would subside, but knowing that it won't. And I don't blame you for feeling that way. I actually feel sorry for you. I really do. Because it's never going to get better. No matter where you go for the rest of your life, you're not going to be able to break free from the pain I've caused. This is never going away."

Alan eased closer. "It's all in your head, Paula. All of it. Wendy didn't drug you. Jacob told me the pills came back clean. Do you accept that?"

"I do."

"Maybe it'd be better if she had. Then you'd have somebody other than yourself to blame. But there isn't anybody else, is there?"

"No, there isn't," she said. "You've read my journal. Every time you look at me, I'll know you see the real me. So there's no place left for us to go, is there?"

After a moment, Alan said, "I'm sorry, Paula. I can't give you what you want."

"What's that?"

"Absolution."

Paula kept her eyes on him. "Maybe that's what I need, but it isn't what I want."

"What do you want?"

The thought returned that had tickled Paula's mind as she'd watched Anthony drive away from the funeral of his murdered wife. It was like a termite, eating its way through a softening piece of wood, embedding itself deeper and deeper. The hole the termite of destruction bore into her was almost deep enough to bury them both, but it was, for now at least, still shallow enough for Alan to climb from. But he could not do so without her help, before the walls came tumbling down for good.

She said, finally, "I want you to be happy."

CHAPTER TWENTY-SIX

IN THE MORNING, the street in front of the house was cleared of reporters. They were like the tide, flowing in and flowing out. And so the tide had shifted, sweeping them elsewhere, but Alan accepted that it would soon shift again and another wave was sure to bring them all back, swamping him anew. Perhaps there were still some lone-wolf paparazzi looking for a shot to sell to one of the scavenger websites, but Alan was no longer interested in picking a fight. Resignation has its benefits.

He left Paula asleep in her room. Much like yelling at the tides, it no longer mattered what he did or didn't do to protect himself from her. Deciding which turn to take to avoid discomfort had become impossible. *If she says this, I'll say that. If she does this, I'll do that.* It made no difference to plan. No, the problem remained exactly as his wife had described the night before. She would constantly surprise him with new ways of blocking his emotional freedom.

It was still early as he walked anonymously across the UCLA campus, carrying several collapsed cardboard boxes. Perhaps some of the forty-five thousand students recognized him, and whispered to their friends as he passed, but nobody made the effort to greet him. It was not until he was inside

Bunche Hall, walking toward his office door, that anyone so much as looked at him.

"Professor Hickman," a student said with surprise as they passed each other.

Alan recognized the young man but could not assign a name. "Good to see you," he said, continuing on.

"Are you coming back?" the student asked, hiking his backpack further up his shoulders.

Alan turned to offer a friendly shrug, but did not stop walking. "Not this year," he said. "Hope everything is going well in class."

Before the sophomore had the opportunity to ask more questions, Alan ducked inside his office and pulled the door closed behind him.

Dropping the collapsed boxes on the narrow desk, he eyed the shelves of the tiny office, stuffed full with books and papers. For a while he studied the sepia-toned map of the world that covered a good portion of the wall opposite him. It was full of red push-pins—all the places his students had been over the years. There were hundreds of pins. A sign he'd created years before hung over the map: *Objects In The World Are Closer Than They Appear.*

No sooner had he sat behind the desk, preparing himself for the emotional task to come, than a knock sounded on the door. Alan sat motionless to keep his incessantly squeaky chair from giving him away, hoping that, whoever the bothersome student was, they would not be so bold as to try entering without an invitation. But the door handle twisted and Alan leaned back heavily in his seat, sounding out a loud squeak of defeat.

"Nice try," Jameson Lynch said, stepping inside and closing the door behind him.

"Nothing personal," Alan said. "I'm just not in the mood to mediate any student complaints at the moment."

"No, I imagine you're not," Jameson said, sitting in the chair opposite him.

"How's Friedman doing?"

"He's settling in, though I hear some rumblings that he isn't following your syllabus."

"It wasn't carved in stone."

Jameson smiled and drew in a preparatory breath. "So," he said.

Alan nodded. "So."

"I'm not going to pretend to have any words to help you through all that's happening with your wife."

"I appreciate the lack of attempt."

"But, as the chair of the department committee, I do have to try, once again, to talk you out of leaving the university."

"On that count, the attempt is appreciated. But my mind's made up."

"It's only been two weeks, Alan. With the stress of everything you've been through, it's impossible to put your work into proper perspective. Not solely as your colleague, but as your friend, I truly believe you shouldn't be making these sorts of decisions right now. The administration is fully behind your taking an extended sabbatical; there's no need to resign."

"I'm afraid this isn't something I'd be readily able to put behind me, Jameson. Not here. My wife has become a rather unsettling part of Los Angeles lore."

"Yes," Jameson said. "Your wife—not you. You're not responsible for what she did or didn't do."

Alan scanned the office that had cocooned him for the past fifteen years. "The truth is, I haven't been happy for a long time."

"I wasn't aware."

"That's not an indictment of the university, or my love of teaching." He looked seriously at Jameson. "My wife has suffered with depression for many years. Perhaps it's unfair to complain about how it's affected me, but, it has. It's as simple as that. I've busied myself with my students, I've improved dramatically on the drums, spent hours at the gym, I've—I've done what I could to maintain a life I hoped would get better. But it's clearly only gotten worse." He was quiet for a moment, contemplating Paula's involvement in the twin deaths of Hannah Mills and Emily Jenkins. "I have no idea how all this is going to play out with Paula, legally or otherwise," he said. "But, whatever happens, my relationship with her is going to end. And I need a change."

Jameson nodded. "You're going to be missed around here," he said.

Alan gave a resigned grin. "Though my syllabi will not."

*

Paula had only pretended to be asleep when her husband left for UCLA. In truth, she had not slept all night. Something in her had shifted. She was connected to something real, something definite, something she could control. Her inner voice, the only voice she trusted anymore, spurred her on.

You're the only one who can end this.

Her eyes had gone dry. She had no tears left. The house was silent, unforgiving. She walked from her bedroom into the living room.

You've caused so much trouble for everyone.

All the pain. The confusion. The sadness. The regret. The insanity. It had all come down upon her. There were no more places to hide. No direction to turn. The madness was everywhere.

Paula doesn't exist anymore. Paula is dead.

Yes, this was the one voice she could trust. Even her own husband no longer trusted her. He had said it, she'd seen it in his fallen expression: Paula was capable of the most heinous crimes.

Everyone sees you now for the monster you are.

She picked up the cordless phone (her cellphone was still in police custody) and walked to the giant window facing the street. Drawing back the drapes, her face was warmed by the morning light. But her heart remained cold, locked away. Dialing the number, she hoped there would be no answer. Her thumb hovered over the off button, just in case.

"I can't take your call," Anthony's recorded voice announced, filling her ear. "Leave a message and I'll get back to you as soon as I can."

The ensuing beep jarred her, but no words came. She continued to stare at the house across the street.

It's because you're weak.

Having taken too long to speak, Paula heard a recorded operator's voice: "If you are satisfied with your message, press two now. To record your message again, press five."

Your weakness ruined everything.

Paula pressed five, her eyes closing.

"I'm sorry," she said into the phone. "I'm sorry for everything I've done. But it's over now. Goodbye, Anthony."

And then she hung up.

They will all be relieved.

Paula left the window and walked through the house like the ghost she had become, finding her way to the backyard. The sun's rays winked on the surface of the pool and the soft ocean breeze lifted the wisps of blonde hair framing her slackened face. She knelt at the pool's edge, momentarily mesmerized by the light reflecting off the water, her reflection a blur. Her inner machinery hummed as her chin fell to her chest and she began a series of deep breaths.

Nothing else is real. This is all that exists.

Her chest rose and fell, her lungs expanded and contracted.

That's right. Breathe.

The sunlight on the water swirled as her lungs squeezed out quicker breaths.

Faster.

The breathing turned to shallow panting. A minute passed. In and out, in and out.

Yes, breathe. Breathe. Faster. Faster.

The carbon dioxide level in her body dropped. Her lungs burned.

Faster. Faster. Faster. This is all there is.

Her gaping mouth went dry. Her lips tingled. Her fingers went numb.

Yes! Yes! I can feel it! I am real. This is real.

The panting breaths turned into a raspy wheeze. Her vision clouded and the light on the water dimmed. Her slow fade to darkness was almost complete.

Do it. Quickly. Do it now.

With no breath left to spend, Paula's body wobbled as she abruptly sprang to her feet. The blood-flow to her brain dropped as if she'd been flung from a catapult, the world spinning into a kaleidoscope of twinkling lights. She lost consciousness and collapsed, falling into the pool. Water displaced with a playful-sounding splash, then washed back over her like a welcoming embrace. With both the carbon dioxide and oxygen levels in her system so depleted, Paula's brain failed to trigger an automatic breathing response. Her larynx relaxed and water flooded down her throat, filling her emptied lungs.

There was no thrashing, no distress.

The breeze picked up and light continued to dance on the surface of the water as Paula sank. The machine wound down. The world, at last, went quiet.

It was peaceful.

*

Paula's limp body was pulled to the surface, dragged to the edge of the pool, and hoisted onto the deck. Two hands landed heavily on her sternum, pressing down with ferocious intensity. After fifteen compressions, air was blown forcefully into her mouth. More compressions and more forced breath animated her body as she began to spew water. Her eyes opened as she was rolled onto her side, allowing the remaining water to be expelled in a series of gurgling eruptions. Disoriented, Paula gasped for air, her heart pounding. Finding her focus, she stared up at the face, dripping wet, looking down upon her.

She had been free, her mind silenced at last. And then she found herself staring up at the distraught face of Anthony Mills.

"Why?" she asked, lacking the energy to say more.

"This isn't the answer," Anthony said, dripping with water as he rolled away, heaving deep breaths.

Lying there, Paula blinked into the sun. All of her senses were heightened, as though the world had become a simulation, a kind of virtual reality displayed in ultra-high definition. Thin clouds exploded white in a sky that was too bright.

Sounds filled the backyard: a mockingbird chirped and another answered, leaves rustled, tree branches rubbed together.

It took a few minutes for Paula to accept that she was alive, that Anthony was actually there, that he had saved her life. She rocked herself to a sitting position. He sat a few feet away, his arms draped over his drawn-up knees. Sunlight sparkled in droplets in his graying hair, his muscular shoulders steady beneath the dark polo shirt molded tightly to his skin.

Her shuddering sigh became tears. Deep sobs punched through her constricted chest, rolling her shoulders, salty tears mixing with the chlorinated pool water dripping down her face. Anthony stared at her, showing no emotion as her body shook until her tears abated and she was able to draw in a succession of deep breaths.

"I'm sorry," she said, sitting up.

"So you said on the phone. What exactly are you sorry for?"

As Paula wiped away the water dripping down her forehead, a small dribble fell from the edge of her left ear, tickling her neck. She shivered. "How can you ask me that?"

"Because it's not clear," Anthony said.

Paula blinked away her residual tears. "I killed her."

It was the first time she'd said the words aloud, and hearing them caused her to tremble again.

Anthony absorbed the confession without so much as a flinch. "Did you?" he asked. "Why?"

Paula stared at the water collecting into a puddle between her legs. She was confused by the question, by Anthony's reticence to accept her confession.

"My mind isn't right," she said.

"Yes, that's certainly what others are saying."

"You're not?"

"I've learned from experience not to put much stock in other people's perceptions. Things aren't always what they seem."

"That's why it's impossible to ever know what's truly real."

"Reality isn't *perception*, Paula," Anthony said, standing. "There is objective truth."

"Yes, I know," she said. "Hannah's dead."

He stood to stand above her, dripping wet, defiant against the starkly blue sky. "That's right. So you *can* see what's real."

"You have no idea!" she shouted up at him. "I believed she looked identical to me. Every last thing about her, every last detail! I *saw* it! And nobody could convince me otherwise. So I went to a fucking therapist who didn't even exist at all! My diseased mind made her up to help me cope with my failing sanity. *That's* the reality. Just like it's the reality that I destroyed Hannah because I couldn't destroy myself. It's the same thing I did to Bunny. God! To *Emily*. She also looked like me. She was blonde, her eyes were blue. And she was so scared, so lost. If I hadn't been invisible—if people could have actually seen me, and not Allyson—they would have thought we were twins. And I did nothing to help her!"

Anthony squatted down in front of Paula, their eyes on the same level. "But you didn't kill Emily, did you. And you have no memory of killing Hannah, do you?"

Paula's tears fell again, rewetting her cheeks. "Why are you doing this to me?"

Anthony stared at her for a long moment, waiting, it seemed, for her to stop crying, which she did. "Because if you kill yourself, the truth will die with you. I can't allow that to happen. I see the real you, right now, Paula. I see what's real. Just as I saw the real you in Allyson. It's why I never gave up on you."

Paula floated. Anthony was different than any other man she'd ever been with. As solid as she was porous. From the very beginning of their relationship, she had tested him for emotional cracks to exploit, as was Allyson's way. But even at age twenty, Anthony Mills was already entirely self-realized—an aphrodisiac like no other. "Why me?" she had asked him on their third date, when he casually mentioned he was no longer interested in seeing other girls. "Because you're interesting," he had said. "Even though you front all the time, with all that makeup and shaving the side of your head like that."

"I'm expressing myself," Allyson had told him, cocking a pierced eyebrow, as if to challenge him to continue deconstructing her.

Anthony laughed. "You're expressing something, all right," he said. "But it ain't yourself."

She had tried to pick a fight. "Fuck you. You don't have me all figured out, asshole."

"I don't have anything about you figured out," he had said, smiling at her. "It seems to me that you don't either, but I can see you're trying. That's why I find you so goddamn interesting."

Boom. Love. Love. Love.

"I *see* you," Anthony said now, his beautiful black skin glistening in the light reflecting off the pool. "The same way I saw the real you shining through Allyson. Look in my eyes, Paula." She did. "I *see* you, and I saw you again through Jill, mother of three, whose husband was gone from her life so much of the time."

Paula's mind sifted Anthony's words, able to hold on to only the larger chunks of information. *Jill. He knows about Jill. No. That can't be.* The emotional implications of that possibility slipped through, falling out of her grasp.

"It was me you were talking to," Anthony said. "It was me talking to Jill."

"You were online…" she said, chasing after the realization.

"Yes," Anthony nodded.

The truth firmed up in Paula's mind. "Who were you?" she asked.

"Brice."

Paula returned at once to the warming persona of Jill Carlson. She had catalogued so many hours over the last years in so many chat rooms, but it was not a task to remember Brice. They had talked for endless hours, steadying each other as their lives and marriages drifted.

"Brice Lawford in San Francisco," she said.

"Jill Carlson in Los Angeles."

"I don't understand."

"I needed something and you gave it to me."

"What?"

"A connection."

She studied him as if seeing him for the first time. "You were so broken, so lost, so unlike how you truly are. Was it all a lie? A game you were playing?"

"No. I did it because it was easier to be my authentic self when I didn't have to put up a front."

She could not abide the absurdity of it all. "But that's exactly what you were doing, pretending to be someone you're not."

"No, that's what I was doing with Hannah. And that's what she was doing with me. We were both so unhappy. You helped us get through that darkness, without even realizing it."

"Not me," Paula insisted. "Jill Carlson."

He shook his head. "You. Paula. The real you."

She shivered. It was too much to comprehend that only a moment before, she'd been prepared to die—was, in fact, dying. And now here she sat, talking with Anthony, or was he Brice Lawford?

"You're wrong," she said, searching his face, so close to hers. "There is no real Paula. There was once, as a child, but she kept getting smaller and smaller, until one day she ceased to exist at all."

Anthony touched her arm, gently, with only the tips of his fingers. "But here you are, right now." He leaned closer, his voice intent. "I *see* you. And if I'm right about you, there's no way you killed Hannah."

CHAPTER TWENTY-SEVEN

STRUGGLING WITH ONE of the larger boxes he'd filled with the detritus of his office at UCLA, Alan set it on the kitchen island. He pulled a Stella from the fridge. Drinking a couple beers each afternoon, before switching to vodka, had become a habit he barely noticed.

"Honey, I'm home," he said under his breath, carrying the box from the kitchen, the bottle of beer dangling precariously between two fingers.

The door to the backyard was open. "Paula?" he called out, but there was no answer.

Setting the box down at the base of the stairs, Alan took another swig of beer and walked outside to investigate. Paula sat in a chair with a beach towel around her shoulders, her hair dry, but her clothes wrinkled and damp. "What're you doing?" Alan asked, not moving any closer than the edge of the patio.

Paula didn't answer. The rock Anthony dropped into her psyche had displaced her emotions, leaving her in its wake, struggling to find equilibrium. She'd been sitting there for over an hour, ever since Anthony left her with a lingering embrace, eliciting a promise that she would not make a second attempt at killing herself. "It would be a third attempt," she had said, her face buried in his chest, his arms enclosing her.

"Everything all right?" Alan asked.

"Not really," she said.

"No," he said, taking another drink from his bottle. "I guess not."

The ensuing silence distracted Paula, making her even more uncomfortable. She looked back toward her husband, but he had left her there, unwilling or unable to give anything more. She was relieved to see him gone. What could she possibly say to him about the unfathomable events of that afternoon? She could barely comprehend them herself. If she could hold on to any one thing, focus on that, it would be easier. But her mind was a prism refracting thoughts in every direction. And then the prism turned, focusing her thoughts to that night at Berkeley twenty-five years ago, the night Emily Jenkins died.

*

"He's a lot better looking than his brother," Bunny said the night of her death. "Nicer, too. Darius can be kind of a dick."

"Then why are you hanging out with him so much?" Paula asked. In her memory, now, Allyson was gone. Paula saw herself as she truly was. *Perception is not reality.*

"Darius can be fun, too, I guess," Bunny shrugged.

"If by fun, you mean trouble."

"As if you don't like to cause trouble," she laughed. "All I'm saying is that Anthony and I would be a better fit, when you think about it."

"I don't want to fucking think about it. And I don't want you to, either."

"It's kinda hard not to," Bunny said, applying another layer of red lipstick in the one mirror the two girls shared in their tiny dorm room. "I probably shouldn't tell you this, but he told me that he likes the way I look. He's obviously attracted to me. What am I supposed to do?"

"You need to get over yourself," Paula said, pulling on her sweatshirt, glancing at Bunny's narrow hips and silently wishing she were fifteen pounds lighter.

Bunny smiled mischievously at Paula in the mirror. "That's exactly what I said to him."

Paula left Bunny at the dorm and met Anthony at the Med Café on Telegraph Avenue for a quick dinner, during which, in the way of insecure eighteen-year-olds, she said nothing regarding her roommate's apparent infatuation with him. She stewed silently and occasionally made passive-aggressive jokes about the sexual appetites of the asshole men at the university. They then went on to the fateful house party over on Hillegass Avenue, along with a hundred or so fellow Golden Bears.

Eventually, she drank enough and danced enough to slough off the layer of insecurity she'd draped over herself, and the night became a whirlwind of escape. But then, as both the house party and Paula reached a fever pitch of pleasure, Bunny arrived, hanging onto Darius, clearly high from whatever substance he'd supplied her with, and it all came crashing down.

Fuming, Paula pulled Darius aside and pleaded with him to leave and to take Bunny with him. Darius was cool with the request—he was, unquestionably, out of his element—but he had four dime bags and two eighths of weed to sell first.

"Anthony's gonna kick your ass if he finds out," Paula warned him.

"I'll be quick. Don't say nothing, all right?"

"You have fifteen minutes, Darius. And then if she's not gone, I'm ratting you out."

Darius smiled. "Shit, these rich white boys'll be halfway through they last joint in fifteen minutes."

Darius left to keep up his end of the deal, and Paula sought out Anthony. She pushed her way through the crowd dancing to Cypress Hill in the living room but couldn't find him. She went to the relative quiet of the kitchen, but nobody had seen him there either. She looked in the backyard, where the party was decidedly quieter, but had no luck. Darius's fifteen minutes came and went, with no sign of Anthony or Bunny. Paula, her face flushed with emotion and tequila shots, was about to lose her mind, when someone in the crowd grabbed her arm.

"Bunny and Anthony just had a major fucking fight!" the girl who had grabbed her said. "She scratched the hell out of his face."

That was the end of the party.

*

"I'll go back to my dorm and straighten this whole fucking thing out," Paula insisted when they got back to Anthony's apartment.

"That's not happening," Anthony said, studying the scratch marks on his cheek and neck in his bathroom mirror. "She's out of her goddamn mind."

"When we gonna hit it?" Darius called out from the other room.

Anthony ignored his brother's impatience and turned to Paula. "Stay here tonight," he said. "I don't want you anywhere near her right now. We'll talk about it after I take D home, all right?"

The raised scratches running down Anthony's face looked

as if they throbbed with each elevated beat of his heart. "Did you do anything with her?" Paula asked, unable to stem the insecurities bubbling to the surface.

"What're you talking about?"

"She likes you. And she told me that you said something about liking the way she looks."

"Oh, please."

"Did you do something, Anthony?"

"You seriously asking me if I raped that girl?"

"That's not what I'm asking, no."

Anthony looked toward the tiny living room where Darius waited. "I can't do this, Allyson. Not right now. Let's talk about it when I get back."

"Why can't we talk about it now?"

"Because I have to get D back to Oakland, and I can see already that the conversation you're insisting we have isn't going to be a short one."

"How long does it take to say yes or no?"

Anthony closed the bathroom door, sealing the two of them off from the rest of the world. "Bunny tried to get with me, okay? She was trying to get me to break up with you and be with her, and she got pissed when I said no. I love you, Allyson. I mean that. I love you. Only you."

Paula searched his eyes, deep pools of glistening black. "I'm going to ask one more time—did you do *anything* with her? Yes or no?"

Anthony's arms opened and he pulled her close to his chest. He held her close, comforting her with his assured embrace. It took a long moment, but he finally said, "No."

*

Allyson had believed him. But Paula did not.

There is objective truth.

Paula stood. She pulled the towel from her shoulders and dropped it onto the vacated patio chair. She had a sour, metallic taste in her mouth. It was as though she'd been an inert piece of machinery that had been plugged in and instantly filled with the energy to operate. Walking into the house, her steps quickened as her mind raced. It was all so clear. Anthony had never been who he'd claimed to be. His self-assuredness was a front—a role he'd cast himself in—insecure Archibald Leach becoming movie-star Cary Grant, the character taking over the man. She'd merely chosen to accept that *version* of him. But what was the truth?

Paula nearly sprinted up the stairs, toward the sound of the shower Alan had turned on, and her thoughts ran faster ahead, whipping through time, all the way back to the detective who looked at her over his reading glasses as he investigated Emily's death. "After their confrontation," he had asked, "did you take Darius home with Anthony?"

"No," Paula said in the reconstructed memory. "Anthony drove him alone. He said it wasn't a good idea for me to go. Oakland is kind of rough, I guess. And his family isn't all that welcoming to me, so Anthony left me at his apartment, told me to wait for him to come back."

"How long was it before he came home?"

"About an hour. I don't really remember, I fell asleep."

As Paula reached the top of the stairs, the twenty-five-year-old lie staggered her. The truth was that she'd been unable to so much as sit still the night Emily died, let alone sleep. Anthony was gone for three hours, not one. Three hours. Hell, he could have driven to Oakland and back five or six times in three hours. Why had it taken him so long? She'd long convinced herself that Anthony had lingered with his family to avoid the conversation that was awaiting him back at his apartment: Violet Mills fussing over the wounds on his face, Devika haranguing him for getting involved with a couple fuckin' crazy-ass white women in the first damn place, and Darius pretending he hadn't been at the party to sell drugs and had only been an innocent bystander in all the drama. Ultimately, all that lingering down in Oakland hadn't mattered, of course—by the time Anthony got back to his apartment, well past two in the morning, Paula was no longer in any mood to argue.

While she never doubted that Anthony was telling the truth about the accusation of rape, over those intervening three hours Paula had extended her assurances to preclude even the *possibility* that anything sexual, mutual or not, had occurred at all between him and Bunny. Anthony was incapable of such betrayal. Anthony was not the type. So Allyson, Paula had decided, wouldn't be the type either. My God, who gives a shit anyway? Even if he had messed around a little, it was no big deal—not really. Allyson was too confident, too self-contained for such childish insecurities. It was girls like Bunny who behaved with irrational jealousy, and Paula was intent on proving she was nothing like Bunny.

She moved through her husband's bedroom to the closed bathroom door, and the prism of her mind turned anew, her thoughts once again rocketing in all directions: Anthony was not who he pretended to be. His entire life was a fraud, perpetrated on everyone he encountered. He was a liar. He was a predator, an online stalker who fantasized a relationship with the woman he'd once loved—who he perhaps still loved. That was why Hannah had been so upset when she'd confronted her in the studio! She was the only one who had known all along who her husband truly was! *Anthony's appetites are not so easily sated.* That's what Hannah had told her. *I may be his main course, but he does love his side dishes.* Hannah knew. And she could no longer play her part in the menagerie Anthony had created. She had confronted him. They'd fought. Paula pulled open her husband's bathroom door as the realization exploded—*Anthony killed his wife. Just like he killed Emily Jenkins.*

CHAPTER TWENTY-EIGHT

Alan stood with one hand holding up the bath towel he'd wrapped around his naked waist, staring at his wife. Paula could barely catch her breath as the words spilled from her mouth with a frenetic attempt to explain the dramatic shift of their shared reality. But the longer she spoke, the clearer it was from Alan's expression that the reality was not actually shared at all.

"You have to believe me, Alan," Paula said, working to bring herself under control. "Anthony is not who he pretends to be, he's—"

Alan held up his free hand and Paula froze, mid-sentence.

"What was Anthony doing here in the first place?" he asked, as if that were somehow more important than the fact that Anthony had killed his wife. "Why did he come over here?"

Paula was annoyed by the question. She had not consciously chosen to omit the tidbit about her attempted suicide, but it seemed secondary to the revelation of Anthony's guilt. "I called him," she said.

Alan's suspicious stare narrowed even more. "Why in the hell would you call him?"

"I was—we hadn't spoken since the night Hannah died and I wanted to reach out to him."

"So you invited him and he just waltzed over here to confess to the murder of his wife?"

"No, that's not what I'm saying. I didn't *invite* him anywhere. He came on his own because I wasn't thinking clearly and— "

"That's enough! You're *still* not thinking clearly, Paula. Jesus, I can see it in your eyes, you're all over the goddamn place. You're clearly having another manic episode, and you're trying to find some order in the chaos you've created, but you're not making any sense."

"No! I'm telling you, he's not who he pretends to be, Alan. He admitted that he stalked me online."

"No! That's what *you* did, Paula! *You* were the online stalker. *You* were the one who created a false identity to worm your way into other people's lives. *You're* the one who invents people. Allyson Clemens, Jill Carlson, that therapist, a Hannah who looks exactly like you. Can't you see what you're doing? This is more of your insanity! You're accusing him of doing exactly what you did!"

"I didn't kill Hannah!" she screamed over the rush of shower water.

"Yes, you did!"

Paula fell silent and Alan reached into the shower and turned off the water. Both of them were perspiring in the gathering moisture of the bathroom.

Alan's voice calmed. "This has to end, Paula."

"You think I don't want this to end? You want the truth? That's why Anthony came over today. He pulled me from the pool as I was dying—drowning myself. It was all finally going to be over. *All of it,*" she screamed. "And I couldn't even control that!"

Alan stood in staggered disbelief as she turned and walked out of the bathroom.

Paula was halfway down the stairs before she realized Alan had no intention of following her. Whatever energy he'd had to keep her afloat in the ever-widening sea of her mind had been depleted, and he could no longer keep even himself above water.

She stared at the box at the base of the stairs. It taunted her as yet another jarring affirmation of objective reality. Her eyes watered as the realization came to her: where Anthony had always worked to be seen as perfect, above petty desires, Alan had been brave enough to reveal himself with all of his insecurities and irritations and helplessness in plain view. For eleven years he had loved her, had supported her, had fought for her. And now he was packing up his life, leaving his work, all because of her.

She picked up the box and turned back. It didn't matter that he didn't believe her about Anthony. She would call Lincoln and the two of them would take care of it. Surely Lincoln would be more than happy to shine the light of guilt someplace else. But first, she would not allow Alan to give up the life he had once cherished. That much she could control. If only that. She would place the box at his feet and tell him to return it to UCLA. If he left UCLA, then they both would remain lost at sea, both drifting. Whatever troubles awaited her with Anthony, they were no longer Alan's to help shoulder. She would leave him, if that was what he wanted. No, what he *needed.* She wanted him to be happy. That remained her most fervent wish. And for him to be happy, he would have to be free. In the end, she was the only one who could give him that freedom.

But halfway up the stairs, the bottom of the box gave way. Files and papers and notebooks dropped with a whooshing sound and swept down the risers.

Stunned by the calamity of the moment, Paula clutched the now empty box and stopped dead in her tracks. The crumpled wreckage of loosened cardboard fell from her hands and she dropped onto the stair riser, crying. Nothing could be done. It was all a cosmic joke. No matter her efforts, there was no way out of the darkness. Her mind was as weak as ever. The tears came silently, a storm washing through her. Then, with a few deliberate inhales, the storm passed as quickly as it had arrived.

She considered the scattered debris in silence. She was utterly alone. Alan would not come: the mess was hers alone to clean up. She began the slow process of collection, reaching for old notebooks and archived newspaper articles and research papers, picking each of them up with the respect they had earned by making it into the box in the first place.

Paying great attention to keeping the collected papers neat, making sure to align them in piles as she made her way back down the stairs, Paula raised a manila folder and something slipped free, falling back to the hardwood of the staircase. It was a two-year-old program for a production of Euripides's play *Helen* at the Little Theatre at UCLA. It was a curious memento to be held for so long, Paula thought, giving it no more attention than a cursory glance. But as she placed it on the pile neatly stacked on the riser behind her, her heart skipped several beats.

She again picked the program up and brought it closer to her disbelieving eyes. And in that one singular moment, everything she'd believed to be the truth was wiped dead away.

"Oh my God," she gasped.

The actress playing Euripides's version of Helen had on a long, honey-brown wig, pulled back from her pretty face. The face was turned at a ninety-degree angle, filling the page with its strikingly forlorn expression.

It was the face of Doctor Claire Horst.

CHAPTER TWENTY-NINE

Paula was hyperventilating. Only this time, it was not by choice. Her vision clouded, the distortion of perception even greater than the moment she'd looked out her living room window and seen herself moving in across the street. She could not comprehend the image staring back at her. Objective reality had left the building entirely. Nothing could be trusted ever again.

"What happened here?" came Alan's voice from the second-floor landing.

His voice more than startled Paula; it frightened her to her core.

She looked up at her husband, standing there in his boxer shorts, still damp from the shower. Unable to manage anything else, Paula raised the program to *Helen* in her shaking hand.

Alan's expression dropped. "Shit," he said.

Paula stood slowly. Her throat swelled. "I don't understand," she said, her voice barely a whisper.

Alan lowered his bare foot to the top step, and Paula took a step backwards down the stairs. He stopped. "I need you to stay calm," he said.

He had asked the impossible. Paula bolted.

Down the staircase she went, moving like a poorly constructed apparatus wobbling on buckled supports, still clasping
the program to *Helen*. Alan's bare feet landed heavily behind
her, covering the remainder of the stairs two at a time. His
hand found Paula's back, and in a blink she was falling, her legs
trailing uselessly behind her as she collapsed to the floor. Alan
watched her the way a hunter watches his prey through a rifle
scope, as Paula labored to pull herself up to her knees, and then,
haltingly, to her feet. "You're not going anywhere right now,"
he said, his voice thick with a warning tone of further harm.

Paula did not turn back to look at him. She stood still, assessing the condition of her knees, which throbbed with a dull pain.

"I'm not going to hurt you," Alan said, moving closer. "I'm
sorry I pushed you. I just want to talk, okay? Can we do that
without getting emotional? We need to figure out what we're
going to do here."

Paula, though, had already decided what she was going to
do. She bolted for the front door. She managed only to turn
the lock and open the door wide enough to see daylight before
Alan's hand landed defiantly on the swinging door, stopping
it dead on its arc.

"No!" she screamed.

Alan slammed the door closed, his body pressed hard
against hers. Paula struggled to break free, but his hold was too
powerful. He dragged her backwards, her feet kicking into the
air. They moved into the living room, Alan holding her tightly
by her torso. She again raised her leg, but this time she did
not kick at the air but slammed her shoe down onto his bare
toes. His grip loosened, but not enough for her to free herself.

"Enough!" he screamed into her ear. With an unforgiving
jerk, he slammed her to the floor.

Paula lay there, stunned by the violence. Rolling onto her back, she looked up at him. He was clearly distraught—his eyes wide, his face flushed. He bent down to grab her and she kicked once more, this time catching his testicles with a solid whap.

He yelped, high-pitched, like a wounded dog, and his knees buckled. As he dropped, his knee landed on her stomach, pining her to the floor. His face twisted as he fought through the radiating pain. A reflexive anger brought his fist up. Paula winced, anticipating the blow, but the clenched fist loosened as he matched her breath for labored breath until the shock to his system had passed. He reached for the program she still clutched in her hand. Once he had it, once the evidence was no longer in her possession, the air left her body, her energy seeping out in all directions, leaving her utterly spent. His knee still on Paula's chest, Alan stared at the now wrinkled picture of Helen of Troy on the program's cover.

Stinging tears fell from the corners of Paula's eyes. "I'm not crazy," she cried.

"Goddammit, Paula," Alan said through clenched teeth. Paula's tears overwhelmed her as Alan's weight came off her chest. He stood over her, his own senses clearly as overwhelmed as hers. "I don't know what to do here," he said, bending over to catch his breath, his hands braced upon his knees.

"Who is she?" Paula asked through her tears.

"Stop talking."

"Tell me who she is."

Alan wobbled backward, half-sitting, half-falling into a nearby chair.

"Tell me!" she screamed.

Alan stared at the crumpled program in his hand for a long moment, as though needing the time to fully resign himself to his new reality. "Her name's Valerie," he said. "She was a student of mine."

Paula's shallow gulps of air deepened, and she regained her bearings. She pushed herself to her knees.

"Stay there," he warned.

"I don't feel well."

He stood irritably, grabbing hold of her arm, and she tensed. "I said I'm not going to hurt you," he said, moving her to the seat he had vacated. "I just need a moment here, okay? Can you give me that? One goddamn moment to think?"

Paula noticed his fingers trembled as he wiped them across his mouth.

"Anthony didn't kill Hannah," Paula said at last. "You did."

His chest continued to rise and fall, rise and fall. "I didn't kill anybody," he said. "Maybe you were right—maybe Anthony did kill his wife." He seemed to smile. "But my money's still on you." He paced back and forth like a caged animal, never getting more than a few steps before some new thought turned him around. There was no escape from the box he'd suddenly found himself in. "Either way, it's all fucked up now."

"What is?" Paula asked, grasping for anything to hold onto.

"Why did you go through my shit?" he screamed, frustration overwhelming him.

"That's not what I was—I was going to apologize. I was trying to make things better."

Her explanation only enraged him further. "Nothing is going to make this better!" he yelled, pulling her from the chair.

"No!" she screamed, trying to break free. "Why are you doing this?"

Alan's hold on her tightened as he dragged her up the stairs and into the master bedroom. His arm curled around her neck like a yoke as he rummaged through a coat draped over a corner chair. He pulled out his cell phone. With his focus briefly elsewhere, Paula lashed out, her nails digging a long trench across his cheek, from his temple to his nose.

He recoiled only briefly, dropping the phone, before his wide palm landed a heavy blow to her cheek. Her ears rang. Mucous filled her nose and eyes.

"This is *your* fault, Paula," Alan seethed, his warm breath spreading across her face. "If you had just fucking killed *yourself* instead of Hannah, Goddammit."

He then pushed her into the bathroom and slammed the door closed behind her.

Paula gasped for air. Her throat stung when she swallowed. The mirror images of what Bunny had done to Anthony's face, and what she'd done to Alan's, flashed like lightning. The two faces, black and white, melded together, making it impossible to tell them apart. Only moments before, she had been so sure that Anthony was guilty of bringing the horror upon everyone, and now Alan had morphed into the monster, revealing its true self. Which was the truth? Was the hidden monster in Anthony? In Alan? Or was it in both of them? And then the devastating thought: was she the hidden monster, looking into the mirror of melding faces, revealing her true self? Alan's words echoed in her head, mocking the debate: *my money's still on you.*

And then his voice sounded outside her thoughts and she pressed her ear to the bathroom door. "It's all a fucking mess," she heard him say. "We have to figure out what we're going to do now." In her mentally enfeebled state, it took a moment to realize he was talking on the phone.

He's talking to her. Helen of Troy. Dr. Claire Horst. Valerie.

Alan's distraught voice moved away and Paula could no

longer make out any of his words. Her hand found the door handle, but the lingering pain of Alan's blow checked her and she did not dare turn it. She backed away, staring at the door, waiting. Another flash of lightening and she sat opposite Dr. Horst in the makeshift office in Pasadena.

Everything's a lie. Nothing is real.

Her stomach lurched and she made it to the toilet in time to vomit into the bowl.

*

After pulling on his Levis and a UCLA t-shirt, Alan sat on the edge of his bed. He'd heard his wife's retching behind the closed door but made no move to attend to her. His customarily keen mind had been so disrupted that he could not effectively put the events of the past hour in order. Everything had indeed gone to shit.

And then things got worse.

The phone rang.

It wasn't the burner phone he'd used to call Valerie (the only one he ever used to speak with her); that one remained silent in his pants pocket. It was the cellphone on the bedside table that vibrated with each piercing ring, lighting up with the name Lincoln Childress.

Alan considered letting it go to voicemail, but decided that was not a good idea. He had to control as much of the narrative as he could before it spiraled entirely out of control. By the fourth ring, a realization formed solidly in his mind: *Paula can never be allowed to speak with anyone ever again.* The plan he had put in motion months prior would have to be sped up. There were no other options remaining. And for it to work successfully, the new groundwork would have to be laid quickly—starting with Lincoln.

"Hello," he said, answering the phone, effectively employing a disinterested tone.

"Are you at home?" Lincoln asked, not bothering with any polite preamble.

"Yes," Alan said, immediately wishing he'd not committed. Perhaps Lincoln was outside his house right then. What then? What possible excuse could there be to not let him in?

"Good, stay there," Lincoln said. "Jacob and I are finishing up here, but we have some things to discuss."

Reprieve. But for how long? "What sort of things?" he asked, unafraid to demonstrate his customary disdain for the lawyer's superior attitude. "I'm not in the mood to argue over the Sullivan estate with you right now, if that's what you have planned."

"Not at the moment. Just sit tight and we'll be there in about an hour, depending on traffic. I swear, the freeways in this city should be put on a terrorist watchlist."

Alan's face warmed. "It's not a good time for you to come over."

"What's the matter?"

"It's Paula, she's acting very strangely," Alan said, focusing his plan. "More than usual, I mean. She was very anxious when I arrived home and wouldn't tell me what caused her to be so upset. The harder I pressed, the more despondent she became; it's hard to tell what's going on with her."

"I'm afraid I might have an idea."

Alan was surprised that his volley of bullshit had elicited a useful response. "What does that mean?"

"Say nothing to Paula," Lincoln instructed. "I'll explain when we get there."

"No. She'll only get more upset if you come here tonight. It's gonna have to wait until tomorrow."

"I'm afraid that's not an option. We'll be there as soon as we can."

Lincoln hung up and Alan's perspiration turned to sweat as he rummaged through the closet, all while dialing the burner phone.

"Change of plans," he said. "I can't meet you. How fast can you get here?"

"I don't want to go there!" Valerie said on the other end.

"How fast?" Alan repeated.

"God, I don't—fifteen, twenty minutes. Why can't you come here?"

"Because I'm about to have company. But Paula can't be here. You're gonna have to take her."

"Take her where?"

Alan's mind spun so fast it was difficult for his words to keep up. "It doesn't matter, we'll figure that out. We'll put her in the trunk."

"In the trunk?" There was a short, expectant silence. Then, "Will she be alive?"

Alan's heat index spiked hotter. "I don't know. Don't worry about that."

"You sound pretty fucking worried to me."

"That's why I need your help."

"My help? I don't know what to do!"

"It's fine, Valerie. Everything's gonna work out. We just have to focus."

Tucking the phone between his ear and shoulder, he pulled a long-sleeved shirt from a hanger and spun it lengthwise before pulling it taut, testing its usefulness.

"Everything is still lined up in our favor," he said, dropping the shirt, discarding it from consideration as a useful tool.

"This is going to end exactly the way we planned. It's gonna be a little difficult for us right now, but we can do this. You don't have to do anything violent, I promise. But you do need to get here as quickly as possible and help me deal with Paula. Can you do that?"

"Yes."

"I love you, Val."

"I love you too."

"Okay, let's do this right, then. If we stay calm and don't make any mistakes, we'll be right back on track. Come here now, quickly, but don't speed—no tickets, right? Don't do anything to bring attention. You don't have to park up on San Vicente this time. Just park a block up the street and then walk down the alley as usual. Do you have one of the wigs or a hat or something?"

"A hat."

"Good, wear it. Text me when you're in the alley, and if I don't respond, then keep going. It means it's too late and they're already here."

"What are you gonna do if they get there before I do?"

"That won't be an issue if you hurry." He stopped searching the closet. "You don't have any rope, do you?"

"Jesus, Alan."

Alan hung up and left the closet, looking helplessly around the bedroom for something of use. And then he saw it. Moving quickly, he unplugged the phone charger from the wall and opened the bathroom door.

"Let's go," he said.

"Please talk to me," Paula said, staying still. "I won't be mad, I promise. Whatever's going on we can— "

"I said get out!"

As Paula walked forward, Alan twisted her arms behind her back and used the charger cord to tie them together. He pulled the knot tight and a sharp jolt of pain spasmed through her shoulders. "You're hurting me," she said, wincing.

"It wasn't supposed to happen like this," Alan said, breathing heavily through his nose.

"What wasn't? What have you done?"

"I've done *everything*! Eleven years of my life taking care of you. I can't do it anymore. I've carried you as far as I can. I'm done."

Paula willed herself not to cry. "I never said you had to stay."

He slammed her face first against the wall, knocking the air from her.

"Yes, you did," he seethed with contempt. "You and that fucking estate you're swaddled in as if you're the second coming of the baby Jesus. But even with all their resources they didn't do a damn thing to help you. Their money didn't keep you safe. *I* did that. I was the *only* one. And they have the fucking gall to tell me if I can't do it any longer—if I can no longer survive being dragged down with you—then I'm free to go with only a few pennies in my pocket? Fuck Jacob and all his self-serving lawyers like Lincoln, who act like they're being so protective of you, when all they're truly concerned with is protecting the money. That's who they really serve. They don't give a shit about you."

The man whom she had once loved, the man whose expansive outlook she had so admired, was gone. Somewhere along the way, he, too, had been replaced by an identical opposite, but she had failed to notice.

"Is that what this is all about?" she cried, despite her effort. "Money?"

He spun her around, his mouth now so close that she could not tell whose breath was whose. "It's about *respect*. Don't you get it? Why the hell do you think they put it in writing that I had to stay fifteen years before I could collect what is rightfully mine? Because they knew something I didn't—that any man who fell for you would never last. Open your eyes, Paula. They disrespected you even more than they did me."

*

The low sun cast long shadows across the neighborhood as Valerie Amoia sat in her Honda Accord, scanning the street for anybody that might notice her. Other than a gardener loading his mower into the back of a rusted pick-up truck half a block away, there was nobody to be concerned with, so she tucked her shoulder-length black hair under her baseball cap, left the car, and headed for the alley at the corner of Seventh and Georgina. Once she reached the alley, her pace quickened. After a few long strides, she broke into a full run; the adrenaline made it impossible to move any slower. As she ran, her hand found the underside of her belly, cradling the soft curve that protected her unborn child.

Arriving at the back fence of the Hickman's house, she pulled the phone from her pocket and texted Alan. A crow cawed in the distance and another answered. A prop plane whined its way across the sky. Valerie glanced at the windows of a neighboring house, paranoid somebody would spot her. Her phone vibrated in response: *Come in. Gate unlocked.*

She always felt like a burglar when she entered through the backyard, but this time the sensation of trespassing was more intense. This time she was not there for a surreptitious romp with Alan, but to finally put an end to the madness they'd been forced to endure since falling in love two years earlier. For a brief moment she allowed herself to imagine what it would be like when the two of them shared a home as beautiful as this—the two of them and their newborn son. If only she'd had more time as Doctor Claire Horst. A few more sessions and she'd have planted the necessary mental and emotional triggers to push Paula over the edge, sending her out of their lives once and for all, by her own hand.

"Val." Alan's voice disrupted her reverie.

He stood beside the ivy-covered pool house. His eyes were rimmed red, tiny strands of hair matted to his forehead. As she came closer, she noticed the puffy scratch down his cheek. "Are you okay?" she asked, moving quickly to hug him.

"I'm fine, now that you're here." Alan hugged her back for a few moments, then pulled away, taking her hands in his. "But we have to do some things differently. I wasn't thinking clearly when I called you. I have a new plan—a better one. You're not going to take her."

"Why not?"

"Too risky. Having her out of the house brings up too many outside variables we can't control. Besides, we can't risk them pulling up when you're leaving."

"I'm sorry I took so long. There was a gardener up the street and I had to wait to make sure—"

Alan used up precious time giving her another lingering hug. "I'm not blaming you for anything. I'm the one who should be apologizing. I was so stupid, saving that fuck-ing program."

"It's okay. Everything's going to work out, just like you said, right?"

Alan kissed her. "If we do everything right, we'll be fine."

"Where is she?"

Alan led her to the music studio. He pushed the door open and Valerie poked her head inside, hesitant to enter. Her eye first caught sight of the serrated kitchen knife resting on the edge of the table by the door. It was clean. No blood yet. She inched her way into the room.

Paula lay on her stomach on the floor, her hands bound behind her back by the white phone-charging chord, head turned, staring up at the two of them. Her face was placid, as if resigned to her fate. Her eyes registered no recognition of the woman who'd once promised to help her fight all her demons.

"Hello, Paula," Valerie said.

Paula stared at her without so much as a blink.

CHAPTER THIRTY

ALAN WAS ALREADY standing in the foyer when the doorbell rang, but he made no move to answer the door. Running through a mental checklist, he made sure everything was all set. His mind had finally recalibrated, his natural inclination towards analytical observation and precise action once again driving him. With a final reset of his expression, he pulled the door open expectantly, then immediately sagged. "Come on in," he said, feigning disappointment, as Lincoln, Jacob, and Heather passed him into the house.

"You all right?" asked Lincoln.

"I was hoping you might be Paula." Alan glanced outside again, then shut the door.

"I don't understand," said Jacob. "She's not here?"

"We had a fight."

"She do that?" Lincoln asked, pointing to the scratch on Alan's cheek.

"I'm afraid so."

Heather's gaze lingered on his face a bit longer than necessary before she glanced around the entryway like a detective at a crime scene.

"What happened?" Jacob asked.

"She was paranoid about why you were coming over." He touched his fingers to his cheek. "I tried to calm her down, but it got pretty heated."

"I asked you to not say anything to her," Lincoln said, not hiding his displeasure.

"Give me a break, would you?" Alan snapped. "I didn't say anything. She was already in a mood, as I told you. But she overheard me on the phone and when I said I didn't know why you were coming, she accused me of betraying her."

"Betraying her how?" Heather asked.

Alan recognized that the young woman was analyzing everything with suspicious caution. It was time to play his next card. He held up his hands as if to hold off their impending judgements. "I'm afraid I haven't been entirely up front with you," he said.

"In what way?" Jacob asked.

Alan sighed wearily. "I'll show you."

Leading them to the living room, Alan crossed to the coffee table. Picking up Paula's journal, he hesitated, looking shamed.

"What's that?" Lincoln asked.

"Paula's journal." He handed it to Lincoln. "My sister found it and gave it to me."

"How long have you had this?" Lincoln asked.

"A week or so."

"A week?" Jacob said, incredulous.

Lincoln continued to stare. "Why did you keep it from us?"

Alan sat down and rubbed his face, making sure his fingers found his eyes to help redden them. "I was trying to protect her."

"From what?" asked Jacob.

"From us?" Lincoln asked.

"From the whole world," Alan said. "Jesus Christ, it's all in that fucking thing—it's filled with anger and violence. She even kept track of Hannah's schedule in there, writing down every time she came and went." As Lincoln read the journal, Alan continued. "I was going to show you eventually—I knew I had to. But I was worried about what it would do to her, how she would react. The smallest things set her off, and that fucking journal is clearly not a small thing. Even tonight, when I told her that you were probably coming over to discuss something about the preliminary hearing, she erupted, convinced that I'd told you about the journal, despite my insistence that I hadn't. I tried to restrain her, but she slapped and kicked me whenever I got close." He again touched the scratch on his face as though in sad contemplation, but despite his effort, was not quite able to force out a tear. "There was no getting through to her. She was afraid of what will happen to her if people find out what she wrote."

"How bad is it?" Jacob asked Lincoln.

Lincoln handed the journal to Heather. "About as bad as it can be, short of her writing a confession that she killed Hannah Mills. Not that the distinction matters. The intent to harm her is implicit enough. This was a serious miscalculation on your part, Alan. What do you think will happen if your sister lets it slip and news of the journal gets out?"

"Wendy isn't going to say anything," Alan insisted.

"That's your *opinion*," Lincoln said. "Which is meaningless, as your judgment has been proven faulty as hell. Heather, get Wendy on the phone, please."

"All my sister wants is for Paula to be left alone!" Alan yelled. "So how 'bout you return the fucking favor and leave her out of it, too? She was dragged through enough shit when Paula accused her of trying to drug her."

"I'm here to do a job!" Lincoln shot back. "Which is to defend Paula. So with all due respect to your sister's goddamn fragile sensibilities, this is exactly the sort of *shit* I'm being paid to wade through."

Heather placed a steadying hand on Lincoln's arm. "Gentlemen, we have more immediate concerns to deal with. Did Paula give any indication where she went?"

"No," Alan said.

"Did she take her car?"

"No," said Alan, standing to seize the opportunity. "She was in no state of mind to be driving. She's a danger to herself. What we need to do is spread out, go in separate cars. We'll have a better chance of finding her before she has the chance to harm herself any further."

Heather and Lincoln shared a knowing glance.

"What is it?" Alan asked, eyes darting from person to person.

"We have reason to believe that she might not have gone very far," said Jacob.

Alan's heart skipped a beat. "I don't understand?"

Lincoln said, "Heather surveilled something this afternoon that—"

"Who did you have under surveillance?" Alan asked.

"It's part of our due diligence to keep track of everyone involved," Lincoln said.

"You mean me?" Alan asked, slipping into a state of panic.

"Everyone," Lincoln said. "You understand that, don't you?"

Alan flashed on every contact he'd had with Valerie over the past few weeks. They'd been so careful. Other than meeting twice at the UCLA food court, they'd only spoken on the phone—surely Heather hadn't discovered the burner cell. *She can't be that good, can she?*

"Alan?" Jacob's fatherly voice cut through.

Alan nodded, his palms dampening. "Of course, I understand."

"This afternoon," Heather said, "while you were cleaning out your office—"

"You knew about that?" Alan interrupted, unable to stay quiet.

"Yes," Heather said. "While you were at UCLA, I was parked up the street here surveilling Anthony Mills's home."

Alan's gut swirled. *Holy shit. Was she still there when Valerie arrived?*

"Approximately thirty minutes after you left, I witnessed Anthony Mills leave his home and enter your backyard, through the side gate."

"What?" Alan said, unsure how much acting was required to sell his shock. "Anthony was here?"

"He stayed for forty-five minutes and then returned to his house," Heather said, not slowing her report. "But as he left, again through the side gate, I witnessed he and Paula hugging each other."

Alan allowed the news to settle in before responding. The plan he'd had in place to get them out of the house had been waylaid, and now, with all eyes upon him, a choice had to be made as to the appropriate response to this new direction. "Anthony and Paula? That doesn't make any sense. Why would he be hugging the woman he thinks killed his wife?"

"Perhaps they've not been entirely truthful about the present nature of their relationship," Jacob said.

"It's still not clear why Mr. Mills was here," Heather jumped back in, showing a flash of annoyance at Jacob's interjection. "Nor is the current status of their relationship clear, so it would be wrong to draw any definitive conclusions. But whatever the reason, his visit was certainly welcomed by your wife."

Alan could no longer hide his worry. He asked Heather, "Did you see Paula leave?"

"No. A few minutes after Anthony returned to his house, Darius Mills left in his car. I followed him, but gained no intel of value, other than confirming that he's very fond of the 4Play strip club over on Cotner Avenue."

Alan was overwhelmed by the euphoric rush of endorphins flooding his system. Heather was gone by the time Valerie arrived. *They don't suspect me of anything!* In fact, it was Paula they suspected. It was not going as he had planned, but everything was falling into place.

"You think she's over there right now?" he said. "With Anthony?"

"It's a distinct possibility," said Lincoln.

"Then what the hell are we waiting for?"

*

The charging cords around Paula's wrists made moving difficult, but she managed to pull herself to a seated position. Yelling for help would make no difference in the sound-proofed studio. Not that it mattered, as she hadn't spoken at all since Alan left to attend to Lincoln, Jacob, and Heather. Valerie spent most of the time walking in and out of the door leading to the pool house, evidently unable to resist the neurotic urge to spy on the main house through a sliver of space between the closed window shutters. Occasionally returning to check on Paula, she offered only a few miserable variations of, "This will all be over soon."

Despite the sun having gone down and the night ocean air cooling the city, the room was hot, the air stale. The air conditioner had not been turned on. Paula figured that was to stave off any possibility of drawing attention. Her back itched, but she could not free her hands to scratch. She closed her eyes and tried to imagine herself walking free, stepping onto the cool grass of the yard in her bare feet. In her mind she ran all the way to the bluffs overlooking the ocean. The wind blew gently and she spread her arms wide, taking in the freedom. But then she realized she was standing where Hannah had died. Everything always came back to Hannah.

Paula pictured Hannah's head bashed in from behind, her wrists cut, the blood. Her eyes sprang open and Valerie was back.

She stood in front of Alan's eight-piece copper-and-black drum set, looking down at her. She was wearing the set of latex gloves Alan had given her and was holding the knife, her arms at her sides. Paula was not concerned, for the moment at least, that the knife would be put to use. It seemed more for Valerie's own protection than anything.

"It looks like they've gone," Valerie said.

Paula's brow furrowed. It took a concentrated effort to not still see the woman standing over her as Doctor Horst, but rather as an actress, her husband's lover. Reality had become the delusion.

"The light went out in the kitchen. They went looking for you, I guess."

Paula looked away.

"I don't want to be here any more than you do," Valerie said. "Well, maybe that's not true, but I never wanted to be Doctor Horst, that's for sure."

Despite the physical and emotional pain, Paula pressed for the truth. "Then why were you?"

Valerie looked surprised that Paula had spoken—uncomfortable even. "That was all Alan's idea. All of this was his idea. I didn't have much of a choice."

"Of course you did."

"I don't care if you believe me or not." She sounded irritated with Paula for the first time. She pulled the seat away from the drum set to sit, facing her. "I didn't say I minded doing it, playing Claire. All I meant was I couldn't see the big picture at first. That's what I admire most about Alan; he's able to see not only the big picture, but every detail. The forest and the trees, right?" She nervously rubbed her left palm across her thigh, her right still clutching the knife. "It's like all that business with the smoothies and the medications. Each little step in the right direction leads to the place you're aiming for."

Paula's eyes narrowed. Of course. Alan only had tea in the mornings, never the smoothie. Every day he'd made her one, always the caring husband. Get those medications in the right combination and they cause all sorts of issues with depression, don't they? Hell—plenty of people have killed themselves because they were depressed. *I was probably the one who gave him the idea to begin with!* Paula marveled at the amount of planning her husband had employed to drive her mad. The realization didn't make her angry, though. It made her sad. "Where did he get the pills?" she asked.

Valerie glanced back to the closed door, as if unsure how much she was allowed to say.

"They're yours, aren't they?"

"What? No," Valerie said, defensively, turning back from the door.

"I don't believe you," Paula said, needling her.

"I don't care what you believe! My mother works as a cashier at a pharmacy. I'd visit her and steal the pills every once in a while—keep the supply coming. Of course we hadn't planned on the delusions they caused you to have. Once you requested seeing a shrink, I had to bone up on all that shit. *Delusion of subjective doubles*. What a fucking trip."

Paula saw it all so clearly now. Of course Valerie was correct; they truly hadn't had a choice. If they had allowed her to see a real doctor, the drugs in her system would have been found. Hell, her getting actual care, actually getting better, would have screwed everything up. Still, one thing didn't make sense. "I *chose* you to be my doctor," Paula said.

"You really don't get how goddamn brilliant Alan is, do you?" Valerie said, her annoyance with Paula returning. "You didn't *choose* Doctor Horst. He *made* you pick her." The more she spoke, the easier the words seemed to come. Like steam under pressure, finally let loose. "You hate doctors. Especially male ones. There was a reason that everyone else on the list he made up was either male or had offices in a hospital."

"He knew I wouldn't have gone to any of them," Paula said, feeling foolish for being so easily manipulated.

Valerie shrugged dismissively. "Even if you had, I'm sure they wouldn't have been available to see new clients when he called to make the arrangements. No. It had to be Claire. And being the brilliant actress I am, I guess I had to be Claire too."

"You are a very good actress, I'll give you that."

The compliment brightened her. "That's how we met, you know. At the theater. He came with some guy from his department whose son was in the play. I used to joke with him that he actually fell in love with Helen of Troy. That was why he kept that program, I suppose. The romance of it all."

Paula hated the sound of this woman's voice. Where once it had been so soothing, now it assaulted her senses, made her sick to her stomach. The more she spoke, the less of Doctor Horst Paula saw. Claire—or whatever her name was—acted so different now. No longer did she remain silent, contemplative, but talked on and on. She was jittery, the outpouring of words like a form of self-soothing. *She's trying to convince herself that everything is still under control.* If Paula were the therapist, she would write that down on her notepad.

"Getting the office space was the most difficult challenge," Valerie went on, as though suddenly proud of all the work that had gone into driving Paula mad. "I drove all the way to Calabasas trying to find a place, but he insisted it had to be in Pasadena because of all that stuff with your parents. It would all have to connect for it to be perfect—all those tiny details that would convince everyone you were unstable. It helped that we could pay cash for the space upfront. God, it was such a pain though. I had to go back, like, four days a week sometimes to make it look legit. I'd get all dressed up in these crazy outfits, with this pixie wig and makeup, and blare my music to make sure I was noticed. Alan even paid a bunch of day laborers he got from the parking lot at Home Depot to make these fake deliveries and hang out with me. Most of them didn't speak any English, so it was awkward as hell dealing with them   my Spanish isn't the greatest. They had no fucking idea what the point was, but they were paid well, so they were happy to be there at all. Alan called them 'extras in our little production.'"

"Turns out he's not a bad actor, either," Paula said.

Valerie laughed. She actually laughed. It was difficult to

watch, and Paula closed her eyes as she listened. "He had a convincing Russian accent, anyway," Valerie said., her words floating on the tide of her nervous giggles. "It was kind of funny, actually. He went all method to prepare. I helped coach him. When he signed the lease for his *daughter's* workspace, he came up with a whole backstory, even wore a wig and fake belly. He was so into it he even looked into getting fake contact lenses. I tried to take a picture of him, but he wouldn't let me."

"You're quite the team," Paula said, unable to sound as derisive as she wanted to be.

"Not that everything was Alan's idea," Valerie said. "The journal was mine. Once you started going off, spouting all those violent thoughts about Hannah Mills, it was obvious that we needed to get it out there. He was so impressed when I told him what I'd done. The truth is, one of my old therapists had me keep one, so it wasn't that difficult to come up with."

Paula recalled the concern Alan had shown, how he'd insisted that he would keep the journal private. The details had indeed been well planned out. But it was impossible to track down each moment, each clue, to Alan's fabrication, because there was only one question looming large in Paula's mind. It rose up like a full moon, illuminating the darkness.

"Was me killing Hannah part of the plan?" she asked.

Valerie's expression slackened; her tone evened out. "You were only supposed to kill yourself. I thought you'd do it, too. Let's be honest, you're pretty unstable, Paula. Sometimes I got so nervous listening to you. But even with everything, we never imagined you killing Hannah. All we wanted was for you to drive yourself crazy and then give up."

I did. All your planning worked. You won, you little bitch. But Anthony saved me.

"So who killed Hannah?" she asked.

Valerie turned the knife in her hands.

"The answer to that," she said, "is the craziest part of all."

CHAPTER THIRTY-ONE

Lincoln did not enter the Mills home.

"Plausible deniability," he called it. "I don't have any knowledge of this taking place."

If he were to question Anthony, it would undoubtedly be used against him by the police and the district attorney. Tampering with a potential witness and all that. So he took a walk around the block, contemplating the next chess move. And wishing, for the first time in eight years, that he hadn't given up smoking.

As they stood on Anthony's doorstep, Heather again argued she should be the only one to see if Paula was inside the Mills home. Jacob continued to insist that, because of his past relationship with Anthony, he alone would be able to get the truth from him. While they were discussing it, Alan went ahead and rang the doorbell.

"What's going on here?" Anthony said when he answered.

It had been hastily decided that Jacob would do the talking, but Alan again took control. "Let me talk to Paula," he said, giving no room for Anthony to deny her presence.

"What the hell does that mean?"

"Get her."

Anthony moved his irritated stare slowly from Alan to Jacob. "What's this about, Jacob?" he asked.

"Paula's gone missing. We have reason to believe that she's here, with you."

"Is that right?" Anthony turned to Heather. "And who're you?

"A friend of the family."

"Not *my* family," Anthony said. "So you all get off my goddamn porch. Paula isn't here."

"You were with her earlier though, weren't you?" Alan asked.

Anthony did not deny it.

"Why did you come to see her this afternoon?" asked Jacob.

"To *see* her? Is that what she told you?"

"She didn't tell us anything," Jacob said.

"I was there," Heather said. "I saw you go in the gate."

Anthony's tone hardened. "If you were there, then why the fuck didn't you do anything to help her?"

"I don't understand," Heather said.

"Were you there or not?" Anthony challenged her.

"Not inside the house, no. I saw you from the street."

Anthony considered the visitors on his porch. "You all have no goddamn idea what the hell's going on here, do you?"

"That's what we're trying to figure out," Jacob said. "Paula was very upset this evening. Because of what Heather saw earlier, we assumed she might have come here. She left without saying where she was going. We're afraid she might hurt herself."

Anthony hesitated. "You have reason to be," he said finally, stepping aside, nodding his assent for them to enter.

Jacob and Heather walked inside the house, followed by

Alan. Anthony watched him silently, then closed the door and followed them into his living room.

*

The night Hannah Mills died, Valerie told Paula, it was his students' fault that Alan was blackout drunk. He had joined them after class, something he almost never did. But they were so young, so carefree, and he was attracted to their recklessness. It had been so long since he'd allowed himself to be reckless, after all. For his students, drinking was more than a social lubricant, it was a way of life. They drank with abandon. They chanted, *Drink! Drink! Drink!* as if it were a mantra, and they cheered each other with each downed shot of tequila. Alan no doubt needed to unwind. But his choice to go out that night was a fateful decision in ways that he could not imagine, even now.

When the drunken, slightly misspelled text came in that he was going to spend the remainder of the evening at Barney's Beanery in Westwood, rather than with her, an emotional chord within Valerie sprang loose, vibrating like a tuning fork throughout her system. The image of her beloved getting drunk with a bunch of twenty-two-year-olds burnished in her the realization that they had lost all control—and control was the one thing that Alan had promised. Hell, up until that moment, he had embodied it. *But if he is always in such goddamn control, why did he get me pregnant?* He didn't have all the answers. He was off getting shit-faced and she was sitting alone in her one-bedroom apartment in Palms, a block off the ten freeway. *Enough! What the hell are we waiting for? It has already been so long!*

The longer it took them to set Paula up, the more problems would arise—that's what Alan had always said. The baby was coming, and they were running out of time. She was not going to be a single mother—a *mistress* for Christ's sake—when her son, *their* son, came into the world. Their true lives together could wait no longer. It had to come to an end right then.

She drove to Santa Monica in a fury.

It had started so simply. Paula was already depressed. Make her more so and she would accomplish what she'd failed to do twenty-five years ago. It was clean. When there's a billion dollars on the table, the argument went, that's the way it has to be. No questions. But Paula fucked that up too, with her strange delusions and her sudden desire to see a therapist. Alan was right, she just couldn't help but make everything more difficult.

As Valerie drove into Santa Monica, the complications grew. She had no clear plan. God, how much Alan would disapprove of that. Perhaps he could be swayed to accept her primal urge to act, but to do so without a clear plan would be unforgivable. Fine. She wouldn't tell him. She'd keep it a secret. She could make it look like a suicide. Slip a bag over her head. Slit her wrists. Maybe Paula could have an accident. Throw her down the stairs and break her fucking neck. God, she was so tired of thinking about Paula.

She parked on San Vicente as she always did and walked down to Georgina Avenue under the cover of darkness. It was after midnight and the streets were empty. It was only her and Paula now. Her, Paula, and the six-inch knife she had tucked into her belt.

Everything made sense in Valerie's frenzied mind. She would walk right up to the house that she so profoundly coveted and ring the doorbell. She would reveal herself. Tell Paula everything. Tell her how much more Alan loved her than he ever did his pathetic little wife. Let the truth finally be unbound.

And then she would strike. In the fantasy she created, Valerie was emboldened by seeing the confusion, the pain, the loss, on Paula's face as she died. How wonderful it would be when this burdensome nightmare was over.

But the closer Valerie drew to the house, the colder the night became. Each footstep landed slower, heavier. The moon split the clouds and illuminated the tears streaming down her face. Reality reasserted itself, as heavy as gravity, pulling her down. By the time she came to stand in front of the Mills home, Valerie could not control her shaking. She could not control anything. Drawing the knife from her belt, she tested its weight in her hand, trying to regain her resolve. But there was nothing left inside. The fever dream had vanished in the cold.

"Paula?" came a woman's voice from across the street.

Valerie's breath caught short.

"Paula!" the woman's voice rang out again, closer, sounding angry, challenging.

Valerie turned and stared into the eyes of Hannah Mills.

*

"You killed her."

Valerie turned the knife in her gloved hands and looked down at Paula.

"Actually, what I did was run. When Hannah realized it wasn't you, she backed away, as if to apologize, and I ran. I was so fucking afraid." Her eyes briefly closed as she remembered. "I'd screwed everything up. She'd seen my face. She saw the knife. She would tell someone and questions would be asked. I got about a block away and then turned back. I couldn't let it happen. All that work, all that planning. Alan would be so mad at me. So I followed her. I followed her all the way to the bluffs."

Paula lowered her head. "I don't want to hear any more," she said.

"Of course you do, Paula," Valerie said, shaking free from the darkness of the memory. "The ending is the best part." Crouching down, she held the knife close to Paula's chest. "You and Hannah were the same, remember? And her ending is going to be your ending, too."

The threat struck Paula like a phantom foreshock to the impending sting of the knife as Valerie's expression darkened. "You see, I didn't have the luxury of not following through, like I had with you. I had to kill her or everything would be ruined, and when she sat down on that bench, I knew it was my only chance. I had to act."

She hunched Paula over to expose the hands tied at her back, the tip of the knife now pressed directly to her wrists. Valerie rested her cheek on Paula's back, like a mother trying to soothe a frightened child. The heat coming off her was palpable. The added weight and the heat, coupled with the lilac scent of her perfume, was claustrophobic. Paula went rigid with stress.

*

Hannah sat, facing the horizon of an ocean that could be heard, faintly, but not seen. Valerie stayed back, hidden by shadows as she surveyed the park. The solar-powered lights of the grand Ferris wheel twinkled in the distance, and arching street lamps, spread thirty or so feet apart, illuminated patches of grass along the empty bluffs. Valerie listened for voices, but heard only the thump of her own heart as she found the rock at her feet. She tested its weight, making sure it was heavy enough to knock Hannah out, or at least daze her enough to slice her open. She had to be quick, and she walked with purpose.

If anyone had been there to witness the death of Hannah Mills, they would have barely registered her attacker, undoubtedly seeing her as one of the countless women in Santa Monica obsessed with burning calories at all hours of the day.

Valerie came up silently behind Hannah, her pulse no longer racing. It was as if she had slipped into a new skin—the way it was when she pretended to be Doctor Horst. She was a different person, capable of things she would never have believed possible. It was always that way when she was on stage, when she was acting; there was always enough belief for it to feel real, to *be* real. And when the moment was over, when the curtain fell, it would all be a memory, a fabrication that had no purchasing power in the real world. It was not, after all, really her.

As she took her last steps to the bench, the plan crystalized in Valerie's mind and the realization that Alan would approve gave her a final boost of confidence. All she had to do was play the part to the best of her abilities and the final act would write itself. In her mind she saw the rock striking Hannah's head, the knife drawing across her flesh, the blood spilling forward. And then she would continue on, back into the shadows, back into real life, unseen.

She came up behind Hannah and raised the rock, ready to strike.

*

"Right then I saw it," Valerie said, pressing the blade harder to Paula's wrist. "A glint of light at her feet. I didn't understand at first, but it was enough to stop me cold. Do you know what it was I saw?"

Sweat dropped into Paula's eyes, stinging them. She shook her head.

Valerie raised her head from Paula's back and whispered in her ear. "I saw a knife, laying at her feet, smeared with blood. The blood was everywhere. She had already done to herself what I was planning to do to her." Valerie violently pulled Paula back, slamming her head against the wall. Her face was only inches away. "Turns out," she said. "You two really were the same."

Paula tried to swallow, but her mouth had gone dry and the effort made her gag. The perspiration kept dropping into her eyes, and the discomfort was turning to pain, so she squeezed them closed. But when she did, all she could see was the image of Hannah slicing open her own wrists. The image nearly drowned her.

"It was absolutely perfect," Valerie said. "Of course it couldn't look like a suicide—that wouldn't have done the trick. So I collected the knife and used the rock to bash her head to make it look like an assault and, voilà—you're a murder suspect, teetering on the edge of sanity. The text was just added insurance, when I saw her phone sticking out of her pocket. I made sure to use my shirt to avoid prints and improvised that final little flourish."

She raised the knife to Paula's face. "And now, the final act writes itself. Eventually, the guilt got to you. You fought with your husband and ran off. While he was out looking for you, you came back home, all the insanity spilling out through the slices you made in your wrists—exactly like the ones you gave to Hannah Mills."

CHAPTER THIRTY-TWO

ANTHONY TENDED TO the little boy who had run from the safety of his bedroom into his father's arms.

"I'm sorry," Violet said, following her grandson into the living room. "He up and bolted out the room before I could get a hold of him. Come here now, child."

"It's fine, Mom," Anthony assured her. "You all right, little man?"

Alex burrowed into his father's chest. Seeing the boy, so small, so innocent, Alan envisioned the child he would have with Valerie, and his love for her expanded in direct proportion to his disgust for Paula and all the turmoil she'd delivered to so many lives.

"Why'd you do it?" Heather asked Anthony. "Why'd you save her?"

Anthony stroked his son's hair. "Because we all deserve to know the truth."

Alan studied him. Anthony, the hero who had no idea it was all a cruel joke. He hadn't saved Paula at all; he had only made her death more pitiful than it needed to be. She wasn't worth saving. She was a monster. He considered spinning some thread surrounding Paula's revelation that Anthony was a liar, a stalker who had possibly murdered two women, but quickly decided against it. Depending on how things went, that card could still be played later. "I'm afraid we already have the truth," he said.

He looked to Jacob, and for the first time he saw confirmation in the old man's eyes.

"Alan," Heather said, a clear warning in her voice for him to say nothing more about the presumed guilt or innocence of his missing wife.

"So where does this leave us?" Jacob asked.

"We need to go find her," Anthony said.

Ignoring Heather's stare, Alan shook his head, saying bitterly, "She obviously doesn't want to be found."

*

There was no other way for it to end. Paula accepted that. Her body was no longer rigid. It flopped loosely on the floor when Valerie pushed her over.

"Alan truly does believe you killed Hannah," Valerie said, rolling her onto her stomach. She straddled her legs, above the backs of her knees, and adjusted her bound hands to expose the wrists. "If you weren't so self-obsessed, you'd realize the amount of pain that gives him. True pain. The guilt has overwhelmed him at times. It's difficult to see, but it's better that way—it's brought us closer, it's made us even more of a team. I've been there for him in ways you never could. It became he and I against the madness of the world."

Paula stared at the wall only a few inches away. She could see nothing else, as the sharp edge of the knife again found her wrist. She welcomed it. Exhaustion had overtaken her. There was no sense in fighting, in prolonging the struggle. There was nobody to come save her this time. This time, it would be final.

"You could ease his guilt by telling him the truth," Paula said.

"Don't act like you suddenly give a shit about him."

Valerie pressed the knife into Paula's wrist and then eased it off—her irritated sighs growing heavier each time she failed to execute the fatal slice. Again the knife pressed down, this time enough to draw blood, but it still did not reach the vein.

A distant thought came to Paula, a tiny ray of light in her dark mind. "I'm happy you're carrying Alan's child," she said, focusing on the sensation of blood dripping into a warm, shallow pool on her upturned palm. She was comforted by it. "It's okay if you don't believe me. But I've taken so much from him, I don't want to take that from him, too."

Valerie hesitated. The knife cut again, more blood dripped, but only deep enough to elicit pain, not to bring the relief of death.

"Let me do it," Paula whispered.

"Shut up, you crazy bitch."

Paula winced as the knife tore away more of her skin, getting ever closer to the vein. "If you do this, then Alan will see you the same way he sees me," she said, stopping the knife's action. "He'd see you as somehow damaged. Once that settles in, eventually he'll come to realize that a woman who could commit such violence wouldn't be worthy of his love."

"I said, shut up!"

"That's why you haven't told him about your plan to kill me that night, or your intention to kill Hannah—you don't want to be seen by him that way. He didn't want you to be a killer; he only wanted me to be a killer, right? So, please, let me do it. Give me the chance to truly go the way Hannah went. On my own terms. Let me finish this."

A moment passed. All Paula could hear was Valerie's stilted breaths cascading. And then the knife lifted away and Valerie's weight came off her legs.

"Sit up and face the wall."

With a strained effort, Paula obeyed, the blood dripping down her forearms. Valerie worked to untie the charger cord from her wrists, saying nothing more. When Paula at last brought her hands around to her stomach, her shoulders, which had throbbed with an aching pain, tingled with relief. It might be, she accepted, the last pleasurable sensation she would ever have. And then, at once, her body tensed. The cord that had bound her wrists was now around her neck, pulled taut. Saliva caught in Paula's throat and she coughed violently. Spit flew from her mouth as Valerie pulled tighter, her opposite arm wrapped around Paula's upper arms, pinning them to her sides.

"Pick up the knife," she said.

Paula blindly felt for it.

"Next to your right leg," Valerie barked.

Paula's fingers stretched and then brought the handle of the blade into her hand.

"Do it now," Valerie spit into her ear. "Or I swear to God, I'll strangle you to death."

Paula considered swinging the knife back, slicing into Valerie's arm, but she could not see her target, and Valerie's hold was strong, restricting her range of motion. If she missed it would be a wasted effort, bringing her only more pain. No. She had to do what she'd contemplated for so long. That was the only way to truly free herself.

She brought the knife to her wrist, lowering it into the trickle of blood.

"Do it!" Valerie ordered.

The ghosts of Hannah and Bunny—Emily—appeared before Paula. They would always be with her. She locked eyes with them, sensed their calming presence. And then, with a deliberate, aggressive movement, she sliced open her vein.

The pain was instant, as blood poured from the throbbing wound. An involuntary gasp convulsed her body and the knife dropped to the floor. As in the pool only a few hours earlier, there was no fighting, no panic—not even with the violence of the cord still pulled around her neck, choking her. She went limp, and the ghosts of Hannah and Bunny retreated— Hannah back to the bench where she opened herself up, and Emily to the roof of the building in Berkeley. Paula observed them both simultaneously, watching them die. Or was it them, watching her die?

The cord around her neck loosened as the blood continued to flow from her. Her body grew ever weaker. Valerie removed the cord and allowed her to fall back the rest of the way to the floor. It took an effort for Paula to open her eyes and look up at the face of the woman who had planned this inevitable moment with Alan. Valerie used her foot to move the knife out of reach, saying nothing, waiting. Paula was not angry with her. In fact, she didn't care about her at all. There was only peace in having the truth at last, in seeing things for how they truly were.

Paula drifted, following Hannah and Emily into the ether. The blood continued to pool beside her, dripping in a steady stream from her slashed wrist. Seeing herself from a distance, it was, she realized, her true self lying there, dying. There were no other personas, no more psychological pain, no more confusion. Only Paula, alone. *Me*, she thought, closing her eyes. *Everything is all right. It is me. I am at peace.*

Time slipped away.

Valerie nervously licked her lips as the reality of the situation slowly overwhelmed her. It felt like sinking into quicksand; the longer she waited, the harder it would be to pull herself out. What the hell was she supposed to do now? What would Alan do? *Focus.* Come up with a plan. Make it look like a suicide. *Yes.* The telephone charging cord. Use it. *Act.*

She removed a guitar from its wall mount above where Paula lay and threaded the cord through the bottom of the mount, tying the loose ends together, yanking twice on the knot to test its hold. That's good. That will work. Paula tried to hang herself, but changed her mind. Or failed. It didn't matter. Either scenario explained the red mark around her neck.

Valerie glanced down, realizing how close she was to stepping into the blood pooling beside Paula's body. "Fuck," she hissed, jumping away. She stumbled slightly, working to fight off the swift arrival of panic, disgusted by the smell of the latex gloves.

When she turned back, Paula's chest was still, her pale face free of animation. Despite all her previous bravado, her prideful recounting of her exploits and intentions, Valerie was shaken to her core. She could no longer act the part. Tears streamed down her face, and she cried openly, without reservation. *This was not really me,* she told herself, repeating it like a mantra as if doing so would make it true. She was not the person she had been pretending to be. She was a caring mother-to-be. A loyal daughter. A devoted lover. She was all those things and not a killer. She hadn't killed anyone. What had happened tonight was not really her. None of this was really her.

She went quickly from the music studio to check the window in the pool house. The lights inside the main house were still off. Another tightening of her stomach brought vomit into her throat. That was all she needed: physical evidence of her being there thrown up all over the room. *Come on, Valerie. Focus.*

Okay. Paula was dead. The hard part was over. There was no reason for her to stay any longer. There was nothing left for her to do. She could just go home and wait. Alan would take care of the rest. He'd return with the others and someone would eventually find Paula's body. Paula was crazy; she had killed Hannah and then she had killed herself. It was all clear. The journal proved her insanity. Yes, it was perfect. There would be no doubts. Eventually, in a few weeks perhaps, maybe a month, Alan would leave Los Angeles and they'd be together, raising their child, living the life they were supposed to have.

But despite all of this mental conjuring, Valerie had yet to learn the most important thing Paula had—that *perceptions* are often a poor reflection of reality.

"Looks like you weren't the only one with a plan."

Valerie wheeled to face Paula standing at the door of the music studio, the knife held in her remaining good hand, the other still dripping blood onto the floor. The fantasy of control Valerie had cocooned herself in vanished, exposing her completely, and she nearly collapsed in shock. Paula took in the anguished reality lighting her eyes with a sad sense of understanding. "Don't be upset," she said, straining to maintain her focus amid the rapid dimming of her energy. "You did the best you could, but your plan's gonna fail, because you forgot one crucial piece of information—*I've done this before.* Even with all of your secrets, in the end I knew something you didn't—it takes a hell of a long time to die from a slit wrist."

"Wait," Valerie begged.

"Unfortunately, I can't wait any longer," Paula said, moving closer. "Eventually I *am* gonna bleed out. So, this has to end now."

"Please, don't," Valerie sobbed, cowering. "I'm so sorry. Please, don't hurt me…"

"I have no choice," Paula said, stepping toward her, raising the knife. She looked at her tormentor with pity, stuck as she was in the wasteland of her own mind. "But don't worry, it's not gonna end the way you think. Like I said, you're not the only one with a plan."

And then she thrust the knife forward.

CHAPTER THIRTY-THREE

LINCOLN HAD WALKED aimlessly, waiting for a return text from Heather with an answer to his question, "Is Paula there or not?" His annoyance with Heather's proclivity for ignoring him until she had a completed report was at a boiling point as he headed back down Georgina Avenue. But when he looked up from his stubbornly silent phone, he finally got his answer.

Paula was in the middle of the street, staggering toward the Mills house.

"My God," he said, breaking into a run to intercept her.

Her feet shuffled forward, barely coming off the pavement with each step. Lincoln was only a few strides from reaching her when she fell forward, onto her hands and knees.

"Paula!" he said, crouching beside her, holding her up.

She said nothing, her body so unexpectedly heavy in his grip, it was difficult to keep her from collapsing all the way to the asphalt. It was then that he noticed the blood. It was not apparent at first where it came from, there seemed to be so much of it.

"What did you do, Paula?" he asked, easing her onto her back.

No answer came as her eyes rolled white, consciousness

slipping away, her face so pale it practically glowed in the dim light. He traced the flow of blood down her arm, quickly tracking the source back to the deeply slit wrist. It gaped at him like a toothless mouth. Pushing his hand down on the wound, he pulled the phone from his pocket and used his thumb to dial 911.

As he explained the situation to the operator, blood seeping between his fingers, Paula's eyes refocused and stared up at him. There was no pleading in them, no fear, as though she were simply watching a performance she had no part in.

"Hang on, Paula," Lincoln said to her, dropping the phone from his ear.

Lincoln pulled off his belt and wrapped it tightly above the gaping wound.

"Stay with me," he said, stroking her hair. "Stay with me."

Minutes passed and her consciousness came and went. And then there were other voices. Her eyes moved across the familiar faces hovering above her like tethered balloons. Her stare glided from one to the other, landing at last on one in particular. As the concerned voices swirled, with the distant wail of an ambulance siren growing ever louder in its rapid approach, Paula's watery eyes remained focused on the terror-stricken face of her husband.

*

"There's no reason for you to go back in there," Jacob insisted. "Lincoln will take care of it. You can ride with me to the hospital."

"No," Alan said between gasps of air. "I'll come later. I can't see her right now."

"You have to, Alan. When she wakes up, she's going to need you."

"I can't!" he wailed.

The two men stood outside the pool house. Lincoln and Heather were still inside, assessing the horrific carnage of Paula's suicide attempt. The trail of blood had been easy enough to follow, but nobody could have been prepared for the scene that awaited them inside.

"It's all right, Jacob," Heather said, stepping out to join them. "I'll stay with Alan and you go on to the hospital. One of you should be there. We'll join you shortly."

"I said I'm not ready to see her," Alan yelled at her.

Since returning to the backyard to find Valerie gone, Alan had been trying to free himself from the others. The burner phone in his pocket continued to vibrate with the distressed beckoning of the woman he loved, but he could not answer it, could not learn what the hell had happened, until he was alone.

"You go on, Jacob," Heather said, calmly, discounting Alan's emotional outburst. "We'll wait here for the police and you take care of—"

"The police?" Alan said. "Why are the police coming?"

"The paramedics filed a report," Heather reminded him. "There'll be an investigation."

"Into what?" he asked, his voice shaking. "She tried to kill herself again. That's all! You heard Anthony, she already tried once earlier today."

Lincoln stepped out to the yard. "There are ears already gathering on the other side of this fence and we need to lower our voices."

Alan bent over; saliva dripped from his mouth. "I'm gonna be sick," he said, which wasn't entirely a lie.

"Go inside the house," Lincoln instructed.

He was already moving away, his pace quickening as he went. He tore into the house and ran upstairs to the master bath. Slamming the door behind him, he didn't bother listening to the four messages Valerie had already left him. He called her directly.

"Alan," she cried into the phone after the first ring.

"Where are you?" he whispered, his voice shrill.

"In my car, outside Saint John's emergency room. I'm sorry, I'm so sorry, I messed everything up."

"What the hell happened?"

Valerie's tears overwhelmed her and she could not get the words out. Listening to her, absorbing her evident despair, Alan's emotions spilled out and he, too, was crying, the two of them suffocating together. The mechanics of how Paula escaped no longer mattered, at least not at the moment. All that mattered was Valerie.

"Are you okay?" he asked, the words barely audible.

"She stabbed me," Valerie said. "I'm hurt so bad."

"Where? Where are you hurt?"

"In my upper chest," she said, her voice choked with tears. "It's really deep, Alan. I'm bleeding a lot. It hurts."

"Okay," Alan said, focusing. "Go into the ER and tell them you were mugged. Tell them you were in the parking lot at the Starbucks on Eleventh and Wilshire and a man came out of nowhere and demanded money. When you hesitated, he stabbed you and ran off, okay? And then you drove right to the hospital, okay? Can you do that?"

"What are we gonna do?" she whimpered. "Oh my God, Alan, what's going to happen to us? To our baby?" The mention of their unborn child sent her into another series of deep sobs.

"Everything's going to be okay," Alan said, despite his mounting realization that nothing at all would be. "You need to get help, that's all you need to worry about right now. Just get taken care of and then go home and wait. I'll call you as soon as I can. Okay, sweetheart?"

There was a long, distressing silence, and then her voice came softly. "Okay," she said.

After hanging up the phone, Alan splashed water on his face. Tensing against the onslaught, he fought back tears as he stared at himself in the mirror. He could barely recognize his own face, contorted with agony. This was not happening. It couldn't be.

"Alan?" Lincoln's voice came through the door.

"Leave me alone, Lincoln," Alan said, tremors wracking his body.

"You need to come downstairs. There are some questions about what happened here tonight."

Lincoln's voice was calm, precise, in that authoritative way that bothered Alan so. It was obvious that he already had all the information needed to convict. He was merely leading the witness, driving the narrative to its inevitable outcome. Alan leaned over the sink as his stomach clamped down, forcing up specks of green bile. He wretched and spat.

"Give me a few more minutes," he managed to say.

"No, Alan. The police are here. Detective Melendez. He's asked to talk with you."

Of course he did! Alan was no fool. Detective Melendez was not downstairs. He was in the bedroom with Lincoln. Lincoln had merely insisted that he would bring his client out safely, would necessarily be there when the detective questioned him about the kidnapping and attempted murder of his wife.

"I'm coming in," Lincoln said, when Alan did not answer.

Before Alan could protest, Lincoln pushed open the bathroom door. There was no escape, nothing he could do. The debilitating image of Valerie, bleeding alone in the ER, surrounded by strangers, darted through his mind. He longed to be with her. If only he could be with her, then everything would be all right. He stumbled backward as Lincoln stepped inside.

"Relax," Lincoln said, raising his hand as if approaching a skittish horse.

But Alan was unequipped to confront the devastation of what his life had, in an instant, become. He could not find his voice, his panic still too present, too disruptive for rational, cognitive consideration. He began to cry.

"Come on, Alan," Lincoln said, inching closer. "This has to be cleared up."

"You don't understand how hard it's been!" Alan screamed through his tears.

"No, I don't," Lincoln said. "I can't imagine the frustration you've been living with, the sacrifices you've had to make just to get through your day. But you can handle this. We're all going to help you get through it."

Alan stared at the tall lawyer, who still had his hand outstretched, still reaching forward to guide him from the bathroom. What the hell did he mean they were going to help him? That was a lie. Lincoln didn't like him any more than he did him, so why was he being so goddamn reassuring in the face of such betrayal?

"Paula's going to need you," Lincoln went on with an encouraging nod. "Now more than ever. We can't allow this to spiral out of control."

Alan's racing mind was still unable to put together what was happening.

"Paula's going to be fine," Lincoln told him. "They've stabilized her and she's out of immediate danger. That's the good news. But with all the trauma, she's evidently had a blackout of some kind."

Alan blinked, his mouth fell open. "Blackout?"

"Jacob has talked to the doctors. They say it's a type of coping mechanism, another way in which she dissociates from herself. So the police need you to fill in the gaps as to what happened today. Now, listen," he said, lowering his already quiet voice to a whisper, "there's no reason to mention the journal, not right now. We'll figure out how we're going to deal with that later. If they ask what you two fought about when she scratched your face, you don't have to lie. Tell them it was about trust issues, her belief that you were not emotionally available to her—that's it. Don't be any more specific than that. They're already aware of Paula's phone call to Anthony and the suicide attempt in the pool, so that's all fair game to discuss. You understand? I am not asking you to lie."

Alan listened in disbelief as Lincoln went on explaining. Detective Melendez had seen the music studio. Suicide attempt, he agreed, an act of violence born from a truly disturbed mind. A failed hanging, followed by a final slash of destruction. There was no indication of foul play.

He followed Lincoln downstairs as if floating. It was all surreal, a lucid dream he struggled to control. He was not a suspect. Paula had told them nothing of Valerie. In fact, when Alan finally made his way outside to be interviewed, the detective seemed more interested in what transpired between Paula and Anthony that afternoon than anything else.

"Do you have any knowledge of other contact between the two of them, before today?" Detective Melendez asked.

"No," Alan said. "But then, Paula is very good at keeping secrets."

It took only fifteen minutes before the detective excused himself and went out to face the bank of camera lights of the media congregating out on Georgina Ave, leaving Alan alone to assess the miracle of deliverance before him.

*

Alan was not a religious man, but as a child he had believed in God. While he never did buy into the notion that there was a specific plan for his life, there were moments—his parents' divorce when he was seven, his mother's death from cancer when he was twenty—when he had leaned on some ethereal concept of a powerful being from whom he could draw strength.

Making his way down the hallway of Santa Monica Hospital, to Paula's room, Alan reflected on the folly of such false beliefs, of such fantasy. God was not real; only he was, himself and the uncompromising love of Valerie, and their unborn child, the physical manifestation of their shared dreams. He had acted only to protect their love. Paula had taken something from him and he had merely fought to get it back. She was the vampire, the evil one, not him. She had bled him of energy, of desire. She had killed Hannah and sat idly by as Bunny had been destroyed, lying to protect Anthony. What else had she lied about? What other acts of destruction was she capable of? It wasn't only his life that would be better off if she no longer existed, the whole world would benefit from her demise. As he opened the door to her hospital room, Alan prayed for Paula's death, to a God he no longer believed in.

"I'm glad you came," Jacob said from Paula's bedside as Alan stepped inside.

"Lincoln's with Heather at the house," Alan said. "They're preparing a media statement."

"He does like to be prepared."

"Is she awake?"

"In and out. They gave her another sedative."

Alan remained by the door. "Do you mind if I talk to her alone?"

Jacob smiled kindly as he stood, pausing briefly by Alan's side to pat his arm, before leaving him with Paula.

Her head was turned away, her breathing slow and steady. The wound on her left wrist had been carefully bandaged, and an IV snaked into her forearm. Her heart and blood pressure were well monitored, the machines faintly beeping and sighing, everything under control.

She turned her face toward him, her eyes alert, despite the sedative.

"I guess I gave everyone another scare," she said.

"Yes, you did," Alan said, staying still.

Paula continued to stare at him as the machines made soothing noises.

"Will you sit with me?" she asked.

Alan did not want to sit with her. He wanted her to drift back to sleep and never wake up.

"Please," she said, reaching for him. "And then I'll let you go, I promise."

With no other option, he crossed the room and sat in the chair by the bed.

"What happened to your face?" she asked, tracing the scratch with her eyes.

He could barely breathe. "You really don't remember anything?"

"Some things," she said, drowsily. "Like, the night we met. Do you remember that?"

"Of course."

"Where was it?" she asked.

Alan held his silence, trying to figure her out, not interested in playing the game.

"Finn McCool's bar," she answered for him.

"That's right."

She smiled, faintly. "Do you remember being nervous?"

Alan stared.

"I was," Paula said. "Because everyone had told me what a brilliant man you were and I was intimidated. But the wonderful thing was, after I was with you, I wasn't intimidated at all. You made everything so easy. We fit so well together."

"That was a long time ago," Alan said.

"Yes, things didn't work out the way we imagined they would, did they? It's like that John Lennon song." She half-sang the lyrics in a dreamy cadence. "*Life is what happens when you're busy making other plans.*"

She laughed gently. Alan did not smile.

"We were happy once," she said. "We were perfect together. There were good things, weren't there?"

It took a moment, but Alan said, "Yes."

She moved her hand over the railing, and he took it into his as though accepting a challenge. "I don't blame you for where we ended up," she said. "So much of the damage to our lives was my fault, too. Hopefully, we've learned from our mistakes. I've certainly learned from mine, and I'm never going to harm myself again. Ever. So there's still time for us to make new memories. Like the way you used to make love to me, how we once held on to each other as if that was all we needed to be happy. And the way you were always encouraging me. The way you encouraged me to open The Little Delicious, to follow my dreams. The way you took care of me." She squeezed his hand tightly, her fingers wrapping around his. "The way you made me a smoothie every morning."

Alan tried to pull his hand free, but she would not let it go.

"And the help you gave me," she said, squeezing ever tighter. "Coming up with that list of doctors, finding the perfect match. And she was. She was absolutely perfect. As if created only with me in mind." She stared, unblinking. "I promise you, Alan. I'll remember it all."

Alan yanked his hand free and jolted to his feet.

"It's all coming back to me," Paula said. "Your love of the arts, of theatre."

"Jesus Christ."

"Yes," she said. "I feel as though by tomorrow morning I'll be able to recall everything. Even the part about how Hannah Mills truly died."

Alan's face paled. "What the fuck is that supposed to mean?"

"It means you should talk to your lover. Evidently she has a few secrets of her own."

"You're insane," Alan said, desperate to regain control. "You've had a series of delusions. Now you're having another one. Nobody's going to believe anything you say."

"An actress from UCLA was attacked last night," Paula calmly said. "She was stabbed in the upper chest. Not deep enough to kill her, though it easily could have been. There'll probably be a report to the police, though there'll definitely be a record of her being treated. Maybe even in this very hospital,

I'm not sure. But it won't be difficult for Heather to track her down. She's so good at her job, isn't she? She'll probably even have a picture of her to show the building manager in Pasadena before the police do."

Alan turned and went to the door but stopped short and spun back around. He had no place to run to, nowhere to hide. "Tell me what you want, and I'll do it."

Her eyes bore into his. "I want you to live a long time, Alan. I want you to always be scared that the next person you meet is going to be the one to see the real you."

"You bitch," he said, his eyes moistening.

"You were already planning on leaving town. You've already quit your job, so there's no more loose ends to tie up. Of course, you'll have to go without the financial stability you'd been counting on. Though I suppose in the morning, when the banks open, if you're very quick, you'll be able to scrounge together a bit. Enough to get you wherever you decide to go. South America perhaps, someplace where it's less expensive to live. Certainly someplace where the police won't easily find you. There'll be so many looking for you. But you'll manage. You're so good at long-term planning."

"Don't do this," Alan said, trying everything he could. "I wasn't in my right mind. I was delusional too, I was. So punish me, if that's what you need to do, but please, leave Valerie out of this. Don't do this to her and our baby."

"But that's the best part of it all," Paula said. "You'll have a new life to live, with your new family. I wonder though, what names you'll use. You certainly can't be Alan Hickman any longer. Alan Hickman is a fugitive from the law. He abused his wife, tortured her, even tried to kill her. Why, he might even have been an accomplice in the murder of Hannah Mills. Is that how you'd like your child to see you? No, you'll have to become somebody new—somebody who looks identical but who's actually entirely different. But I'll make you a promise. I promise that I'm going to live a long, long time. And I will never forget. I'll always remember the real you."

CHAPTER THIRTY-FOUR

PAULA WAS STILL not used to the attention. She never would be. Ever since the news broke of her kidnapping and torture, the media interest in her story had exploded anew. That was why, even after six months in seclusion, she kept her impending move a secret. It was better to fade away without telling anyone where she was going. She'd told a few people, of course. Lincoln helped organize the logistics, though Paula figured Heather did most of the actual work.

"How long?" Jacob asked.

"A few years," Paula said. "There's no real plan. But you can come visit any time you'd like, and stay as long as you want. And I hope you will, Jacob."

"You can count on it," he told her. "You're the only family I've got."

Paula cried in his arms then, but they were happy tears.

After months in intensive therapy, getting her emotions sorted out and her system back in check with a low-dose anti-depressant, Paula was looking forward to her new life.

"Where will you be?" Wendy asked.

Paula trusted Wendy, but she decided it was better to create a little emotional space between them, along with the physical distance. "I'll be in a better place," was all she offered.

To her credit, Wendy didn't push. Perhaps she hadn't any energy left. It had all been so hard on her. Alan was her only sibling and he was gone from her life without so much as a goodbye. He and Valerie had thrown together what they could in the middle of the night and driven off in her Honda. The police had traced their whereabouts to the Bank of America on Wilshire Boulevard in Santa Monica first thing the following morning, where Alan had withdrawn just shy of four thousand dollars from a checking account. According to the detectives assigned to the case, that money, combined with whatever he already had in his wallet, along with the eight hundred dollars Valerie had withdrawn from a saving's account at Wells Fargo, was all they had between them when Valerie's car was spotted on a surveillance camera as it drove across the Mexican border a few hours later.

"I blame that woman," Wendy insisted, still unable to use Valerie's name. "She seduced him and got pregnant on purpose. She twisted him all up. I mean, she was obviously the one who really killed Hannah, despite that bullshit story she told you about suicide. It was all her doing, I'm sure of it."

It was certainly an angle that had played well on the television news shows, and Paula did not argue against the possibility—what would be the point? Everyone enjoyed the game, and dissecting the tabloid-ready relationship between the scheming professor and the failed actress was entertaining and lucrative for everyone involved. Even, as it turned out, for Wendy. There were only a few loose ends for Paula to tie up before she left, the biggest being what to do with The Little Delicious on Montana Avenue. Ever since the truth had come out, customers had returned in force, and closing it seemed an unnecessary waste. So it gave her a smile when Lincoln reported back that Wendy nearly fainted from shock when the offer of sale was presented. Paula thought she might even frame the dollar bill Wendy had used to buy it outright.

And now, as gaffers manipulated the fill lights surrounding her and the cameraman attended to his last-minute duties before they would start running tape, Paula thought of Anthony Mills. She hadn't spoken to him since the day he pulled her from the pool. There was a letter, but it had yet to be mailed. That would be the last piece of business before she boarded the plane. She was not convinced that if she saw him in person she'd be able to keep her destination a secret, the way she had with Wendy. So a letter it was. She was sure, though, that Anthony would not be able to find her until she was ready to be found. She wasn't taking a computer; her interest in chatroom discussions was over. It pleased her to envision Anthony with little Alex, playing together, discovering new things, leaning on each other for support. She wished peace for him. It had been so long since he'd had it, if he ever did.

"Are you ready, Ms. Sullivan?" a production assistant asked.

Paula smiled and nodded that she was. A makeup artist came in and rechecked her face, but made no adjustments. The ten or so other production people from CNN settled and the living room fell quiet as the light above the camera came on. Paula fidgeted in her seat, picking at the thin paper wrapped around the water bottle another production assistant had given her. The sound it made reminded her of the crinkly pages of her grandmother's Bible.

"You're going to do fine," the silver-haired reporter sitting opposite her said, kindly. "We'll just talk for a while and you'll tell your story."

"Okay," Paula smiled, setting the water bottle down by her foot.

"All right, everybody." The reporter nodded to the room. "Let's begin."

The camera focused intently on every nuance of Paula's placid expression, recording the facts as she relayed them. She talked a bit about the beginning of her relationship with Alan, how they truly had been in love once, about her long battle with depression and the toll it took on their lives.

"My husband once joked that opening a bakery was the most expensive and time-intensive group therapy session ever devised. But there was something about the gathering of ingredients, the measuring, the molding, the precise oven temperature, that focused my mind and evened out my emotions—connected me to both time and place. That's all I ever wanted. That's all anyone with depression wants—to simply breathe in and out without a sense of disconnection."

The reporter nodded. "Of course we've learned over these past months that Hannah Mills suffered from depression as well."

"Too many people do, and they do it in silence."

"And that's why you've started the foundation, correct? To offer hope to those who find themselves in that situation?"

"Yes," Paula said. "We've already committed ten million dollars to get it up and running. It's called Emily's Voice. It's named for a girl I knew in college, who thought the same thing as Hannah. The same thing I once did. She was a beautiful young lady, and I let her down. Maybe through the foundation created in her honor, we can see to it that the next young girl isn't."

"Eventually, this story will be aired across the world. If your husband is out there watching, what would you like to say to him?"

The camera pushed close on Paula, her pensive face filling

the screen. Where Alan was, she did not have any idea. What he was doing, or how he survived, she could not guess. But he was out there, hiding from the world, scared, forced to be someone he wasn't. Whatever the circumstance, he was undoubtedly trapped in his own delusion of who he truly was. Paula smiled. "I have nothing left to say to him," she said at last. "I'm sure I wouldn't even recognize him at all."

*

It was a long flight to Italy, followed by a winding car ride along the Amalfitana, the highway that hugged the shoulder of the Amalfi Coast. Paula kept the window down, the fresh breeze on her face all the way to the seaside town of Ravello. The house Heather had found for her was small, only two bedrooms. But it was perfect. The terrace was surrounded by green grass and lush gardens, with a sloping path to the white-sand beach far below. It was close to the town of Sorrento, where Paula had already arranged for a weekly session with a well-regarded therapist named Lauretta Moretti, who had been trained in Switzerland and had promised to help her in her continued quest to find mental and emotional peace.

The afternoon Paula arrived at her new home in Ravello, she took only one item from her suitcase. She had found it in a store along Ocean Park Avenue in Santa Monica, after her final lunch at Thyme Café with Wendy. It was called a Matryoshka but was better known as a Russian nesting doll. The Russian angle amused her, in light of Alan's predicament. Paula opened the colorful outer shell and removed the identical, smaller doll from inside it, then placed the biggest one on the reclaimed wood mantle above the fireplace. She took the smaller figure with her as she went outside.

Standing on the edge of the cliff overlooking the white-capped azure-blue Mediterranean, she practically floated in the breeze. One by one, Paula opened the progressively smaller nesting dolls, removing each identical figure from inside the other. Each time she drew a new one out, she threw it over the edge of the cliff, watching it disappear into the wind and ocean, until there were none left.

"You're new here," an old man's voice came from behind her.

"Yes," Paula said, turning to face the man, who wore a red sweater and a grey wool Borsalino cap. "I am."

"I saw you arrive," he said, leaning on a walking stick for support, his accent thick, but his English very good. "We heard that the house was sold to an American."

"It's even more beautiful than I imagined."

"Do you have any family with you?"

"No," Paula said. "It's only me."

"Ah. And do you speak Italian?"

"Not yet," Paula said.

"Not yet! I like that answer. It means you are still learning new things. I live up the road with my wife. Not too far. We can help you learn, if you'd like."

Paula smiled. "I'd like that very much, thank you."

"I am Marcello," the old man said, removing his hat. "It is a pleasure to meet you."

"The pleasure's mine," she answered, her smile widening, lighting her eyes.

She pushed aside the blond hair blowing across her face so he could better see her.

"My name's Paula."

ACKNOWLEDGMENTS

My continued thanks and appreciation to Jennifer Silva Redmond for her insight and editorial expertise. And to Mary Vensel White, Nick May, and Katherine Flitch for their invaluable contributions to making sure I don't embarrass myself too badly. Finally, to Sergeant Ed Nevill for helping me with police procedure.

ABOUT THE AUTHOR

Photo By Chad Savage

Clay Savage is a writer and voice-over actor whose voice has been heard on hundreds of television shows and movies. He lives with his family in Santa Monica, California.

Visit Clay at Theclaysavage.com